PRAISE FOR THE BEAT MATCH:

"Fun to read, while also delivering a satisfying, sometimes tear-inducing, and heartfelt love story. Do yourself a favor and *read this book!*" ~ Bookgasms Book Blog

"A friends-to-lovers and older-brother's-best-friend book that will blow you away." ~ Reads and Reviews

"This romance flits between grin-inducing banter and hypnotic dance scenes. Annie and Wes are a couple to remember!" ~ author Michelle Hazen

"The writing is delicious and Kelly's voice is vibrant." ~ author Mary Ann Marlowe

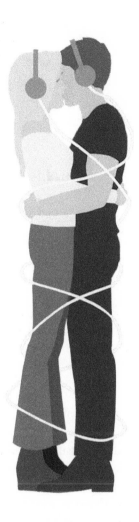

First edition: CD Books September 2020

The author is not responsible for websites (or their content) that are not owned by the author.

ISBN 978-1-988937-14-4 (ebook edition)

ISBN 978-1-988937-13-7 (paperback)

❀ Created with Vellum

ALSO BY KELLY SISKIND

Chasing Crazy

Showmen Series:

New Orleans Rush

Don't Go Stealing My Heart

The Beat Match

Over the Top Series:

My Perfect Mistake

A Fine Mess

Hooked on Trouble

One Wild Wish Series:

He's Going Down

Off-Limits Crush

36 Hour Date

Visit Kelly's website and join her newsletter for great giveaways and never miss an update!

www.kellysiskind.com

THE BEAT MATCH

ALEXA —
HEARTS & HUGS TO
YOU! ♡

Kelly Siskind

1

WESTON ALDRICH always dressed for success, from the shined tips of his Berluti shoes, to the crisp knot of his Christian Lacroix tie. Failure in business was for lesser men. A last-minute fumble when applying for a pharmaceutical patent? Fixed with a well-placed phone call and courtside Knicks or US Open tickets. An investor getting cold feet? He could sweet talk a vegan into buying a cattle ranch. He walked through life prepared, his mental rolodex one flip from solving the unsolvable. Which made his father's shocking statement all the harder to compute.

"Biotrell is entertaining an offer from DLP," Victor S. Aldrich repeated.

Weston stared at his father's stark expression as those horrifying words sank in. The prospect was so absurd it was laughable. He'd been working toward the Biotrell merger for two years. Planning. Maneuvering. Clocking more hours than a video game junkie urinating in a bottle to secure a win. Like hell they'd lose this deal to anyone, let alone those shady bastards at DLP. "You must have heard wrong."

His father straightened to his full six-foot-two height, his custom-made suit creasing as he crossed his arms. "Since I heard it from the horse's mouth, I'd say my sources are accurate."

Weston blinked, at a loss for words. An anomaly. His words usually worked just fine. They were pretty damn clever, actually. Up until one minute ago. "We're the right company for this deal," he said, his tie suddenly a boa constrictor around his neck. He jammed his finger into the knot and yanked it down. "Biotrell will remain intact if they merge with us. DLP will tear them apart. They must realize that."

"DLP has promised to keep all their employees on."

"Because they'll say whatever they need to get the deal done." Lie. Steal. Cheat. They made cesspool pond scum look appetizing.

"They may have found ways around promises before, but they're saying all the right things now. And Mr. Farzad's listening. But he still wants Biotrell under our umbrella. Seems he also wants something else, and he's using talks with DLP to entice us to up the ante."

Frustrated, Weston stared through the window, the sprawling Manhattan views doing zilch to calm his rising agitation. They'd been nothing but accommodating with Biotrell, working with their timelines, ensuring their workers wouldn't lose wages, offering them enough cash to keep five generations of Farzads living like kings. This would be one of the largest pharmaceutical mergers in history. Why toss a wrench into their plans now? "If they want more cash, we'll be hard-pressed to find it."

His father joined him by the window, their polished shoes parallel, matching starched shirts as stiff as their stances. Their resemblance didn't end there, as people never failed to remind Weston. They both had thick heads of hair—his father's more gray than black these days; their blue-eyed glares could cut diamonds, and the Aldrich jaw was sledgehammer strong. They had bodies built for athletics and minds sharpened for business. Weston had been groomed to steer their company into the future, to take over when his father eventually stepped down.

Whatever had Biotrell playing hard to get had to be fixable.

"There's no derailing this merger," Weston said, unsure why his father was stalling. Victor S. Aldrich was as direct as a compass and twice as obstinate. "We'll close this deal no matter what it takes."

His father nodded sharply. "I'm glad you feel that way, son. It seems Mr. Farzad wants a personal favor from you."

Now things were getting downright bizarre. "What do you mean *personal*?"

"You know his daughter Rosanna?"

"Yes," he said slowly, the wheels in his head spinning to get ahead of this quagmire. Rosanna was a few years younger than Weston, founder of some cosmetics business, beautiful with a full mouth, dark hair, and striking eyes. A hellcat on wheels, last he heard. Something about a salacious video going viral tickled his memory. "What does Rosanna have to do with a deal that's already been negotiated and tentatively agreed upon?"

His father stayed facing the window, his only movement a gentle tug on his jacket cuff. "Karim Farzad is a proud man, but all men are willing to admit weakness if it means helping their children. It appears Rosanna is heading down a bad path and Karim thinks you can help."

Weston had no doubt Rosanna was one bad decision away from landing on a seedy reality show, but his father's "helping children" comment had him biting his tongue. Aside from lavishing his wife with affection before Weston's mother passed away, the man was as sentimental as a slab of granite. "How exactly does Karim think I can help his daughter?"

"He'd like you to ask her out."

Weston sputtered out a laugh. "Excuse me?"

"You're an upstanding man with an impeccable reputation. You have excellent connections and a bright future. Any father would be honored to call you his son-in-law."

Weston searched the streamlined wood cabinets, his contemporary sculpture collection, the leather seating area around his coffee table, looking for a hidden camera or microphone or any explanation for this insanity. Surely this was some kind of sick joke. "I'm not marrying some girl I barely know. This merger's a smart business move for both our companies. Karim knows that. His demand is nothing short of ludicrous."

His father faced him, unruffled, serious as ever. "Marriage is the long game, if it suits you both. Karim's only asking that you be open to the idea. But I'm not asking. I'm telling. Take her on some dates. Spend time together. She's a beautiful girl. Asking her out is no hardship. She just needs a positive, stable presence in her life. Someone who enjoys quiet nights, not wild parties."

Well, wasn't that the kicker? If his father knew how Weston spent his nights, the man would have an embolism, or disown him, or both. If Biotrell knew, they'd have squashed this deal months ago, and Karim Farzad would never have made this insane proposal. Thankfully, that secret would never get out, but this request was appalling. "Women aren't business pawns."

"Rosanna's aware of the proposal and has agreed to go out with you."

Jesus. This was like some kind of villainous matchmaking, with Weston's father pimping his son out to secure their financial future and market share.

Weston stalked to his chair and gripped the back of it, digging his fingers into the leather. His desk was tidy, papers neatly stacked, pens tucked into unobtrusive holders, keyboard and cell phone parallel with the dark mahogany edge. Everything organized and uncluttered, exactly like his apartment and daily life. Only two framed photos suggested Weston had a beating heart inside his chest: his best friend, Leo, who died nearly thirteen years ago, and his mother, who died a year later.

Weston had no intention of ever marrying. Losing the people closest to him had taught him one paramount lesson: love always ended in pain. He'd been forced to attend therapy. He knew the drill, why he still kept people at arm's length. Emotional distance, fear of abandonment. He was so textbook the textbooks were jealous of him.

Label him whatever you wanted, Weston planned on a long life of bachelorhood, most of it spent in this towering office. But dating wasn't marriage, and Karim couldn't force the couple into a union that would end in divorce. Sealing this deal was Weston's chance to make his mark on Aldrich Pharma. Prove he deserved to take over the family business and appease shareholders who worried he was being gifted the reins.

"Fine," he told his father, still angry about this change in circumstance. Business should be business. Dating to secure a merger made this personal. "Tell Karim I'll try—"

His cell phone rang, cutting him short. The number wasn't familiar, but it was an excuse to kick his father out and seethe in private. "I need to take this. I'll ask Rosanna out in the next couple of weeks, once I get my head around it all."

"See to it that you do, and that you do it soon." Victor's heavy jaw clamped shut.

Weston didn't bother replying or watching him leave. He picked up his phone. "Hello?"

"Hey, Wes. It's Annie."

He frowned. It was definitely Annie, but her name should've flashed on his screen. "Why aren't you using your phone?"

"There's been an incident, and I need a favor."

"What kind of incident, Anthea?" If she lost her phone, he'd have to get her a new one. He didn't like the idea of her being without that safety net.

She made an annoyed growly sound. "How many times do I have to tell you to stop calling me Anthea?"

"Sorry, *Anthea*, but it's hard to hear you over the whine in your voice."

"God, you're annoying."

He chuckled at her irritation. Needling Annie with her full name was the only thing that could amuse him on a day like today. "Well then, *Squirrel*, do fill me in on this favor."

Another growl. Something snarky under her breath. She enjoyed his nickname for her as much as her given name. Instead of biting back, she said, "I need a lift."

"Did you forget how to use the subway? Are you allergic to taxis? Did your Uber app malfunction?"

An exasperated sigh slipped through the line. "I lost my keys and my purse is locked in my apartment."

"So ask your landlord to let you in."

"It's more complicated than that, and I need to get to work. So can you pick me up or not? This is an emergency."

Everything with Annie was an emergency. The night she ran out of glue for her obsessive scrapbooking hobby and dialed 9-1-1 had been a special level of absurd. The time she spotted a vintage purse she just had to have and bolted from his still-moving car had been stroke inducing. Anthea—*Annie*—Ward had the attention span of a fruit fly and was as organized as a Black Friday sale. He had no clue how she made it through each day. "Tell me where you are and I'll rescue you before the sky falls."

He felt her trademark evil stare as she barked out the address and hung up.

He shook his head at Leo's photo. "When you told me to look out for your little sister, you didn't tell me she'd be this big of a pain in my ass."

He smiled sadly, wishing Leo could bust his gut laughing, or punch Weston's arm and tell him to suck it up. He wished Annie had more people to rely on. As it stood, he barely had time to sleep, let alone nag her to stick with a job longer than a month, or go back to school for a useful degree.

Weston snatched his keys and wallet from his desk drawer and left his office. After quick instructions to his secretary to divert his calls, he cracked his neck and jabbed the elevator button twice. *Go on a date to secure a merger. Be a son-in-law for hire.* It was unprofessional. Exploitative. His vision turned spotty as he marched into the opening elevator.

Duncan Ruffolo slipped in before the doors slid shut and nodded at Weston. "Hey."

Weston grunted.

Duncan rocked back on his heels, hands clasped over a new, astronomically expensive suit. Weston of all people would know. Where some fathers played ball with their sons or shared laughs and shouts over a sport telecast, Victor S. Aldrich dragged Weston to his tailor to be poked and measured and told to stand straighter. "The suit doesn't make the man," his father would say. "The suit reinforces the man's greatness."

If Weston didn't know better, he'd say Duncan was wearing a Guanashina suit, the luxurious fabric exceeding greatness. The blend of guanaco, baby cashmere, and kid pashmina was so fine it felt like silk against the skin. At fifteen thousand dollars a pop, it sure as hell better feel like heaven.

"Have we given you a raise?" Weston pressed the button for the parking garage.

Duncan chuckled. "Only you would notice the suit. And no, sadly, you haven't. My father came into some cash, spread it around his kids. Thought I'd have some fun with it instead of saving." He brushed non-existent lint from his lapel. "I also ordered a new bed," he said, smug.

Duncan was an exceptional executive assistant, flexible with senior managers and shrewd enough to anticipate needs. Resourceful and efficient when coordinating events and arranging travel. He was personable and well-liked by all the staff. He was also well-liked by most of New York's female population, as he never failed to boast.

"Careful putting those notches on the bedposts," Weston said. "You might weaken the structure."

Duncan smirked. "Crashing would only heighten the fun."

Normally Weston laughed at Duncan's jokes, but he wasn't in a laughing mood. And he didn't envy Duncan's player status. Weston may not be relationship bound, but he believed in treating women with the respect they deserved. With Duncan's All-American blond hair and quarterback build, his once-and-done attitude often left a trail of unhappy women in his wake.

"Saw your father leaving your office," Duncan said. "He looked pleased about something."

Weston sure as hell wasn't pleased. "You mean he wasn't scowling."

"The man won't be hired for a toothpaste ad anytime soon. But, yeah, he seemed less lethal than usual."

"Well, he shouldn't be. Not when—" Weston cut himself off before launching into a tirade about Karim Farzad and this merger turning into a Match.com slumber party.

Duncan had proven he could be counted on and was as discreet as employees came, but no one could know how low

Weston was sinking to get this deal done. "Some final things are snagging the merger's momentum, but nothing detrimental. My father was just filling me in."

Duncan studied him as the elevator hit the garage floor. "Care to join me for a Scotch at Leverage tonight? Looks like you need to unload."

What Weston needed was to fit ten hours of work into five, clear his head for tonight's *non*-pharmaceutical job, and prep for an unwanted date with Farzad's daughter. "Thanks, but I've got to work."

"All work and no play makes for a dull life," Duncan said as they headed for their cars. "When does the great Weston Aldrich make time for fun?"

"Fun is overrated." Weston waved vaguely as he unlocked his Audi and slid into the driver's seat.

Duncan's version of fun—dating, socializing, relaxing on weekends—was reserved for a different kind of person. Accomplishment drove Weston, professional strides and goals reached, which made the merger's latest obstacle all the more infuriating.

His car nearly stalled as he decelerated down the garage ramp. He almost sideswiped one of the support columns. *Date Karim's daughter. Hopefully marry her.* Rosanna's awareness of the request made the sham even more confusing. The longer he ruminated, the more erratic his driving became, the city's gridlock shredding Weston's already frazzled nerves.

By the time he pulled up to the curb where Annie should've been, his grip was close to crushing his steering wheel. He searched the busy sidewalk for a girl in layers of vintage clothing, long blond hair tied into a knot on her head. He often told Annie she was one oversized sweater shy of looking like a tree-hugging hippie. She'd roll her eyes and tell him he wouldn't know chic style if it bit him in the ass. His designer-filled closet proved otherwise, and there was no sign of Annie or her eccentric wardrobe anywhere on the bustling street.

Then a woman stood from where she'd been sitting on the stairs of the pizza shop, and his heart two-stepped. What in the actual hell?

This woman was definitely Annie. The birthmark above the left corner of her upper lip and striking hazel eyes, so much like her brother's, were unmistakable. But this Annie's lace top pushed up her breasts and bared her abdomen. Her black skirt showed more leg than a Radio City Rockette, and her tall black boots had every passing male licking his lips.

This Annie was about to get an earful.

He left his Audi, closed the distance between them swiftly, and removed his suit jacket, swinging it around her. He steered her toward his car, away from the man who'd just winked at him knowingly. Goddamn creeps in this city.

Annie dug her heels into the sidewalk, nearly toppling them both. "Aggressive much, Wes? Are you trying to break my legs?"

"I'm trying to get you into my car before someone offers you a key to a room that rents by the hour."

She shoved him and his jacket off. "Are you for real?"

Was she trying to give him a coronary? "Since when do you dress like...this?" He motioned to her skimpy outfit, then sneered at a preppy jerk giving her the once-over. "If you value your face, buddy, keep it pointed ahead."

The idiot snickered and walked on. Weston tried to shield Annie with his body.

She tipped her head back and sighed. "You are such an overbearing asshole sometimes."

Honestly, this girl. He hadn't driven through ungodly traffic, instead of poring over this merger disaster, for the pure joy of it.

"If my memory serves me correctly, and it usually does, you're the one who called me. Something about an emergency."

Her face turned serious. "I was dying for one of those amazing gyros from that place around the block, but when I got to the restaurant I realized I'd snatched my keys but forgot my purse. And I *may* have left those keys in their bathroom and now they're gone. Since there's the teeny, tiny issue of me being late on rent, I can't speak to my landlord today, and when I explained my situation to the nice man waiting for his gyro, he loaned me his phone so I could call you. Small mercies, right? So I'll have enough cash for rent after tonight's shift, *but* I'm cashless and cardless until then and can't be late for my new job, so we really need to get a move on. I'll also need to borrow your key to my place."

He counted to five, making sure her verbal deluge had ended. Annie had three settings: Chatty Cathy, sarcastic comedienne, and pit bull. "What do you mean you're late on rent?"

"It's nothing. Just a small setback. All will be well tomorrow."

"This isn't a small setback. This is irresponsibility."

She planted her hands her hips. "I don't need you to lecture me, Wes."

"No. You need me to rescue you."

She added an eye roll to her confrontational pose. "I only called you because everyone else I know has a real job."

Well, wasn't that the cherry on this shit-flavored day. "Did you hit your head this morning? Is there some kind of frontal lobe damage I should be aware of?"

It would explain the wardrobe malfunction and the asinine comment. Annie knew Weston clocked upwards of eighty hours of work a week. She was well aware he ate, drank, and breathed his job. Aside from fitting in hours at his home gym, squeezing in dinner with her every couple of weeks, and the evening activities she'd never know about, his life revolved around Aldrich Pharma.

She sassed out her hip, a move that hiked her miniskirt farther up her thigh. A bike messenger whistled at her. Weston gave him the finger as the moron plowed into a parked car.

"Let's dissect this, shall we?" Annie said, oblivious to the male chaos she was creating. "Did you have to tell someone, a boss for instance, you had to leave work?"

He glared at her, and she smirked.

"Are you worried," she went on, smug as a Cheshire cat, "you might get in trouble for sneaking off? Be given a warning? Lose your job?"

He curled his lip at the implication. Just because he had freedom to come and go as he pleased didn't make the demands of his job any less real. Or less stressful. He was being told to date, hopefully marry, a woman for God's sake. But there was no point explaining his responsibilities to someone who flitted from job to job, barely making rent, quitting when anything got too tough. "Don't talk about things you don't understand, *Anthea*."

"Come on, Weston Ald*rich*. The word 'rich' is in your freaking name. You don't know from real work." The pit bull unleashed.

"And this outfit you're wearing," he said, unsure why he was getting so angry, "is that for a real job? One that won't have your brother rolling over in his—"

Annie flinched, just enough for shame to silence him. Mentioning Leo was a low blow. Too low. They never outright fought. Ragged on each other, sure. Went out of their way to tease and torment. Something was different today, though—her outfit, this weird protectiveness that had him wanting to build a castle around her. With a moat. And sharks.

During the thirteen years since her brother's death, he'd watched Annie grow out of her gawky limbs and boyish figure, into this...woman. He wasn't sure when the change had fully struck him. It felt gradual, yet sudden. Expected, yet feared. Forward momentum he was powerless to control. The past year he'd found himself staring at her occasionally as she'd fuss over one of her scrapbooks, her teeth lodged into her bottom lip, T-shirt carelessly slipping off her shoulder. He'd forget himself when she'd laugh, the sound huskier than he remembered, her head tipped back and her throat open, so much easy joy in the sound.

Yeah, he'd noticed the burgeoning beauty in Anthea Ward, little sister of Leonardo Ward—*in a totally platonic way*—which meant other men had noticed, too. And here he was, tasked by her brother to ensure some idiot didn't hurt her or take advantage. Near impossible in her current outfit.

"Just...please get in the car, Squirrel. We can yell at each other in there while you tell me about your new job."

Annie didn't glower or snark back at him. "Sure," she said softly, her fierce eyes oddly downcast. A weird ache pinched the center of his chest.

2

WES'S CAR still had that fancy new-car smell, like it smelled of money. Come to think of it, everything about Wes had a distinct scent: his cologne/soap mix conjured scenes of snow-drenched pines, a roaring fire, and a cocky man wearing an extravagant smoking jacket. His stark loft apartment was almost odorless, save for hints of lemon and lavender and subtle whiffs of ostentation.

Annie clicked on her seat belt and melted into his new Audi's expensive-smelling leather. They probably stuffed hundreds into the cushioning for extra-special comfort.

"So," Wes said, his hands on the wheel, eyes dead ahead, the car still in park. "Why are you late on rent?"

She rolled her head over the headrest and faced his stern profile. "That aromatherapy course set me back."

"You told me you had money to pay for that course."

"Yeah, but there's a new craft store on 6ᵗʰ and it's like being in a scrapbooking wonderland. I mean, only a cyborg would leave there without five bags of glitter and glue, and you should have seen their bowls of buttons." Buttons so cute they'd be the envy of her online scrapbooking group. Craft supplies outweighed adulting times a million. You couldn't put a dollar value on that level of awesome.

Wes shook his head. "Are you even planning to use the aromatherapy training? Or was that as big of a waste of money as your glass blowing class?"

"Neither of those felt right in the end. Not everyone needs to have their lives planned out by age five."

He gestured wildly at the busy street. "You're stranded without a purse because you can't pay your landlord. Don't you think it's time you started acting your age? Take some responsibility for your life."

Weston's holier-than-thou attitude was long past tiresome. From his first appearance at the shelter Leo and Annie had called home, he'd walked around like he'd been better than everyone. Not a stretch back then. Wes was rich. Smart. Swoon-worthy to most girls, or certain guys—really anyone who had a faint pulse. Including a twelve-year-old Annie.

Until she'd learned his volunteer hours had been an ultimatum laid down by his mother. Until he'd hung around Leo more often, the two boys leaving her out. Until Leo had died while partying with Wes, and Wes had made it his mission to be Annie's stand-in brother.

She appreciated how hard he tried to look out for her. She really did. It was sweet when he wasn't driving her up the freaking wall. She knew he still harbored guilt for being there the night Leo died. She understood the responsibility he felt toward her. But why did he have to make her feel so inept? So young? Like a charity case he'd been saddled with.

At twenty-seven, she didn't need to be anyone's pity sister. "How about I start adulting when you quit acting like a constipated eighty-year-old."

The corner of his lips twitched. "I was going for ninety, so I must be off my game. And do you want to tell me again why you're wearing...*that*?"

She bristled at the disdain in his voice. "I don't recall telling you a first time."

"Why are you always so difficult?"

"Why are you always so tyrannical?"

"Honestly, *Anthea*."

"Honestly, *Weston*." She deepened her voice to mimic his.

He looked ready to smack his forehead on his steering wheel, and she laughed. Okay, sometimes it was fun sparring with his overbearing self. "I'm sorry. You're just too easy to rile up. I have a new bartending gig at a hot spot in the Meatpacking District. Tight clothing means more tips."

The car remained parked. He opened his mouth and closed it, hopefully thinking before spewing more judgmental nonsense. "What happened to the waitressing job at that"—he squinted through the windshield—"sports bar?"

"I got tired of smelling like chicken wings. And I may have dumped a beer on a regular who thought my butt was a hand rest."

Weston's knuckles whitened on the wheel. "You have to tell me when you need help. They can't fire you over that."

"They didn't fire me. I quit. And I can take care of myself. I've been doing it since I was fourteen."

He sighed and slumped slightly, the defeated pose so unlike Weston Aldrich, and guilt pressed on her lungs. She really had been more defensive lately, mainly with Wes. He was just so meddlesome. And infuriating. Unbelievably controlling. The way he'd sneered at her clothes hadn't helped. She didn't like her outfit much more than him. Not because it was revealing. The skimpy halter-skirt combo was typical clubbing attire, which made her think of carefree kids dancing to a DJ's beats, which made her think of Leo, which made her think about the approaching anniversary of his death, which made her sad and crabby.

"Can we start driving so I'm not late for my new job?" she asked as she tugged down her skirt.

His eyes flicked to her thighs, then quickly away. Without replying, he turned the ignition and waited for a break in traffic.

Wes didn't tease her about starting yet another job as he drove. She didn't taunt him about his one-dimensional life, which revolved around work, work, and more work. He seemed stuck in his head, the tight clench of his jaw hinting at an internal yelling match. About her? His job? There was no reading Weston's mind. Especially when she was eyeball deep in her own frustrations.

This new job wasn't going to be much better than her last one. She would reek of booze and sweat instead of chicken wings and beer. Men would make sloppy advances. Her feet would hurt from hustling all night. She knew these jobs didn't utilize her creative energy, as Wes never failed to mention. What he didn't know was she had a plan.

And a piano.

The eight hundred dollar used Yamaha upright would be all hers tomorrow. She was excited and nervous, but mostly nervous. Piano had been Leo's thing: learning to play, then learning bass, then drums, then tinkering with DJ mixers and controllers, anything that made sound, spending hours in his high school's music room and music stores, earphones on, boasting that he'd be a huge DJ someday. He'd even found a rec center with a piano. They'd never complained when Leo used it to teach Annie.

She hadn't touched a keyboard since the night Leo died.

Last month, everything had changed.

A couple of glasses of wine in her system, she'd sauntered

into the subway station and could have sworn she'd heard Leo playing. It hadn't been him, obviously. But the sound had drawn her, along with the strangest urge to play. Ten dollars placed in the busker's hat, she'd asked if she could tickle his ivories.

"You can tickle anything of mine you like," he'd said with a friendly wink. He'd stepped back while fanning his hand toward his electric keyboard, and she'd taken what had felt like her first breath in thirteen years.

She had played. Couldn't believe she remembered how. Leo had told her she'd been a natural. She *had* felt something special as a twelve-year-old, closing her eyes, the cold-firm press of the keys beneath her fingers, the vibration traveling up her wrists as the notes spilled from her hands. All to impress her big brother. For two years they'd played as often as possible, her skills surprising even Leo. That same rush had blindsided her last month, the addictive pull to play, be closer to her brother.

Now she owned a piano that would be delivered tomorrow. She planned to practice until she could teach beginners the way Leo had taught her. What she wouldn't do was tell Wes craft supplies hadn't been the only purchase she'd made in lieu of paying rent. If he told her teaching piano was yet another dead-end job, it would cut deep. She didn't want to defend her choice or put into words how she thought Leo would hear her if she played. She wasn't sure why it had taken her thirteen years to touch a piano again.

"I thought you said you were worried about being late," Wes said.

Annie looked out the window. She hadn't noticed Wes pull over, but they were at her newest gig. A job that would pay the bills (and cover emergency craft-shop purchases) while her new plans marinated.

She unclicked her seat belt. Wes did the same. Which was odd. When he opened his door and his intentions sank in, she reached over him and yanked his door shut. "What do you think you're doing?"

He cast a derisive glance at the bar. "I'm not letting you walk in there on your own."

Imogen's did look seedy in the light of day. Cigarettes and garbage littered the sidewalk. Buildings were in various states of decay, this section of the Meatpacking District less gentrified. Still nicer than the streets she'd once called home. She could handle herself anywhere, anytime. What she couldn't handle was explaining to her coworkers that she'd needed a chaperone her first day. "You're not *letting* me do anything. I'm doing this on my own because I'm a functioning adult who doesn't need an escort."

"A functioning adult wouldn't be locked out of her apartment."

Oh, man, he was cruising for a bruising.

His phone rang from the center console, and Duncan's name flashed on the screen. She'd met the dashing blond at last year's company Christmas party. Wes invited her to the event every year. After a handful, she'd begun declining.

The Aldrich Pharma staff knew Wes had met her while volunteering at a shelter, doing his Good Samaritan work. They'd seen Leo's picture on his desk. Their pitying looks made her feel like she was Wes's philanthropic project. Last year, free booze and food had outweighed her pride, and Duncan had introduced himself with a kiss to her hand, flirtation oozing through his bedroom voice. Wes had warned her to stay away from him *after* dragging Duncan away by the elbow. If Wes wanted to unleash his inner control freak, she'd have to fight dirty.

She grabbed Wes's ringing phone and hit Talk. "Hey,

Duncan! It's me, Annie. We met at the Aldrich Pharma Christmas bash."

"Must be my lucky day," Duncan said, his cheerful voice a contrast to Wes's scathing look. "To what do I owe the honor?" Duncan asked.

"I'm with Wes and your name popped up on his phone. I remembered how nice it was chatting with you, and I simply couldn't resist answering."

Scowling, Wes grabbed for the phone. She dodged the control freak, but his hand swiped her boob, and he pulled back, as though horrified. He didn't try again, and a strange tingling spread up her neck. And down her thighs.

The tight space suddenly felt tighter.

"Anyway," she said, slightly off balance, "I need to head into work, but it was nice hearing your voice again."

"The pleasure was all mine. You sound as pretty as I remember."

She laughed effusively, loudly, giving her best flirty girl impression, then she shoved the phone at Wes. "Thanks for the lift, *Weston*. I can take it from here."

He looked about to lace into her, but he pulled out his keys and wallet and tried to hand her a wad of cash. "Use this for a cab home. Please don't take the subway at night. And if you need my help with rent, call."

He must really think she was still fourteen. She took his copy of her key and grabbed the cash. "I'll make enough tips to get home on my own, but there's someone who could use this. Say goodbye to Duncan for me," she called loudly, hoping Duncan would hear. Wes's cheeks turned her favorite shade of furious.

She shimmied out of the car, twisting awkwardly to avoid flashing Wes or the homeless man on the street corner. She closed the door as Wes barked, "Annie is *off*-limits," into the phone.

Pleased with her ability to ruffle the unrufflable Weston Aldrich, Annie walked over to the homeless man, crouched in front of him, and gave him Weston's cash. "I hope you have a good night."

She made eye contact with him until he gave her a lopsided grin. His expression was loose and sloppy, but it was a smile nonetheless. When living on the street, Annie hadn't understood why people wouldn't look at her. Fear. Guilt. Disgust. The only thing worse than disdain had been invisibility.

"*Annie*," Wes called from the car, using his *be careful* tone. He often warned her away from homeless people. Told her not everyone was safe. Then he'd drop a fifty into someone's outstretched hand, covering her meager one or five.

She stood and blew Wes a kiss, then pushed into Imogen's. The dank bar felt cavernous and smelled slightly sour, the floor so scuffed it looked like a Jackson Pollock painting. The high-top tables had seen better days, and the two pool tables and small stage at the back were a little worse for wear. Imogen's rep as a "new" hot spot seemed suspect.

A beautiful Korean woman with a pixie-cut, who looked too young to work at a bar, was scanning bottles of alcohol and writing on a clipboard. When she noticed Annie, she waved. "I'm Vivian. You must be the new girl."

"That would be me—Annie. Just tell me what needs doing, and it's done."

Eight hours later Annie's predictions had come true. She was sweaty, she smelled of booze, her feet ached, and one slurring man had told her she had nice eyes, while staring at her boobs. Surprisingly, the "hot spot" label had also proved accurate. Dim lighting, electro jazz tunes, and a boisterous mid-twenties crowd had transformed Imogen's from shabby to chic. Aside from her sore feet and less-than appealing smell, she felt energized.

Annie slid a whiskey sour to a tattooed woman along the bar.

Vivian caught Annie's eye. "Selma said we can punch out at midnight." She raised her voice over the music, dancing as she spoke. "The later shift will close."

"You won't hear me complaining." Annie collected cash from her customer, grooving along with Vivian, and pocketed her tip. "Is it always this busy?" Thursdays at her last job had been hit or miss.

Vivian scanned the animated room. "Pretty much. Weekends are even better. And they'll be more bearable with you here. The guy you replaced was slow as a slug."

"Never hire a man to do a woman's job."

"Truth." Vivian shook her hips as she gathered dirty shot glasses. "You should come out tonight. There's a killer DJ playing a late-night set at a new Brooklyn joint."

At the word *DJ*, queasiness curdled Annie's stomach. "I don't have ID. It's locked in my apartment."

"Not an issue. I know the bouncer."

So much for an easy out.

Besides playing piano, Annie hadn't visited a club or watched a DJ in thirteen years. Not difficult during her late teens, but it had been a concerted effort since turning twenty-one. She interacted online in music forums, but visiting a club reminded her too much of Leo's death.

She should politely decline Vivian's offer, head home, take a long bath, rest her sore feet. Get some sleep so she could be fresh and bright for tomorrow's piano delivery, *after* paying her landlord this month's rent. But she was wired from her shift, and buying that piano had been about feeling more connected to her brother. Walking into a club would be hard. Listening to the music live could trigger memories she tried to forget.

It could also be like that moment her fingers had touched the busker's piano, filling her up in unexpected ways.

"Count me in," she told Vivian quickly.

"Oh, fun!" Vivian clapped. "I'm meeting a date. It'll be nice not to go alone."

"As long as you're sure I won't be a third wheel."

"It's a first date, so you'll be doing me a favor. We'll come up with a save-me-before-I-die signal."

"You're going to a club at one a.m. for a first date?" Annie's dates had generally been mundane affairs at restaurants and quiet pubs. Except that one time she'd been dragged to an underground poker game and the cops had raided the place. Calling Wes to bail her out of jail had almost been amusing. The color of his cheeks had been more livid than furious that night.

Vivian ran her hands along her black bustier, her suctioned leather pants and stilettos making Annie's skirt and high boots look matronly. "Clubs mean I can dress to impress, and if she can't hack the scene, she's not for me."

Annie hadn't expected the "she" but loved that Vivian owned who she was, down to her partier status and the type of woman she wanted to date. Annie had no clue who she wanted to date, or if she had a type. Of her two boyfriends, one had been nice and quiet, most of their evenings spent watching movies on the couch, often falling asleep there. The other had been loud and fun, snapping social media photos every chance he'd gotten, dragging her to parties and double dates, rarely spending time alone with her.

Both had gotten on her nerves around month three.

"Meet me out front in fifteen," Vivian said.

Annie nodded and worked to clean her area, moving,

wiping, trying not to think too hard about how it would feel walking into a club. Already, though, images of Leo were sneaking up on her. She may not have been there the night he'd been shot, but that didn't keep her imagination from conjuring horrifying images: blood splatter, strangled screams, lifeless eyes.

She blinked hard.

Hopefully this outing wasn't a horrible idea. Hopefully it wouldn't end with a wallow session on her floral couch as she drowned her sadness in salt and vinegar chips while scrapbooking until her fingers hurt.

3

THE CLUB'S atmosphere was like plugging Annie's fingers into a light socket. Energy blasted from the speakers. Tons of it. A massive heartbeat wrapping her in its intensity as club goers bopped and grinned. A wave of sorrow didn't drag her under as she'd expected. Instead the deep bass pounded in her chest, awakening memories of Leo's smile and roaring laugh and killer dance moves.

The potency built as she followed Vivian through the standing-room-only space. Lights flashed. They got jostled a few times before they found the bar.

"This place is nuts," she yelled to Vivian.

"Wait until you hear the last DJ. He goes by Falcon and will blow your mind. If it gets wild and we get separated, let's meet at the exit at two thirty." Vivian shook her shoulders to the beat while trying to flag a bartender. Fat chance with this crush of people. "So, boyfriend? Girlfriend? Single?" Vivian asked.

"Would be a boyfriend, but very single. If I don't break my dry spell, my body might petrify."

"That's an appetizing visual." Vivian wrinkled her nose.

"If we lived in Egyptian times, they'd mummify my deprived body and pull out my brains through my nose with a hook."

Vivian looked mildly horrified, then she smiled. "If my date sucks, that'll be our signal."

"You want me to have my brains yanked out with a hook?"

"Although that would be fascinating, no. But you could pretend your hand's a hook and jab at your nose." She mimed the hook-nose move.

"Are you trying to make me look like an idiot?"

"Busted." She grinned. "But we need to do something about this catastrophic dry spell. Wouldn't want you shriveling up and rotting in the middle of a shift. And stay on the lookout for a half-Korean blond-haired woman in a red shirt. I told Sarah to meet me by the bar."

Annie was tall enough in her high boots to scan the club for Vivian's date. No luck, but talk of her dry spell made her think of the hand-boob incident in Wes's car, and the strange tingle she'd felt afterward. Her lack of male company was clearly an issue. She was so deprived, even Wes, a man who treated her like a child, could spark her libido with nothing but an accidental brush.

Vivian wrangled them a couple of bright blue drinks, and they clinked glasses.

"Did you grow up in New York?" Vivian asked.

Annie sipped her drink, which was stronger than expected, delaying her reply. Aside from casual work colleagues, most of Annie's friends were online: her scrapbooking group, the members of her BOOMpop music app, her Vintage Anonymous forum. In the online world, no one knew her mother had died with a needle in her arm, or that her alcoholic father had tucked tail and run before she'd been born. They didn't know Leo had bribed homeless people to pretend to be their parents while moving from shelter to shelter, determined to stay together and keep them out of the foster system. In that world, Leo hadn't been killed in a random club shooting.

"Yeah," she shouted to Vivian, "I grew up here." She pointed to her drink. "This is awesome. What do they call it?"

They talked about their favorite cocktails until Vivian's date arrived, and Annie gave herself a mental high-five for redirecting their conversation away from personal topics. If she could turn that skill into a job, money would be a non-issue.

Sarah and Vivian leaned close to talk over the noise, clearly comfortable with their proximity. Where Vivian was slim and petite, Sarah was curvier and tall with long blond hair pulled into a sleek ponytail. She was also a private detective.

"Does that mean you did a background check on Vivian before tonight?" Annie asked.

Sarah gave Vivian the once-over. "That happens after a couple dates. No point wasting my time if things fall flat."

Vivian struck a sexy pose and fluttered her eyelashes. "Is that a challenge?"

The duo moved closer together, talking too low for Annie to hear over the electronic tunes pumping from the stage. Annie caught Vivian's eye from behind Sarah and mimed picking her nose with a hooked finger. Vivian laughed and shook her head. Looked like the date was off to a good start.

Preferring not to intrude, she people watched. The eclectic crowd was dressed in everything from skimpy dresses to T-shirts and jeans. All music lovers, closing their eyes and moving to the infectious beat. The music drifted from techno to cosmic to disco funk. Some dancers looked high as a kite, or drunk, or both, but the atmosphere was positive and upbeat. She ordered and finished a second drink while dancing quietly in her own little spot.

Vivian caught her eye, tapped her watch and mouthed *two*

thirty, then disappeared with Sarah to an upstairs section. They would meet at the exit as planned, and Annie kind of liked being in the club alone, free to dance and drink, no personal questions asked.

After a while, the neon lights dimmed. A hush spread through the crowd, followed by a few whistles. When a figure moved onto the stage, cheers exploded.

It was too dark to see much detail, but the guy looked tall, wearing some kind of feathered mask. Maybe he was the last DJ, Falcon, starting his set—the one Vivian had wanted to hear. More random whistles. Shouts echoed through the club. He didn't engage with the audience, just stood there, statue still. His mysterious aura electrified the crowd even more, and Annie leaned forward, maneuvering slightly to get a better view, anticipation building in her chest.

Then a violin crooned.

Slow and lush, the quivering melody flowed through the speakers, swelling. A contrast to the heavy bass from before, the notes full of sorrow and hope, peace and agitation. A flash of light and burst of symphony followed, there then gone.

More violin hummed, its rhythm and speed building. Another flash, brighter with a blast of sound, fragments feeding off one another, invigorating the packed room. Annie couldn't quite catch the beat, but its elusive quality was mesmerizing, the need to chase it impossible to ignore. Her hips moved and her chest popped, finding the beat, losing it, getting closer. Everyone in the club was feeling it, too, the growing crescendo about to erupt.

Then *bam*.

A solid beat blended with the classical music. The lights turned high, and the bodies around her jumped. People waved glow sticks. Many held water bottles, high on more than the music. The song had a dark-wave vibe with electro pop mixed in. She started jumping, too, so much joy spilling through her wide smile.

She had avoided clubs so long for fear of missing Leo too much or being forced to envision his death, but all she could think about was how much he'd have loved this. *She* loved this, the blend of old and new, the raw energy—enough wattage to send her to the moon.

She moved closer to the stage, danced next to two women, who seemed happy to have her join them. Anonymous. Just people out for a good time. The lights were dim, occasionally flashing, but bright enough to better make out the DJ. His mysterious status was still high. He wore dark jeans and a black long-sleeved shirt. An elaborate mask covered his face—the features of a wild bird in glittery turquoise, yellows, and greens. Only his mouth and lower jaw were visible. He danced as he hovered over the controller, using hand signals to slow the crowd down and speed them up.

A new hypnotic beat chased the first, blending, teasing, then taking over.

The beat match.

She remembered Leo explaining that term. Manipulating the beats, stretching or shifting one song until it perfectly synchronized with another. She moved closer to the stage, danced harder, absorbed the heat wrapping her in happiness. A trickle of sweat slid down her back. The crowd fed off every note shaking the floors.

This DJ was the real deal, and she was captivated.

WESTON LAID down the next track, built the electricity in the room, just him and his beats feeding the frenzy. The club was perfection tonight, exactly what Weston needed. Upbeat. No bullshit or drama.

And it was a packed house.

His DJ gigs the past few months had gotten busier, momentum growing along with his fan base. Aldrich Pharma was a functioning beast of its own, fifty thousand employees who lived on his family's dime, many supporting others through their business. That corporation was in his blood. His mind needed the intellectual chess match it provided. DJing provided something different.

"If you tune out the rest of the world," his mother had said when he'd work too hard at school, barely going out, "you'll end up alone. Detached from the real world. If you don't let yourself care about others, you'll only live half a life."

Like your father, she hadn't said, but he'd later understood the implication. She hadn't wanted Weston to turn out cold and calculating, driven solely by financial success.

No mistake about it, Weston was driven by ambition, but he'd volunteered at soup kitchens and shelters, initially at his mother's insistence, later because it felt good. Making a difference had made *him* feel like the best version of himself, and meeting Leo was no small twist of fate. From that first day, doing dishes together, laughing as Weston's fancy clothes had gotten drenched in sudsy water, their friendship had been easy. Authentic and real. Nothing like the preening between his private school buddies, who cared more about showing off than looking out for one another.

Leo had introduced Weston to the underground music scene, the two of them, fake IDs in hand, walking into clubs, hitting on girls too old for them, and dreaming of being on stage.

All of it shattered one fateful night.

Weston still had music, even if he was distracted tonight. He *was* the music, he reminded himself. The center of this writhing organ, pumping life into the room, giving people an escape for the length of a song, an hour, a night to feel nothing but the beat. It wasn't as altruistic as working the soup-kitchen line, his philanthropic efforts these days doled out through dollars spent. But he loved working the room and, more important, he owed a debt: if Leo couldn't live his dream, Weston would live it for them both.

He moved as he mixed, tried not to think about the mess with Karim's daughter, or Annie's latest antics: blowing off paying her rent, her barely-there outfit, that stunt with Duncan. He particularly didn't want to think about how close they'd gotten while fumbling for his phone. The tiniest brush against her breast. Weston's sudden urge to feel more.

So wrong. Too wrong to even contemplate.

He shook his head, the slight itch of his mask a reminder he wasn't at some club for his own enjoyment. He had a job to do, and a crowd to please.

He got into the rhythm, felt a punch of adrenaline as he scoped the floor. The scene was riled. Already shaking the walls. Instead of threading in mellower songs, longer sections that would gradually build, he combined four or five tracks into one, taking dancers on a journey, signaling them to get lower or jump higher with the beats and his hands, tipping the scales into a natural euphoria. Not so natural for many club kids, but for him, always.

He conducted the crush of people. Pushed. Pulled. Elevated. A handful wore T-shirts printed with "Freed by the Falcon" on the front. He wasn't sure who'd initiated the pseudo merchandise. He'd noticed it two months ago, one girl dancing near his stage. Then a couple here, a few there, an organic growth of a brand he hadn't initiated.

Freed by the Falcon.

Leo would have loved it.

Weston gave them what they craved, his music exploding from the speakers. His blood pumped in time to the bass. Humidity hung in the dense air. He let his gaze skim the floor, his attention locking on various dancers. Connection was key, making them feel part of his show. Weston nodded at a purple-haired dude, adjusted the frequency and volume, added a kick of reverb, and lifted the background drums. The kid punched the air to the beat.

Weston's gaze slid to the left...and air jammed in his lungs.

Someone who looked a hell of a lot like Annie was dancing. Not just dancing. She was glowing, her arms up, head tilted back, hips and upper body swaying suggestively.

His blood pumped harder. Yeah, it was definitely her, still in that skimpy outfit. He glared at the group around her. Was she on a date? At this hour? Was some dude hoping he'd score big? But she was dancing on her own mainly, occasionally interacting with others on the floor. She didn't seem to be with anyone specific.

Was she alone? At a late-night club, hoping for a hookup?

Agitation edged his movements. Frustration fogged his focus. If he hadn't launched into a new track, he'd have fumbled the transition.

He kept one eye on her and one on his equipment, berating himself for the possessiveness firing in his gut. Annie was twenty-seven. She wasn't the kid he'd promised to watch over. She was an adult free to party and date. Seeing her out and happy shouldn't unbalance him like this. But clubs were unpredictable. All it took was one grudge, one weapon, and all hell could break loose. Or a man could think he was entitled to something that wasn't his.

A new urge Weston couldn't name drove him. He tested out a new song, a swell of pleasure building when she picked up the rhythm, a secret smile on her face like she knew he'd chosen the song for her. She couldn't know. No one ever could or would.

He used a burner phone for all DJ business. He'd hired a roadie anonymously. Hank set up and stored his equipment for a generous fee. Weston showed up minutes before gigs, wearing his mask, a black outfit, casual shoes, and a different cologne, disguised down to his smell. He gave strict instructions limiting interaction and bailed the second his set finished. In and out. No talking to the audience. No talking to fans. He wasn't doing it for personal glory.

He was doing it for Leo.

Annie didn't know Weston was the man controlling her body now, but he knew he was the one making her move like that, and a strange warmth filled his chest. Her neck glistened with sweat. Her curves moved with his mix.

He played the rest of his set for her, and for Leo. Always for Leo. He'd love seeing his sister like this, truly happy, even with him gone. One song, then another. Weston was on fire. Annie was glorious. It was his best gig, hands down.

With his last note reverberating in the air, the crowd went nuts, and he pumped his fist for his screaming fans, stealing one last glance at her. She seemed to be trying to catch his attention, mouthing something he couldn't make out. For one freaked out second, he wondered if she recognized him, but it was impossible.

He strutted off the stage. A couple of guys congratulated him, but most knew to stay away. His disappearing acts didn't seem to hurt his bookings. If anything, being eccentric and mysterious upped his appeal.

He pushed out the back exit and almost smacked into a small group.

"That show was sick." A guy waved, moving to block

Weston's path. He was thin as a beanstalk but taller than Weston. One of the others wore a Freed by the Falcon T-shirt. They all started badgering him for autographs.

This had never happened before. He'd leisurely grab a cab after a show, remove his mask and get dropped off a few blocks from his condo. Not so easy tonight.

He pressed his fingers to his lips, then to his heart. Hopefully a sign these fans would understand as *thank you*. Then he busted into a run.

Footfalls trailed him, but not for long. "Love you, man!" one of them called.

At least they didn't sound angry.

He hailed a cab and hopped in.

"Costume party?" the cabbie asked once they were on their way.

Weston adjusted his mask, but didn't take it off. "Something like that."

"The wife and I went to a masquerade party once. Crazy thing one Halloween. Not my scene, but the wife loved it. Said she liked pretending to be someone else. Kind of talked different that night, too. More outgoing and stuff." The cabbie glanced at him in his rearview mirror. "You find that? That you're, I don't know—more open with that thing on?"

"It definitely gives you freedom to do things you wouldn't normally do." Like live a secret double life.

"Guess it's a rush for some folks."

Not exactly how Weston would describe his live sets. Sure, DJing pumped him with adrenaline, but the outlet served a purpose. Clubs paid him through online transfers to a numbered account. The money he made got funneled into campaigns that pushed for stronger gun control, in memory of Leo. All of it for Leo. Weston owed that guy everything. Including his life. But, lately, DJing the way Leo had imagined and tossing money at charities hadn't felt like enough. Hands-off philanthropic work wasn't the same as working in a soup kitchen, touching people directly.

For now he'd have to rethink his transportation. Maybe hire a personal driver. Avoid future fan ambushes. Get picked up and dropped off discreetly. *Discreet* being the operative word. One whiff of his evening activities and he'd be ousted from his family business. No one would trust a Chief Operating Officer who DJed at night, a scene well known for drugs and bad decisions. Even though he was there for the music, not the partying, his credibility would nose-dive. His father would be the first to cut him loose.

Weston closed his eyes for the rest of the ride.

When he finally made it home, he tossed his bag on his sectional and pounded back a glass of water. He plunked his cup down on the concrete counter. The resounding silence in his loft apartment made his ears ring. The modernized industrial space felt sparser than usual, the salvaged brick walls barer, even though he'd recently acquired an exquisite Trudy Benson painting. The space was pristine and timeless; an architectural masterpiece, the ceiling soaring three stories high.

Over the ringing quiet, all he heard was Annie her first time in the place, saying, "It's stunning and funky. It just feels more like a museum than a home."

He rubbed his sternum and headed to his Falcon Cave, a name Leo would have loved. The guy had been obsessed with Batman: the comics, the movies, the gadgets, how a regular guy could be a superhero without powers. Weston had razzed him about it. Now he moonlighted as Falcon and spent hours in his Falcon Cave, aka his sound room.

He unlocked his studio, grabbed his laptop, and sank into the leather couch. He surfed through music sites, read an article about this year's Ultra Music Festival, left a comment suggesting they put Grid Girl on the main stage—that woman dropped a serious beat. He browsed his latest research projections afterward, his mind flipping from music to pharmaceuticals and back on a dime.

Switching between two lives was exhausting at times, but multitasking was *his* superpower. What he didn't want was for his mind to keep drifting to Annie, her relaxed body as she'd danced to his beats, her hips and chest rolling, sexy as sin.

He was glad she'd enjoyed herself, but sin was the real takeaway there. There were umpteen reasons he had to box, chain, and burn his unwelcome thoughts. None of which he wanted to unpack. He needed to focus on the Biotrell merger, not his late best friend's little sister. He would ask Rosanna Farzad on a date. The move was good for business and maybe for his personal life, too. A way to squash these unwanted images of Annie.

4

ANNIE WAS HIGH. Not literally, of course. With her family history, drugs were a hard no. That music, though? It had been a hit of euphoria injected straight into her veins. She closed her apartment door, still vibrating. She was restless, wired. Even at 3:30 a.m., sleep couldn't be further from her mind. She eyed the dirty dishes in the sink, the laundry she hadn't put away, the craft supplies littering her coffee table and purple carpet.

If Wes were here, he'd take one glance at the controlled chaos and say her apartment looked like a garage sale. "How do you even find the couch?" he often asked, familiar judgment lacing his words. The same tone he'd used when criticizing tonight's wardrobe.

She could use her excess energy to tidy up. Get her place ready for tomorrow's piano delivery. *Or* she could pull out her secret Weston Aldrich scrapbook and add a new page.

Scrapbooking won out, obviously. She grabbed her laptop and clicked on the most serious, stuck-up, holier-than-thou photo of Wes she could find. Once the grim picture printed, she maneuvered her secret book from below her floral couch.

She'd started this treasure on her sixteenth birthday. That fateful day, she'd been invited to a Lil Wayne concert and had shared the awesome news with Wes while out to lunch, too excited to keep it bottled up. The self-righteous dictator had said, "*No.*"

He may not have been her official guardian, but he'd insinuated himself into that role. At twenty-one, he'd seemed so much older than her sixteen years, and she'd been too afraid of losing him, controlling or not, to push him away.

He'd told her she was too young to go to the concert, that it wasn't safe, droning on while looking down at her from his ivory tower, clueless to how valuable those concert tickets had been. Normally she'd have told him to screw off and gone anyway, but he'd taken it upon himself to call her friend's mother. The ticket had been given to someone who didn't have a tyrannical pseudo-brother/father controlling her life.

Thus began the Weston Aldrich secret scrapbook.

Some of his photos had been defaced with horns and mustaches, the backgrounds tastefully decorated with colored paper, butterflies, and flowers. One special page had cutouts of dog poop shoved into his mouth, with the tagline: *Weston is full of shit.*

Defacing Wes pictures had become a soothing hobby. She hummed as she cut his face from the new photo and pasted it on a fresh page. She then gave him long pink hair, a sexy dress, and thigh-high boots like the ones she'd worn tonight. She even added a sparkly purse.

The caption read: *The dress makes the man.*

Scrapbook closed and hidden, she got ready for bed. It was insanely late, or crazy early. She still wasn't tired. She was excited about the piano arriving—the idea of playing again and working toward a new job. She also kept reliving the thrill of the club, the beat moving through her as she'd danced. She wasn't sure why she'd tried to catch the DJ's attention afterward. To thank him maybe, ask him what it felt like to pilot the crowd, fill hearts with happiness and the club with intoxicating energy. Maybe to know how Leo would have felt if it had been him.

Too jazzed to stay horizontal, she picked up one of her Sudoku puzzle books. She had twenty-odd books scattered around her apartment, their various states of progress another point of contention with Wes. Every time he visited her, he'd pick one up and shake it in the air, hollering, "Why don't you finish these? You don't get points for giving up."

"Simple," she'd say, loving his irritation. "Hobbies are supposed to be enjoyable. When I get stumped, I get frustrated and probably look like you with your resting brood face. So I move on. I keep the hobby *fun*." Knowing the half-finished pages annoyed Wes was an added bonus.

He wasn't here to annoy her tonight, and the math puzzles weren't making her sleepy. She retrieved her laptop from the living room, sat on her bed, covers pulled up to her waist, as she powered up her Punchies page. She signed into her online scrapbooking group as Harley Quinn—badass comic book aliases for the win—and scanned the screen for her favorite online friend. Pegasus's icon was lit.

Harley Quinn: **Surprised you're up at this hour.**

Pegasus: **Working different shifts. Nights are days and days are nights.**

Harley Quinn: **No rest for the wicked.**

Pegasus: **Wicked as in we're super cool or perversely evil?**

Harley Quinn: **Let's go with cool.**

Pegasus: **BORING**

Harley Quinn: **Perversely evil?**

Pegasus: **Now you're just unoriginal.**

Harley Quinn: **I'm trying to remember why we're friends, but I'm coming up blank.**

Pegasus: **It's my winning personality. And my embossing skills.**

They chatted about Pegasus's new matting technique for framing her photos, but Annie's mind kept snagging on tonight's wild club, the music, how it felt like another piece of herself had clicked into place.

Harley Quinn: **What makes a person fulfilled?**

Pegasus: **Since when do we do deep thoughts?**

Harley Quinn: **Since I'm overtired and overthinking.**

Pegasus: **I hear you on overtired. As for the question, I think fulfillment is different for everyone. I'm good at my job. It fulfills me in many ways, but it's not all about financial success.**

Annie had no clue what Pegasus did for work or if Pegasus was a man or woman. She assumed woman, but like with all her online friends, they didn't ask personal questions. They talked shop and joked. Kept their interactions light and easy. Tonight, as she relived the energy in the club, the music and all the memories it had unearthed, she couldn't resist delving deeper.

Harley Quinn: **I don't mean jobwise. I'm not even sure I'm talking about fulfillment, exactly. Have you ever avoided something for a long time, but when you actually did it, you realize it's not as scary as you thought it would be?**

Pegasus: **Are we talking about laundry?**

Annie laughed while eyeing the mountain by her closet.

Harley Quinn: **Not laundry. Something bigger you thought would make you sad, but it actually made you happy. It made you realize you need more from life.**

Pegasus: **Thinking about things can be more intimidating than doing them.**

Harley Quinn: **Exactly. But this thing I did, it feels different, like a turning point. Like I've opened the door to Narnia and have to choose to stay in this life or walk into another.**

Awareness struck Annie as she wrote, just how deeply tonight's DJ had affected her. The piano purchase was one thing, but the club scene had been something else entirely. Another way to feel closer to Leo. She'd never been to clubs with him. She'd been too young, but he'd get back from a night out, glowing, full of energy, talking nonstop about how alive he felt. She finally understood. The buzz in her chest hadn't relented since she'd gotten home. She'd loved those beats, had wanted to jump into the notes and let them explode out through her limbs.

Not just as a dancer. On stage. Being the power source for everyone's joy. Doing what Leo would have done.

Pegasus: **I guess you have to decide which you'll regret more, missing the world you know or never exploring the one that scares you.**

Fear was there, all right, under the slight tremble in her fingers. Many events had defined Annie's life, most of them on the devastating side of unfortunate. Still, she didn't consider her current life bad, and her foster homes had been better than most. She'd moved through three of them, none rough or dangerous. The other foster kids had been decent enough, everyone keen to keep their heads down and power on. There had been one girl in particular she'd loved. Clementine: cute pigtails, freckled nose. Older than Annie, but so shy and scared she'd seemed younger. Annie had made it her mission to make Clementine smile, chatting about comic book characters and acting silly.

They hadn't kept in touch in the end, but Annie didn't need close friends, not with her online communities and coworkers.

She also had Wes for company, even though he could drive a teetotaler to drink. She waitressed enough to support her various hobbies and vintage clothing obsession. She dated sporadically, though not recently. She liked living in Queens, even with her tiny apartment and not-so-tiny commute. She was happy in her day-to-day life.

She just wasn't sure she was *fulfilled*.

Harley Quinn: **I think there's a side to myself I haven't explored.**

Pegasus: **The first step is recognizing it. The second is going after it, no matter what the people in your life think. If this is something you want, don't let anyone or anything stop you.**

She hadn't mentioned wanting to be a DJ. She hadn't entertained the notion before tonight, but the prospect was suddenly all she could see. Like there was no *maybe* or *we'll see* or *I could try* standing in Annie's way. Life was short. She didn't need to ponder and research to decide if DJing was a viable option. That wasn't how she rolled. She was the sort who quit jobs when they didn't suit her. She breezed through half-finished Sudoku puzzles, bought used pianos after avoiding music for thirteen years. If she was any good at DJing, she could even quit waitressing. Teach piano during the day, DJ at night.

The first step to making this a reality was taking DJ lessons, which required cash, and only one bank would never turn her away. The Bank of Weston Aldrich. But the request would have to be covert. If he caught wind of her piano and DJ plans, his head would explode, epically, loudly. He'd berate her for buying the piano and then hopping to another pursuit.

He'd call her Squirrel.

He loved that nickname, always joking that her shifting attention span was like a dog whose mind blanked at the sight of a running squirrel. This wasn't her sometimes-flighty behavior, though. In her mind, teaching piano and DJing were linked. Different expressions of the same goal. And Wes was on a need-to-know basis. He had offered to help pay her rent. She simply had to convince him she needed a few months' buffer, use the excess money for a DJ course or equipment, then pay back every penny.

Her second step was finding Falcon.

Taking a class was one thing. She wanted to learn from the best, and Falcon had set the bar high. She'd figure out where he was playing next. Flag him down or ambush him and plead her case. Ask to be his apprentice. As Pegasus suggested, she wouldn't let anyone or anything stop her.

5

"CLINICAL TESTS NEED to be pushed back." Saanvi removed her glasses and polished the lenses, her movements small and precise. "We need more time. We're not where we hoped we'd be."

If Weston had a penny for every time a research team asked for more time, he'd be able to end world hunger. "The investors need specifics, not generalities. Give me something to keep them on the hook."

Saanvi slid on her glasses. "Tell them the inhibitors are cleaving the APP proteins into fragments, limiting beta-amyloid deposits, as hoped, but results are inconsistent. We still believe in the treatment's viability."

With the millions they'd sunk into the research, she better believe in it. Not that Aldrich Pharma was alone in their unending quest to cure Alzheimer's. Every pharmaceutical company in the world had teams trying and failing to develop treatments. Except Biotrell, who was trying more than failing. Karim Farzad's company was closer to success than any of them. If their merger went through—no, *when* their merger went through—the life-altering breakthrough would belong to Aldrich Pharma. Hence tonight's date with Rosanna.

Weston left Saanvi to her work and rode the elevator to his office floor. He should be thinking about the board meeting he had to arrange, the words he'd need to finesse. Instead his mind was stuck on tonight's impending date and all he stood to lose.

He left the elevator as Duncan emerged from the conference room.

Duncan nodded. "How'd the R&D chat go?"

"Frustrating as always."

"You need me to help with damage control?" Duncan matched Weston's brisk stride.

"We might have to arrange a last-minute meeting in Chicago. Sweet talk those investors into loosening their wallets."

"Say the word, and it's done." Duncan slowed as they neared Weston's office. "I haven't heard from Annie since our nice chat. What's she been up to?"

Weston stopped dead, his chest rising and falling too fast. He knew some of what Annie had been up to the past three weeks. She'd been at all four of his last DJ shows, by herself, dancing in front of him, trying to catch his attention. An effort she didn't need to exert. When she rocked her hips and tossed her long blond hair, he couldn't look anywhere else. He just didn't know why she was so intent on *Falcon*.

The anniversary of Leo's death wasn't far. Hitting clubs and partying could be her way to forget. She wasn't a hardcore drinker, but dancing and music were powerful distractions. None of it explained her infuriating attempts to corner him after the shows.

Her persistence was troubling. Hearing her name on Duncan's lips was doubly distressing. "I thought I told you she was off-limits."

Duncan held up his hands in mock surrender. "I was asking *about* her, not asking for her hand in marriage. And, if I remember, she was the one who answered my call."

Because Annie lived to exasperate Weston. Even now, her antics were infecting his office. They were standing near Weston's secretary. Marjory hadn't glanced up from her work, but he'd guess she was eavesdropping on their conversation. She was gossip central at Aldrich Pharma.

Weston lowered his voice. "If you value your pretty face, you'll forget Annie's name."

Duncan laughed. "It's sweet how protective you are of her. Unless..." He made a show of leaning back and studying Weston's face. "Is there something going on with—"

"*No,*" Weston barked out the word, his voice ringing off the marble floors and glass-walled offices. So much for discretion. A few employees stopped mid-stride. His secretary *did* glance up, Marjory's eyebrows disappearing beneath her bangs.

Duncan looked amused as hell. "I'm glad you still spend time with her. If you won't go for drinks with me, I hope you at least talk with Annie. The merger stress must be taking its toll."

Everything was taking its toll these days. He had another gig this weekend and couldn't handle seeing Annie again. Last weekend, the urge to dance with her had blindsided him. Along with a kick of attraction. Impulses he couldn't indulge. Annie was off-limits, and she could never know he was Falcon. Weston also had another woman to wine and dine.

He had to find a way to keep Annie busy, away from his shows.

Away from Duncan.

"Like I said," he told his executive assistant, "I suggest you forget Annie's name."

"As you wish." Duncan winked, purposely antagonizing him.

Weston glared at the man's back as he walked away.

Marjory poked her head around her computer. "You make it too easy."

Weston slid his scowl to his secretary. "I make what too easy?"

His disgruntled tone was far from pleasant, but she stared back, placid as ever. "You'll know when you know," was all she said.

Infuriatingly typical. The fifty-three-year-old woman had answered to Victor S. Aldrich before working for Weston. She had been present for most of their personal and professional highs and lows, often stepping in when others turned a blind eye. Marjory had been the one to insist Weston seek counseling following Leo and his mother's deaths. The feisty woman had faced his father and said, "He goes or I quit."

It took more than one hard look to fluster Marjory Edelstein, and Weston hated how she always seemed to know something he didn't. "Shouldn't you be working right now?"

She held his gaze while typing. "I never stopped."

Infuriatingly typical.

Weston tried to forget Duncan's impish smirk and Marjory's cryptic comment as he closed his office door and exhaled.

Annie was a big girl. She'd always been able to handle herself and would never date a guy like Duncan. The bigger issue was her obsession with his Falcon alter ego. He couldn't avoid her during a set, and giving her the slip afterward was getting tricky. That left ensuring she never showed up, something he'd deal with before his next gig. Tonight was all about winning over Karim Farzad's daughter, hopefully an easier task than avoiding his late best friend's little sister.

As it turned out, dating Rosanna was as tedious as avoiding Annie. Weston cleared his throat—a feeble attempt to draw Rosanna's attention away from the phone glued to her hand. "Our waiter wants to know if you'd like dessert or coffee."

She peeled her eyes off her device, casting a derisive glance at their patient waiter and her impatient date. "Coffee. Black." She returned to texting or tweeting or whatever it was self-obsessed women did.

She'd paid more attention to her phone than Weston all night, blatantly ignoring him at times. She hadn't smiled once. Since she'd agreed to this setup, her rudeness made no sense.

"An espresso for me, thank you," he told the waiter *kindly*.

The man gave Weston a pitying look as he left, and Weston's temper flared. "I know tonight's date wasn't our idea, but you could at least make an effort. Put your phone down for half a second."

Rosanna's dark eyes shot up, her hands still clutching her precious device. "Talk to me once you've lived under my father's thumb for a while. Until then, I suggest you keep your thoughts to yourself."

An absolute treasure, this one. "And you think my father's all hearts and rainbows? You think you're the only person whose life isn't perfect?" If she'd walked a day in Annie's shoes growing up, she'd be shaking in a corner.

Rosanna rolled her eyes. "What I'm saying is I'm my own person. I like my alcohol hard, my men dangerous, and my parties loud. Monogamy isn't my game plan, and neither is dating a trust-fund boy who's sucking up to my father."

"So why'd you agree to this date?"

Her narrow shoulders sagged slightly, her gaze flitting as though people might listen in. Not a stretch. Rosanna was beautiful and notorious. He hadn't realized how in-the-news she was until he'd googled her. Her pictures were splashed on tabloids and gossip blogs. Tonight, the second she'd walked into the restaurant, people had pointed and whispered. It could be her dark hair flowing enticingly around her shoulders, the deep-V plunging down the front and back of her pink mini-dress. With what he'd researched, odds were these gawkers were after juicy gossip.

"I owe my father money for an...incident," she said. "But I'm thinking I'd rather be in debt than do this." She gestured vaguely between them.

Her open distaste for him wasn't subtle, but parental blackmail was something concrete he could handle. "How much do you owe him?"

She leaned into her chair and re-crossed her legs, her phone momentarily forgotten. "One hundred million dollars," she said smugly. Like she was proud of the astronomical amount, no hint of joking on her face.

Weston tried not to cough up his sip of wine. "What the hell did you do?"

"I threw a party on his yacht, which is now at the bottom of the Atlantic."

"You sank his yacht?" She was more off the rails than he'd thought.

She shrugged. "It was an epic party."

Weston looked at this unapologetic woman, who kind of hated him and didn't give a damn about consequences, and he laughed. Under his breath at first, then harder, covering his face with his hand as he shook. The only person who made him laugh like this was Annie when she danced around her chaotic apartment singing into her hair brush, trying to loosen him up.

This was a different kind of laughter—defeated, tired.

By the time he recovered, Rosanna had her elbows on the white tablecloth, her lips quirked into a half-smile. Her phone was face-down on the table. "I guess you won't be offering to pay my debt."

He scrubbed his hand over his mouth as their waiter returned with their coffees. Paying off that monstrous screw-up was a hard no, and nothing about Rosanna would be easy. But she was in a pickle, as was he.

"Why haven't I read about the incident?" Weston asked.

She traced the lip of her mug. "No one was hurt, and my father called in some favors. Then he called you."

"Actually, he didn't call me. He called *my* father. It seems we're both pawns in their game." It was Weston's game as much as his father's, but the softening of Rosanna's mouth meant he'd said the right thing. "Can I make a suggestion?"

She blew on her coffee, took a sip, then licked her lips. "Depends on the suggestion."

"How much do you know about your father's business plans?"

"I know he wants to retire in the next few years and has a tentative merger set with your company."

"That he does, and everything was going full-steam ahead, until you, apparently, sank his yacht." He held up a hand as Rosanna shot him a scathing look. "Problem is your father's entertaining another offer. I'm not sure if you've heard of DLP?"

"Davis-Lane Pharmaceuticals." She watched him intently now, leaning slightly forward, a spark in her eyes. Another tidbit he'd learned while googling Rosanna Farzad: she'd built her cosmetics company from the ground up. With her father's money likely, but she helmed the growing business—avant-garde makeup geared toward bold men and women. Her accolades proved Rosanna was as shrewd as her father, her wild ways notwithstanding.

"You may not want to date me," Weston said, "but I can assure you Aldrich Pharma is a business built on integrity. If we make promises, we keep them, which includes keeping Biotrell's employees on our payroll. DLP has offered the same, but I've seen them break agreements. They also have a reputation for underhanded dealings."

"That's all well and good, but I have no intention of settling down and living behind a white picket fence for a business deal."

"What if we make our own deal?"

She straightened on her seat and gave her hair a flirty flip. "I'm listening."

"We pretend to date. Make sure we're seen together enough to make it believable. Your wild parties would be on hold, and there could be no social media stunts, but you could still date your dangerous men, as long as you keep it quiet. After the merger's signed and your father's over your yacht stunt, we call it quits publicly."

She tapped her fingers on the table. "What if marriage to a steady guy is the only way to appease my father?"

"Marriage is off the table." A line drawn in permanent ink. "It's up to you to sell him on your changed ways. Convince the man you're happier and won't cause him more grief."

"And if my father signs with DLP?"

"Then we part ways having done what we could."

She scanned the room, brazenly making eye-contact with onlookers, who glanced away quickly. Her attention finally dragged back to him. "You seriously won't care if I date other guys behind your back?"

"It won't be behind my back if I know about it. And I'm free to do the same."

Another flash of Annie dancing caught him off-guard. It had been voyeuristic, observing her from a distance while in disguise. Her moves, the music, the secrecy—it had awakened something in him. Uncomfortable thoughts he wished hadn't surfaced, not when his track record with women was painful. There was also the small fact that he'd lied to her about how Leo had died.

Rosanna smiled genuinely for the first time all night, her natural beauty impossible to deny, *when* she wasn't obsessing over her phone. "Then, Mr. Aldrich, I think we have ourselves a deal."

He breathed easier, one step closer to finalizing this merger. Next on his list was keeping Annie away from his DJ gigs.

No matter his late nights, his daytime focus had been fine before she'd started showing up at clubs, and quitting the DJ scene wasn't an option for him. Not yet, at least. Since that cabbie had asked him about the rush of wearing a mask, he'd been thinking more about using his Falcon status to provoke change. But he'd need time to figure it out, and Annie had recently borrowed money.

Significantly more than needed for covering rent in Queens.

She was using the rest for something else. He wasn't sure to what end, and he hadn't questioned her about it. The obstinately independent Annie asking for help was a small miracle. It also meant she owed him a favor. He sipped his espresso as an idea bloomed. Not a long-term solution, but it could buy him time. Keep her away from his next gig at least. The more he spun the thought, the more ridiculous the idea seemed, but Annie was all about ridiculous and only so many things would occupy her late at night.

6

Teaching piano wasn't all roses. It was more like half-dead tulips struggling to live while sucking water from the bottom of a crusty vase. Granted, Annie's one and only client was a tone-deaf eighty-two-year-old determined to cross piano off her bucket list, not a child prodigy, but it kind of hurt her ears.

"That was lovely, Joyce," she fibbed with gusto. One tone-deaf client was still a client, and Annie was nowhere near ready for an experienced student. "You'll be playing Beethoven by next week."

Joyce patted Annie's thigh. "You don't get paid extra for lying, dear."

"Okay, not Beethoven. But your sitting position's much better. We'll work on fingering next week." Joyce raised a penciled-in eyebrow, and Annie's cheeks flamed. "I mean finger work. Hand positions. Not *fingering*, fingering. We'll work on positioning your fingers. On the keys. On the piano."

Joyce cackled, and Annie dropped her head forward. She'd just told her client they'd work on *fingering*. Thank god it had been a senior with a sense of humor, not a snarky teen.

Joyce left with a promise to return next week, but Annie's embarrassment lingered. Her dry spell must be affecting her brain, or maybe it was her lusty dreams as of late, all of them centered around a certain masked DJ.

The more out-of-reach Falcon felt, the more determined Annie had become. She was desperate to talk with him, learn from him, but she hadn't expected to develop a growing crush on the mysterious man. Some nights she'd swear he was watching her as she danced, his music sliding over her damp skin, dominating her body. She'd wonder if he was feeling this strange connection, too. Then he'd point at another guy or girl, raise the beats, and she'd feel foolish.

Of course he hadn't noticed her. She was fixated.

For the first time in her adult life, she had a *goal*.

As annoying as Wes's Squirrel nickname was, he wasn't completely off the mark. She often got bored and switched tracks. Planning and thinking ahead weren't her fortes, but this impulse felt different, purposeful. A vision of herself on stage, blasting music, her vibrations shaking the floor. She wouldn't let Falcon's elusiveness, or her hefty crush on him, throw her off. She'd even debated telling Pegasus about her plans, asking her online friend to help pin down the mysterious DJ, but that would mean breaking their fourth wall. She'd lose the easy anonymity their friendship provided.

One way or another, she'd do this on her own. She'd be Falcon's apprentice. He just didn't know it yet. She might even corner him at tonight's show.

With a quick glance at the clock, she knotted her long hair on her head and chose a patchwork purse from her collection. Wallet, phone, and sunglasses shoved inside, she hurried for the door. As pumped as she was to see Falcon play tonight, Thursdays in general had become her favorite day of the week. No waitressing to exhaust her. She practiced piano all morning, taught her one client, then headed to her DJ lesson, thanks to the Bank of Weston Aldrich.

His cash donation had paid for eight sessions. This would be session three, but it had only taken one minute with her hands on the equipment and Leo in the back of her mind to know this was what she was meant to do.

Her cell phone rang as she closed the door. At the sight of Wes's name, she almost didn't answer. He hadn't needled her about the sum of money she'd borrowed. Large to her, a drop in an ocean-sized bucket to him. Still, he'd been quick to help her out, and she felt guilty for lying about the circumstances.

She locked her door, double checking she still had her purse and wallet, then answered her phone. "Hey, Herbert."

"...Who's Herbert?"

"The eighty-year-old, constipated man on the other end of this line."

He laughed, a deep sound that made her limbs feel loose. "Well, this old man needs a favor. You have a minute to talk?"

She paused on her apartment stairs, paranoia clamping her fingers around her phone. Wes had agreed to her loan easily. So easily he could have had an ulterior motive. He wasn't the favor-asking sort. He was a planner who mostly relied on himself. "What, pray tell, might this favor be?"

"I need you to bunny sit."

She scanned the walls for a clue to decipher the odd request. All she saw was flaking white paint, a ripped Honda-for-sale flyer, and a bunch of skid marks. "Is 'bunny sit' code for some weird new-age meditation because you've spent thousands on a life coach who's promised to teach you the art of having fun, but you've realized he's a quack who looks like a bunny and you need someone to distract him while you escape? Or, oh—is it some kind of kinky sex thing?"

She almost swallowed her tongue. She and Wes didn't joke

about sex. Innuendo wasn't part of their repartee. Even worse was the sharp clench of her thighs at a sudden image: Wes hovering over her, one of his large hands braced by her head, the other...

Nope. She shook her head, unnerved. Weston was like a brother. An annoying one at that. Her steamy Falcon dreams had usurped her mind.

A strangled cough rattled through the line. "I'm talking about an actual rabbit, Squirrel. I need you to watch it for me."

"What's a rabbit-squirrel? If you've been experimenting on animals in some secret underground laboratory in your offices, I'll have no choice but to send out a bat signal and come down on your ass. You know my stance on animal testing."

The line was dead silent, but she pictured him cursing or banging his head on a wall. A better visual than him dragging his hand up...*ugh*. She blinked repeatedly.

"I have a *rabbit*," he said, the fact absurd enough to focus her uncooperative brain. "A bunny rabbit that needs watching. His name is Felix. Your name is Squirrel."

"My name isn't Squirrel, Herbert."

"Oh my god. You're impossible."

"Or amazing. I'd go with option two."

Again with that deep laugh. "I don't know why I bother with you."

Pleased with Wes's annoyance, and their quick detour away from innuendo land, she continued outside and slipped on sunglasses as the sun hit her face. "You bother because I'm the only one who doesn't kiss your designer behind. And why exactly do you have a bunny?"

"It's a neighbor's. He's heading out of town for a couple of days and asked me to look after it, but I have a last-minute meeting tonight. A dinner with an investor that will go late."

"But you hate pets."

"It's a one-time favor."

"So leave the rabbit-squirrel at home. Unless you're worried he'll chew through the cage with his mutant teeth and tear apart your pristine condo." She hoofed it down the sidewalk, dodging pedestrians, the summer breeze ruffling her lace skirt. Exhaust mingled with the smell of street meat, followed by a whiff of curry, then a blast of cinnamon goodness. The city streets were a life-sized scratch-and-sniff book.

"As amusing as you are," Wes said, "that's not the problem. This rabbit has abandonment issues. He was rescued from an abusive home and can't be left alone."

"Abandonment issues."

"That's what I said."

"And he can't be left alone?"

"Did you accidentally stab yourself in the ear while scrapbooking?"

"No, but I might slip and stab you next time you're over." Or more likely add another page to her Weston Aldrich scrapbook. This favor was getting more bizarre by the second. "So what do you do with Felix during the day?"

"He comes to the office with me and stays with Marjory."

Oh, man, this was too good. "Do you walk your rabbit-squirrel on a leash during your lunch break? Feed your new baby at your desk?"

"I'm going out," he said, a growl to his voice. "I need you to take Felix for the night. In case you misunderstood, your answer should be a simple *yes*."

"Not when I have plans tonight." She was thankful he'd loaned her cash, but missing Falcon's performance wasn't up for discussion. And going out wasn't only about cornering the elusive DJ. No matter how much time had passed, the anniversary of Leo's death always flattened her. Not just the date. The lead-up, knowing it was approaching, a premonition of heartbreak ahead. Staying home alone, with or without a mentally disturbed bunny, wouldn't do her any favors.

"You'll have to cancel your plans," Wes said, reprising his role as Captain Ego. Like his life was more important than everyone else's.

Her carefree walk turned into an angry march. "I can't."

"You have to."

"Ask Marjory to rabbit-squirrel sit tonight. I can't do it."

"She's busy."

"Find someone else." She stepped off the sidewalk without looking. A car horn blasted, and her breath caught as the car zipped past. She'd almost been creamed by a Porsche, thanks to Weston's irrational demands. "I wasn't put on this planet to serve you."

A rough grunt sounded. "I didn't question you when you asked to borrow money. I helped, because that's what we do for each other. We help when it's needed. You don't waitress on Thursdays, so whatever plans you have, they can be rearranged. Marjory's at the office until six p.m. I expect you to pick Felix up from her before then."

The bastard hung up.

Annie couldn't remember walking the last ten blocks to her lesson. She couldn't recall stomping up the stairs to Julio's apartment or jabbing his entry buzzer. Her head felt like a comic book filled with thought bubbles and expletives, all written in shouty-caps, with not-so-creative insults like *you're such an asshole, even the assholes are jealous.*

She was going to have a blast on Weston's next scrapbook page. She could turn him into a baby with a pacifier and diapers. Add a bonnet on his too-big head. Yeah, that would take the edge off her fury while she babysat Felix the rabbit-squirrel.

"Did someone piss in your coffee?" Julio Suárez had his

apartment door open, one pierced eyebrow raised. Three piercings decorated his face; eleven dangled off his ears. He had blue hair, a tattooed neck, and a natural curl to his lip that should be intimidating, but he was the one stepping back warily.

She probably looked as lethal as she felt. "In a manner of speaking." She inhaled deeply, then released her breath in a rush. Wes may have ruined her night, but he couldn't ruin her DJ lesson. The one he'd unknowingly paid for.

"Bring on the beats," she said, channeling her irritation into concentration.

Today's lesson was about phrasing. Choosing the optimal place to seamlessly mix one song into another by recognizing the beginning and end of a phrase: a drum fill, a new instrument introduced, breakdowns, buildups. Technology had simplified DJing. An entire mix could be displayed on a laptop, lining up songs to cut in perfectly. Paint-by-numbers style of mixing. Julio believed in teaching old school methods first, technology second.

Annie was all over it.

"How does that sound to you?" Julio asked as he played back a recording of her mix.

"It's crap." Clunky and embarrassing.

"Not crap, but it's messy. Tell me why."

It had been crap. If Leo were here, he'd wail and pretend he'd blown an eardrum. But Leo wasn't here. He hadn't been here for a long time. Twelve years, three hundred, and sixty days, to be exact. She had five days left to think about that approaching anniversary: Wes walking into the shelter she'd called home, his face bone white, tears leaking out of his eyes. Her excruciating wail. Five days left, then another year gone, another one beginning, and she couldn't dance those memories away tonight, thanks to Weston Aldrich.

She swallowed roughly and replayed the recording, listened for the beats. "The phrasing in the second track is slightly ahead of the first. I started the second song too early."

"Bingo." Julio punctuated the word by beatboxing, his mouth an instrument of its own. "Your new track's gotta hit on the first beat of the eight-bar phrase. Do it again."

She did. Three times before she nailed it, her sadness ebbing with the efforts. Julio didn't have Falcon's creative brilliance, but the man was a great teacher, and she wanted to understand the fundamentals, do more than push random buttons. She wanted to be the mistress of her music.

Julio high-fived her and played a sick new tune. *Elevator One.* She bopped to the syncopated beats, closed her eyes as the vocals distorted slightly. The song had tons of layers, the power of it building in her chest, so much density to the sound. Fast. Full. Fresh. She smiled, letting herself be happy in this space Leo would have loved.

By the end of the session, she felt rejuvenated. Until she saw a text on her phone.

Wes: **Felix will be waiting for you with Marjory. Don't be late.**

Her blood returned to a deface-Weston-scrapbook boil.

"Remind me not to get on your bad side," Julio said.

This from a dude with a tattooed neck. "I don't have a bad side." She was pleasant and fun. She got along with all her coworkers.

"Tell that to the phone you're glaring at. Your boyfriend forget your birthday or something?"

"He is *not* my boyfriend. His name is Weston and he's a royal pain in my ass."

"Casual hookup, then?"

She tipped her head back and laughed with an exaggerated girly lilt, then pressed her hand to her chest as though she were an amused debutante. "If nuclear testing wipes out humankind and vampires take over the earth after battling an army of mangy werewolves, and we're the only hope for repopulation, the answer would still be a resounding *no*."

Julio whistled a tune, something old-fashioned and sweet, completely out of character for him. "From my experience, women only do that die-motherfucker look when they're emotionally or physically involved with a guy. Just sayin'."

Yeah, she was emotionally involved with Weston, all right. In a *he-makes-me-irrationally-irate* kind of way. That must be why her cheeks were scorching hot right now. It was a fury blush. Except that wasn't completely fair.

Wes was everywhere in her life—one helpful call away or demanding favors, cluelessly funding her dream or calling her *Squirrel* in his condescending tone. He was the good and bad in her day, the last link to her brother. Her momentary fantasies today had been ridiculously out of character. She'd just felt confused, addled. So many changes going on at once. She needed to focus on music. On the mysterious Falcon she'd no longer see tonight.

Annie marched out of Julio's apartment, his comment rattling around her head with each footfall. Emotionally or physically involved? With Weston Aldrich? Wes couldn't be further from her type. Not that she had a type. But if she did, he wouldn't be it.

By the time she hopped off the subway at Wes's office, she was grinding her teeth. Wes was as overbearing as his towering building. So much glass and steel reaching for the sky, marble walkways inside, new flower arrangements daily—shades of white, all stark and serene. She walked past an abstract painting that oozed wealth, the grotesquely simple kind with a white line drawn on black canvas, as though saying: *we're so powerful we pay millions for the mundane.*

If she didn't know Wes loved to eat Cup Noodles soup on her couch, his silk tie tossed on the cushions, she'd think he was as rigid as every surface in here. But she'd seen him laugh until tears streamed from his eyes, thanks to her lip-syncing performances. When she was younger, he'd let her dress him for Halloween with fake blood and makeup, even dying his hair pink once. He often tried to talk to her about modern art and shoved stinky cheese in her face, telling her she needed to expand her horizons, but he also listened when she bitched about work or when she got excited about a clothing purchase or scrapbooking accomplishment.

They didn't talk about Leo, or the parents they'd lost. They teased, they joked, they got on each other's last nerves, the messiness of their relationship making Julio's comment even more farfetched. Yet, she couldn't let it go.

She'd been so vehement in her defensiveness. The type of quick retort rooted in denial. And it wasn't just Julio's chiding. With Wes's constant meddling, she didn't want to dissect the way he'd brushed against her breast in his car, how she'd felt it down to her toes, or untangle why she'd been blushing more when talking to him or about him. She couldn't *like him*, like him. He was part of her foundation. The mortar to her bricks, and complicated feelings had the power to blast those supports to smithereens. Not that it mattered. She'd always been a charity case to Wes. A responsibility. He'd only ever see her as his late best friend's little sister, a foster girl who used to live on the streets.

She stepped off the elevator on his floor and, in her confused haze, slammed into the man himself.

Weston steadied her, one hand on her lower back, the other on her shoulder. Instantly, her body awakened, melting and tensing at once. She leaned farther into him, and his fingers dug deeper into her hip. Neither of them moved for a prolonged second. Could he feel how quickly she was breathing? The shakiness of her hands? And why did he smell so *good*?

Flummoxed, she laughed awkwardly and eased out of his hold. "You do an excellent impression of a brick wall."

"Your zoned out zombie routine isn't half bad, either." His eyes darted to her, then skipped across the floor. "I need to make my meeting, so I'll see you later. Tomorrow. Thanks for watching Felix." A surprising blush dusted his cheeks, and he didn't move to go.

For a second, she wondered if their contact had affected him, too. Then she remembered he'd been rushing to a meeting. He must have worked up a bit of a sweat hurrying from somewhere.

"I didn't have much choice in the animal rescue," she said, internally chastising herself for her unacceptable reaction. "At least I'll be able to put it on my résumé: Rabbit-Squirrel Sitter. I'll be a shoo-in when I run for senate."

He smiled fully, his easy composure returned. "You'll have my vote."

When the elevator doors closed behind Wes, she slouched and pinched her nose. *What in the ever loving hell is wrong with me?* It wasn't just her mind anymore. Her body and sense of smell were betraying her, reacting to all things Wes. And why was she joking about his stupid rabbit? This favor was the last thing she wanted to do.

She counted to five and slowly exhaled. There was no denying Weston's curb appeal. He was like a Hamptons mansion, fun to look at but out of reach. For many reasons. And she'd been off lately, frustrated with her lack of dating and unrequited Falcon crush. This office was real and grounding, regular folks working their nine-to-fives, or more likely five-to-nines, the halls still buzzing with activity. So many people under Weston's employ.

She'd never asked him if that was overwhelming, so much responsibility on his shoulders. She should really ask him. Talking work and business would help her bury this weird new attraction.

When she spotted a cage by Marjory's desk, her irritation resurfaced and all she wanted was to spike Wes's next Cup Noodles with habanero extract.

Annie sauntered over to Marjory and eyed the white and gray bunny nibbling on hay. "Bet you never thought bunny sitting would be part of your job requirements."

Marjory swiveled on her chair and gestured to Weston's closed door. "I never expected to work for a man whose diapers I changed."

"You changed Weston's diapers?"

"He never failed to pee on me."

Annie clamped her hand over her mouth to keep from cackling. "I'm sorry," she said through her fingers. "It's not even the peeing. I'm picturing him in a mini Armani suit, wearing diapers underneath." Even when she'd first met Weston, he'd shown up at the shelter in slacks and a dress shirt. Mr. Posh Begosh.

"I often remind him I've seen him naked." Marjory grinned. Her orange-red lipstick matched her curly hair, her pointed nose somehow matching her nasally voice—a voice that often reprimanded her boss.

Annie had been wrong before, telling Wes she was the only one who didn't kiss his designer behind. Marjory was part of the Annoy Wes Club. "He had some nerve asking me to watch this ridiculous rabbit," Annie said. "He didn't even care I had plans tonight. Just gave his demands, like he runs the world. He must think I have no life."

"You get under his skin, is all. Always have."

Something in Marjory's tone made Annie feel exposed. She

crossed her arms. "The feeling's mutual." Awareness of Wes was becoming a sliver under *her* skin, digging deeper, impossible to ignore.

"I'd take the critter," Marjory said, "but I'm hosting canasta at my house, and a couple of the women are allergic."

"No worries." Annie blew a flyaway hair away from her face. "I owe him anyway."

"In that case, I need to run. And Annie?" Marjory's brown eyes softened. "Be patient with him."

Annie watched Marjory gather her things, unsure if she was referring to Weston or Felix the rabbit-squirrel. Probably the rabbit, considering his separation anxiety.

"You seem fine to me," she told the bunny once they were on their own. He really did. Not stressed or panicked. She could take the little dude home and sneak out. Leave him in her room with the lights on. Weston would never know. But she would. He rarely asked her for favors, and she did owe him. For more than the cash he'd loaned her.

"As I live and breathe."

Annie turned. Duncan was beaming at her, his bright teeth flashing. Some dentist somewhere had earned a few bucks straightening and whitening those suckers. "Fancy meeting you here," she said, pleased to have a distraction from her frustrations.

"Considering I work here, it's not a stretch. And I see you've met Weston's new fur child. A striking resemblance, if you ask me."

The bunny twitched its cute nose. "They have the same eyes."

"So..." Duncan circled her, a panther on the prowl. He propped his hip on Marjory's desk. "Did you stop by to see me?"

"Unfortunately, no. I'm on rabbit-squirrel duty." She pointed at the animal.

"What's a rabbit-squirrel?"

"Just go with it."

He nodded, unperturbed by her oddness. "Well, I consider this my lucky day. This finally gives me a chance to ask you out."

She laughed at his boldness. She might have flirted on the phone, but the prospect of them dating was comical. He was as stylish as Weston, all done up in a charcoal suit and silk tie. She wore knee-high leggings under her lace skirt, a floral tank blouse on top. Her striped scarf was knotted around her neck, with funky ankle boots and a pink purse rounding out her whimsical outfit. Bohemian style next to his swanky elegance. Pretty much how she looked next to Wes. The thought made her frown.

"Let me guess—Weston warned you away from me?" Duncan didn't look annoyed. Amusement lit his eyes.

"He did. But he warns me away from most things."

Duncan twisted his cufflink, aligning it slowly. "Does his controlling nature bother you?"

"Sometimes." *Always.*

He released his cufflink and met her eyes, unabashed. "So go out with me."

This guy was too much. "As what? A way to get back at him?"

"For whatever reason you want. But I'll warn you in advance, I'm pretty killer on a date. Once we're out, I can't be responsible for you falling for me."

"Aren't you a cocky one?"

He shrugged. Total player, like Weston worried, but Duncan was straightforward, and he was easy on the eyes. This brash routine of his would get old, but she could handle a guy like him for a date or two. Even better, saying yes could help her get that elevator altercation off her mind: the weight of Wes's hand on her back, the slight dig of his fingers into her skin. *Ugh.*

"Why not," she said quickly. "Let me know when you're free."

He stood from the desk edge and inched closer. "I'm free tonight."

"You don't waste time, do you?"

"Not when I'm talking to a beautiful woman."

Yep, player central. She sidestepped him and fanned her hand toward the cage. "Unfortunately, I'll be busy watching the rabbit-squirrel tonight. And before you ask, he's not allowed to be left alone." She mouthed the words *abandonment issues* in case the bunny understood human.

"I won't pretend like any of that makes sense, but I could come over and keep you company." He dragged his gaze down her body.

Casanova needed to dial down his hormones. "You're nice enough, Duncan, but I don't do first dates in my apartment. Or second dates." She hadn't lost her street smarts when she quit living on the streets.

"What if I can get you a rabbit-squirrel sitter?"

Now that had promise. A sitter meant she could see Falcon after all. "Seriously? Who?"

"I have a step-sister who'd love the little bugger. She'd be thrilled."

Agreeing and chasing Falcon would mean bringing Duncan to the club with her. Not ideal. She'd rather not tell him about her DJing plans, and she couldn't picture him dancing in a club. Never mind that the maneuver was utterly selfish. But he'd said he didn't care why she agreed to a date, and she could ask Vivian to tag along as a buffer. "Fine, but I'm making the plans. I'll text you the address to a club. Seedier area, so don't flash your money or fancy clothes around. Meet me there at eleven. Unless clubbing isn't your speed."

He hesitated a moment, then raked his hand through his country-club hair. "If you're there, beautiful, it's my speed."

Duncan was in for a hefty surprise, and so was Falcon. Tonight would be the night she finally spoke with him. She was tired of chasing a ghost. She would not be deterred. Until then, she'd listen to music, get pumped for the club. She'd forget about whatever had zinged through her when touching Wes. She even had a sexy outfit ready to impress Falcon.

7

VIVIAN WAS at the bar when Annie arrived, unexpectedly chatting with Sarah—the same private eye from several weeks ago. Lots of close talking, subtle touching. Still into each other.

Annie dodged a few people and joined them. "Looks like you two have been here awhile."

Vivian cozied up to Sarah's side. "We're celebrating. I got myself background checked and passed with flying colors."

Sarah raised a dubious eyebrow. "I overlooked her college arrest. And the vandalism incident."

"Graffiti art isn't vandalism." Vivian danced as she spoke, cozying up to Sarah.

"Tell that to the gas station you decorated with *Kama Sutra* poses."

Vivian pouted. "It's not fair. All I can do is stalk her on social media."

"Y'all are too cute, digging up dirt on each other." Annie ordered a margarita and settled against the long bar, facing out to watch the action. "I'm guessing this place used to be a theater."

"With that kind of attention to detail," Sarah said, "you could be my assistant."

As much as Annie enjoyed detective shows, a private eye she was not. She'd get bored in the middle of a stakeout and miss the big event. It wasn't tough to see the history in this remodeled club, though. Whatever seats had lined the auditorium had been removed, but the soaring embossed ceiling was still extravagant, the stage breathtakingly broad. A crimson curtain hung behind the current DJ. The woman playing was knocking out some funky beats, but she was no Falcon.

"When's your date showing?" Vivian asked.

"Eleven-ish. And don't laugh when you see him. He'll be a fish out of water in here." For the life of her, she couldn't picture Duncan mingling with this crowd. Half of them had neon makeup painted on their faces, some wore threadbare clothes and Freed by the Falcon T-shirts. Others looked like they'd raided a spandex factory.

"You certainly dressed to impress."

"What? This old thing?" Annie was totally on the prowl, but Duncan wasn't the man set in her sights. She'd pulled out all the stops and shimmied into a mini skirt and a gold sequined tank, red thigh-high boots completing her look.

She loved piecing together thrift-store outfits, feeling chic and comfy when out and about. Her club style was tapping into another side of her she'd never explored. Wearing skimpier attire at bars made her feel sexy, confident. Her inner vixen unleashed. She'd used her newfound feminine wiles to sweet-talk a bouncer tonight, ensuring she'd be let backstage after the show.

"I'm here for the music," she told Vivian. She was about to admit she'd been taking DJ lessons and planned to work with

Falcon, but a woman, who looked *exactly* like Sarah, waved their way. "Did you know you're dating a clone?"

Vivian followed Annie's wide eyes and laughed. "That's her twin. They even dress similar and love all the same stuff, spend tons of time together. My sister and I are lucky to see each other on holidays."

"I can't tell them apart."

"Yeah, it's nuts. What about you? Any siblings? An identical twin with stunning hazel eyes and a sexy birthmark by her lips?"

Annie glanced down, feigning embarrassment. Compliments made her blush, but this wasn't self-consciousness. All these years later, she never knew if she should save people the awkward interlude and tell them she didn't have a sibling. Or smile and say she had a brother, or admit he'd been killed in a club like this. On July 27th. Twelve years, three hundred, and sixty days ago.

Her breathing turned shallow. Heat stung her eyes, the sudden rise of emotion horrifying. She never cried. Keeping herself together was a well-honed skill. Yet the urge to blow past Vivian and escape to the bathroom had her tensing.

"There she is," Duncan said, his head appearing over Vivian's shoulder.

Annie let out a shaky breath. She never imagined she'd be this thrilled to see her date.

"Glad you showed." She walked over and kissed his cheek. His potent cologne made her eyes water more.

He flashed his white teeth. "Told you I would. And you look..." He whistled.

Everyone introduced themselves. Duncan's black slacks and slicked hair stood out as expected, but he seemed at ease, chatting easily with the girls. Slowly, Annie sloughed off her discomfort.

He linked his elbow through hers and led them back to the bar. From behind him, Vivian mimed picking her nose with a hooked finger—their save-me-before-I-die signal. Annie shook her head. She didn't need an escape, but it was nice having a friend nearby, and even nicer that the personal questions had ceased. Duncan knew enough about her past to hopefully steer clear of that minefield.

"So, Annie Ward, this is your thing." He leaned on the bar, close enough to brush arms.

She tried to avoid deep whiffs of his spicy cologne. "If you mean the club scene, then yeah. I'm guessing it's not yours."

"Not at first glance, but I'm a believer in stepping out of my comfort zone. Just wouldn't have pegged you for a club rat."

"Why's that?"

"Although you look stunning tonight, you don't normally dress the part. And I figured..." He scanned the space, swallowed twice. "With your history, I figured you'd stay away."

Her history. Leo's death. The club shooting.

Instead of avoiding that minefield, Duncan had stepped right in it.

She often wondered what it would be like to just leave. Start fresh in a new town where people didn't know her. A blank slate in a blank life she could fill the way she filled her scrapbooks, with hope and happiness. The non-deface-Weston-style of scrapbook. But Wes lived in New York. No matter his faults and her recent troubling fantasies, she couldn't picture her life without him. Plus moving wouldn't keep innocent questions like Vivian's at bay.

"I got into this scene recently," she told Duncan. The truth. "If you let memories haunt you, they control you." Talking about them was a different story. "How about a drink?"

He waved a credit card at the bartender and handed it over.

"Start us a tab. Martini extra dry for me. And the lady will have..."

"Another margarita," she finished. "You don't have to buy my drinks, though."

"I told you, I'm basically a professional dater. Just try to resist me."

"So, that makes you a male escort?"

He recoiled. "Me? No. That's ludicrous."

The guy made it too easy. "Professional implies paid services."

He paused, narrowed his eyes, then laughed. "Quick on the jabs, Ward. I see why Weston likes you so much."

"Weston likes me as much as he can control me." If he knew she wasn't home rabbit-squirrel sitting, or that she was on a date with Duncan, his head would implode. But she didn't want to talk about Wes. Part of this date was about pushing thoughts of him from her mind.

"You should give the guy a break," Duncan said. "You know how much he works. I've actually been worried about him lately."

Something in Annie's chest pinched. "Worried how?"

Duncan shrugged.

The DJ was finishing her set while another guy set up. Annie didn't imagine Falcon would play in that narrow section of stage. He was likely setting up behind the curtain, would add a theatrical element to his performance. He was creative like that. She should watch the stage in case he appeared early and she could flag him. Instead she angled her back to the action and searched Duncan's face. "Wes is used to working hard. It's his motto. Why would you be worried?"

"You know about the merger?"

"Only that it's a big deal to him."

"Well, it's getting complicated. Wearing him down. He looks

more tired than usual and seems distracted. I've tried talking to him, but he brushes me off. I was hoping he'd confided in you."

Weston didn't lean on others. He was his own pillar of strength, one *she'd* leaned on more times than she could count. If she really thought about it, their relationship was pretty one-sided: him giving, her taking. His generosity often came in the form of orders, advice, and money, but it was because he cared. Yet he'd asked her for a favor today and she'd pawned it off on Duncan's step-sister the first chance she'd gotten, all while Wes stretched himself thin to keep his moving pieces in check.

She pictured his busy office building, the floors filled with thousands of employees. And that was just New York. Aldrich Pharma had offices in multiple cities, all those employees relying on Wes and his team. The strain on him must be incredible. "I'll talk to him. But I'm not sure I can help."

"Just talking might help, and you can always come to me. I know what he's dealing with. I might have some insight you can relay to him."

She pressed her hand to Duncan's forearm. "Thanks. I'm glad Wes has you in his corner."

Duncan's eyes darted to her lips. He moved closer. She stepped back, needing distance from him and all that cologne. She sipped her drink, savored the kick of lime and salt, tried not to picture Wes at his late-night meeting, then home alone, sleepless, stressing over a million worries. Nothing she could do about it tonight.

"On a happier note," she said, "you're in for a treat. The last DJ is in*sane*."

"Can't say dance music is my jam, but this place has atmosphere." Duncan raised his voice. "And it's loud."

"It helps you feel the beat better. And if you don't dig this, what music is your jam?"

"Whatever's on the radio, I guess."

Someone jostled her from behind. Her drink spilled a little. Hopefully the fumble distracted Duncan from her pinched "judgy" face, as Wes called it. She didn't understand how people existed without music in their hearts. "What about hobbies? What makes you tick?"

"Golf, golf, and golf." He grinned. "Got myself a new set of clubs that are smooth as silk."

He talked over the music, droning on about the weight and balance of the clubs, the swanky courses he'd played and a trip he'd booked. She zoned out and scanned the room. A guy walked by wearing a beaded necklace similar to one Leo had owned, and her eyes stung again. She bit her cheek and checked the stage for Falcon.

"I also play racquetball," Duncan said, yelling in her ear as people crowded them. "And I love talking with beautiful women."

She snort-laughed. Yeah, no. She was feeling zero attraction to Duncan. The guy was all-American attractive, but her intellectual interest was falling faster than an under-baked soufflé. Hopefully he'd at least dance with her when Falcon played, and his concern over Wes had been sweet. They could say a friendly goodbye afterward, no future dates in store.

Another drink and more mundane chitchat later, the lights dimmed. The crowd roared. Annie's heart beat wildly. *Falcon.*

"Let's get closer to the stage." Without waiting for his reply, she grabbed Duncan's hand and dragged him as she elbowed her way closer. No points for kindness when her favorite DJ played, and she wasn't the only one in pursuit. She lost Duncan's hand in the crush. They got separated. She should turn and find him, but the first wave of violin trilled. Immediately, she was entranced, staring at the crimson curtain as lights danced and people cheered. The next segment of music was different. Melancholy. An emotional cello filling the space.

People quieted. Shivers sailed down her neck.

She closed her eyes, felt more than heard his transitions, gusts of sound breezing around the room. The soaring melody made her throat burn, as though the notes had been written for her, a soundtrack to that approaching anniversary. Sorrow bleeding into healing, coming out the other end hopeful, but still sad.

The bass cut in. She opened her eyes.

The curtain lifted and...*wow*.

As always, Falcon was a beast on stage, tall and commanding, a bird of prey surveying his domain. The stage was a different story. TV screens filled the space, different sizes at various heights arranged in a dramatic pattern. Images flashed to the beats: falcons swooping in slow motion, weather footage whipping through the sky—hail and wind and rain. The scenes moved from one monitor to the next, as though crashing through the room.

All went black. The music paused.

A new song exploded, sunshine beamed and flowers grew in a hypnotic time-lapse sequence, and...wait, *was that?* She whooped. He was playing the new song she'd heard at her DJ lesson. It was sensory overload.

Falcon pumped his hand in the air, head tipped up slightly, that stunning mask making him look like a feral king.

She tossed up her hands and danced. Let the rhythm slide through her bones, every troubling thought shaking out of her head. His gaze swept the floor as it often did, and her body loosened, moving just for him. She forgot about Leo's anniversary, Vivian's and Duncan's tough questions. She didn't worry about losing Falcon again tonight. She let everything go but the music. Until a hard body lined up behind her.

She tensed, ready to stomp on some dude's foot, then she smelled that heavy, familiar cologne. Duncan. He was closer than she liked, but there wasn't much room with this crowd, and it wasn't fair to ditch him again. He danced with more rhythm than expected, his hips and torso rocking behind her. She matched his moves. Relaxed while *maybe* picturing Falcon behind her instead. She imagined turning, pressing closer to him, digging her fingers into his thick shoulders, licking a line up his neck, lifting his mask for a peek at his face. She closed her eyes, reveled in the fantasy...and saw Weston.

The wrong face. The wrong daydream.

A-freaking-gain.

She whipped her eyes open, searched the stage for the man she was allowed to crush on. Falcon was safe. He was infatuation material. His gaze suddenly locked on hers, and the song screeched to a stop.

8

WESTON'S VISION WENT DARK. Everything blackened except for one woman and the man behind her, the scene so wrong anger clouded his eyes and his finger snagged on the volume. Just a second. That was all it took to fuck up his set. Silence flared. A boulder lodged in his stomach. He realigned the music with the video feed, then normalized the volume.

There was nothing normal about the angry kick of his pulse.

Annie was here. A quick glimpse of her lower body revealed sinful red boots, a micro-mini skirt, exquisite legs. Her sequined halter top caught the flashing lights, as bright and beautiful as the woman lost to his music.

But she wasn't supposed to be here. She was supposed to be at home with Felix, the emotionally stunted rabbit-squirrel. A foolish plan he shouldn't have implemented. Idiotic or not, she'd lied to him. Ignored his request. All of which was enough to bring his blood to a boil. Seeing Duncan with her made him seethe.

He'd told Duncan to forget Annie's name. He'd told Annie

the guy was trouble. He wasn't sure who'd initiated this little outing, but the sight of Duncan's hands on Annie's hips, his body moving against hers—fuck *no*. Not okay.

Tonight was supposed to be about playing with the video feeds. Sussing out the effect on the crowd, testing if the gimmick could be used to say something more meaningful. Make a bigger difference like when he'd volunteered as a kid. People didn't listen to lyrics if they didn't like the beat. They didn't pay attention to the world's problems if they didn't feel connected to them. The video stage was a first step toward a larger vision.

All he could do was watch Annie.

He played his set by rote, feeling disconnected from the crowd, furious at Duncan, at Annie, but mostly at himself. He couldn't quit picturing himself dancing with her, letting his hands roam over her curves, stealing touches of her the way he'd gripped her tightly when she'd plowed into him from the elevator. A tantalizing feel he shouldn't have stolen. He shouldn't feel this roar of attraction now, but there was no denying the hard pump of his blood.

He swallowed roughly, forced himself to remember why this was wrong.

"Take care of Annie," Leo had whispered the night he'd died. Weston had pressed his hands to the bullet wound, shaking, telling his best friend over and over he'd be okay. The blood had seeped everywhere, through his fingers, onto the floor. The sharp bite of copper had stung his nose.

"She has no one," Leo had croaked. "You gotta keep her safe. And don't...don't you dare let her date an asshole like you." Because only he'd crack a joke as he struggled to breathe. But it was his last choppy words that would forever keep Weston awake some nights.

I'm scared.

Don't wanna die.

Please. Oh, God...please. It hurts.

Can't leave her.

You gotta...

Then he was gone. All because Weston was a selfish bastard.

He was pretty sure "Don't you dare let her date an asshole like you" was equivalent to "don't date my sister." Not that it mattered. Weston couldn't date Annie when he'd lied to her about her brother's death. She'd never forgive him for his deception, and Weston didn't do relationships. The one time he'd tried had been a Titanic-sized disaster. And he needed Annie in his life. Someone to argue with, to ground him, let him eat Cup Noodles on her couch, no judgment. With her, he imagined his mother smiling down on him, pleased her son had a place he could relax, laugh, and bicker teasingly. Forget about work for a minute.

Aldrich Pharma gave him purpose. DJing eased his guilt over the past. Annie Ward gave him peace, *when* she wasn't antagonizing him. Adding intimacy was a fast track to losing her.

He struggled through his set, one of his worst to date, even with the video feed. The crowd sensed when a DJ's head wasn't in the game. The energy was lower. People left the dance floor. He cursed when Duncan used the space to turn Annie around. They were face-to-face, and Duncan grabbed her ass. Weston's adrenaline slammed into fifth gear.

He was half a second from jumping off the stage, but Annie wiggled out of his grip—*good girl*—and swiveled back to face the stage. Duncan didn't take the hint. He pushed up behind her, grabbed her waist.

Weston snapped.

He pointed at Annie and crooked his finger, motioning for

her to join him on stage. Because he'd apparently lost his mind. Avoiding fans was how he kept this secret, and Annie was no ordinary fan. But he was beyond rational thought, only needing her away from Duncan.

The crowd, reenergized by this new development, cheered and parted for her. Excitement lit her face, so genuine a crush of pleasure swamped him.

She's looking at Falcon, he reminded himself. Not him. And he was doing this to get her away from Duncan, not to work out this unrelenting attraction.

People helped her on stage while his mind spun ahead to the end of the night. Duncan would invite her to his condo, show her his fancy new bed. A growl rumbled low in Weston's throat.

He grabbed the paper and pen he kept by his equipment. The notepad was a place to jot down thoughts during a set. Quick points he'd use when analyzing and modifying his playlist later. He scribbled the only thing that would keep Annie away from Duncan tonight and tucked it in his pocket.

She ran to his side, breathless, her cheeks flushed. Goddamn beautiful. He didn't speak. If she heard his voice, she might guess who was behind the mask. He was thankful he went as far as wearing different cologne, but he found himself at a loss. He suddenly wanted to confess he'd been thinking about her, wanting her, this woman who anchored his world. Then tell her all the reasons it couldn't happen, drill that reality into *his* uncooperative brain, anything to squash this growing urge to slam his lips on hers.

Buying himself a minute, he lined up his last song, not trusting himself to work spontaneously.

She shifted nervously beside him. "I've been dying to talk to you." Her eyes flitted between him and his equipment. "I'm a

DJ, too. Not yet. Actually, not at all. But I will be. I'm a quick study. Which is why I've been trying to catch your attention."

She was glowing with excitement, and affection caught him square in the chest. The DJ comment, however, was a surprise. It explained her relentless pursuit of him. It hadn't been attraction. She hadn't felt the connection between them, hadn't been dancing for his pleasure. His relief should be palpable. All he felt was disappointment.

She waited on him to speak. Not happening. Duncan moved to the side of the dance floor and glared at them, arms crossed.

Suck it, buddy.

Without many options, Weston danced. He couldn't let Annie leave the stage yet, not when Duncan might pull her into another hip grind. Annie responded eagerly, respecting his distance at first, then closing the space between them. She didn't put her hands on his body, but her hips bumped against his, her breasts brushed his chest. Her head lolled as her hands wove up into the sultry air.

He was radioactive, an atom about to split.

"I've been chasing you for weeks," she yelled over the speakers. "Trying to ask if you'd teach me. I want to be your apprentice. I'll do anything. I won't be a bother. I just...I really need this."

The desperation in her voice was unfamiliar. The Annie he knew was Wonder Woman strong. She'd gone into foster care after Leo's death with her chin ticked up. Weston had tried convincing his father to take her in, but that had been a lost cause. She'd moved through three families, never once complaining or breaking down. She'd finished high school on the honor roll and got along with everyone and had a thousand hobbies to feed her natural creativity. To be this well-adjusted was no small feat. She was also a walking hurricane, flitting from job to job, her endless chatter and flighty nature beyond maddening, but she was so incredibly resilient.

Maybe this music did for her what it did for him, kept memories of Leo alive. A connection to the past. Unfortunately, he couldn't be the one to give her that gift.

He maneuvered them in front of the TV monitors, gave the club a show. Blooming nature behind them, two dancers to watch. He only had eyes for Annie: the subtle curve of her lips, that birthmark sinking into the crease by her luscious mouth, the lazy sweep of her eyelids, like she was drunk on him. Annie's hazel eyes often shifted colors. Sometimes they were vivid shamrock, fun and mischievous. Other times they were woven with slivers of gingerbread, sweet and daring. Tonight they were a seductive hit of chocolate-laced jade.

The room faded. Heat built between them. Her familiar smell of sage and honey mixed with the sweat-tinged air. He didn't know when he'd pressed his hand to her lower back, drawing her to him. He hadn't been aware of his erection rubbing against her belly, only the hot throb of his blood as they moved together. Those eyes. Those lips.

The curtain came down in front of them. Timing he'd arranged with his tech guy. The crowd cheered. His music blended into the usual after-performance song, a steady beat, slower but still catchy. Annie stopped dancing. He couldn't catch his breath. He should step away, let her go. He slammed his mouth against hers.

He wrapped her in his arms, hauled her lithe body against his bulk. He swept his tongue between her lips and groaned. She tasted like lime and salt and sinful heaven. He dove in deeper. She made a pained sound as the edge of his mask caught her cheek. Worried, he moved to pull back, but she dug her fingers into his shoulders. Her lips moved greedily, their tongues swirling, a sensual rhythm that rolled over him in a massive head rush. This was Annie. His Annie. Leo's Annie. A woman he shouldn't want. A woman who had no clue who she was kissing.

That reality had him wrenching away.

Her lips looked plump and well used. Her cheek was red from his mask. She oozed satisfaction, then her eyes flared and she flinched. He wanted to ask her what was wrong. Instead he dug the note he'd written from his pocket and thrust it into her hand. He stalked past her, desperate to get away from whatever the hell he'd just let happen.

ANNIE STOOD ON THE STAGE, stunned. She'd kissed Falcon. Or he'd kissed her. Kissing had just happened, and it had been a-*mazing*. Her body still tingled, so much unquenched pleasure pulsing below her skin. Falcon hadn't been satisfied, either. Not judging by the hard ridge that had jammed into her stomach.

And that kiss? She was ruined for all future mortals.

The only downfall had been that split second where his eyes had looked familiar. In that instant she'd imagined Falcon as Wes. She'd pictured dragging him in for a deeper kiss, his body pounding into her. She'd flinched, and Falcon had up and split. Now she was ditched. And annoyed. She had to stop thinking about Wes. It was becoming a problem, and her hesitation had spooked Falcon. She should run after him, get his contact. She was too discombobulated to move.

A guy with muttonchops walked around her and began packing up Falcon's equipment. She lifted the note in her hand and read it. *Ditch your date. Meet me at the back exit in fifteen.*

"Yes!"

The equipment guy looked at her and laughed. She grinned like a loon.

Falcon had gone from ditching her at every chance, to hauling her on stage and mauling her. Did he want to be her DJ instructor? Her kissing instructor? Either would be fine with her, as long as she squelched those dastardly Wes flashes. For now, she had to speak with Duncan, explain their date was over. He would be pissed. He probably *was* pissed. She'd left him high and dry to dance with another man. At least he hadn't seen the kiss.

Still feeling flushed, she peered through the curtain's edge. Vivian and Sarah, and Sarah's twin, were at the bar. Duncan was beside them, typing aggressively into his phone. Complaining about his graceless date, likely. She took a fortifying breath and hopped off the stage.

Two steps out, a girl ambushed her. "Oh my God, that was so cool." Fluorescent makeup lit up her eyelids and lips. "Did he talk to you? What does his voice sound like? Did you see his face?"

Based on her Freed by the Falcon shirt, this groupie wanted Falcon gossip. All Annie had was kissing intel—ovary exploding—which she wasn't about to share. "We just danced. And I need to catch my friends."

Two more groupies assaulted her before she made it to Duncan. He looked up and fumbled his phone, quickly shoving it into his pocket. He'd for sure been texting crap about her. Not that she could fault him. She'd have done the same. "I'm so sorry. That was unexpected and rude of me. I shouldn't have left you in the lurch. It's just, I've been trying to talk with Falcon for weeks."

Duncan waved his hand casually. "No worries. You seemed like you were having fun up there. But..." He examined her face. "Looks like you scratched your cheek."

"I must have grazed it on the curtain." She touched the spot, remembered Falcon's masculine grunts, their burst of passion.

She'd done more than graze her cheek. Duncan wouldn't know about that tonsil tennis, but he was surprisingly unruffled. "I'm still sorry for leaving you. It wasn't nice."

"Don't give it another thought. Besides, the night isn't over yet." He waggled his eyebrows.

"Actually, it kind of is." She glanced at Vivian, who was watching her from a few feet away. Vivian pointed at the stage, swayed her hips suggestively, then flapped her arms like a human bird. Her version of charades: Annie dancing with Falcon. As absurdly hilarious as those moves were, Annie needed saving, not awkward charades.

She could do the hook-nose signal, flag Vivian for some help. She opted for honesty. "Thing is," she told Duncan, "what I said before about trying to talk to Falcon was true. I've been taking DJ lessons and am dying to learn from him. He invited me to meet him tonight, and I can't pass this up."

Duncan's cheekbones sharpened, darkness flashing in his hollowed cheeks. The irritation she deserved. "You trust this guy to meet him alone?"

She replayed the kiss, how he'd been the one to pull back first, put on the brakes. It had been her who'd taken charge afterward, deepened their kiss. He hadn't been pushy or overly aggressive, and being alone with him was the best way to talk music. "I trust him."

He studied her, then deflated slightly. "Can't say I'm pleased, but I get it. We'll just have to do this again sometime."

He smiled his player smile, and her stomach clenched. Turning a person down was never easy. "As nice as this has been, I'll have to decline. I think we work better as friends."

"That's because I was out of my element. Let me take you out next week."

So much for blunt honesty.

Out of options, Annie crooked her finger and jabbed at her

nose. Duncan squinted at her. She looked like a nutcase, but she wasn't the one hitting on an uninterested party.

Vivian spotted the signal and hurried over. "Annie, darling, didn't you say you had to get up early tomorrow?"

"Nope. You must have me confused with Sarah's sister. I'm actually meeting Falcon in..." She pulled her phone from the top of her thigh-high boot and cringed at the time. "In one minute, so I need to run. Maybe you can hang with Duncan?"

"At least let me walk you." Duncan was gunning for Clueless Man of the Year award.

"I'm good, thanks."

"We were actually just talking about you." Vivian took hold of Duncan's elbow. "You've got to tell me what dentist you use. I was thinking of having my teeth whitened. Or maybe getting fang implants." She led a confused Duncan away, but glanced back at Annie and mouthed *ohmygod Falcon.*

There would be questions later.

Already a minute late, Annie rushed to the back exit, a slick of guilt coating her stomach as she hurried. Meeting Falcon had been a success, but she'd pawned off Wes's favor to make it work, she'd used and ditched Duncan, and she'd kissed Falcon while on a date. Becoming a DJ was important to her, but this selfishness wasn't cool. She'd have to apologize to Duncan again. Find a way to balance this growing music obsession so it didn't turn her into a monster. For now, she had a mysterious DJ to meet.

She leaned into the door's release bar and shoved it open, inhaling the warm night air. An overflowing garbage bin made her regret that deep inhale. People were lined up at a club across the way. Freed by the Falcon groupies smoked in cliques, chatting about tonight's show. They weren't griping about Falcon's lackluster performance. They were talking about the video screens, the visual images, and her being dragged on stage.

The bouncer she'd chatted up earlier stood nearby, towering over the scene. He saw her and ambled over while cracking his knuckles. Gold rings glinted on his fingers. "Falcon told me to tell you he had to split."

Her shoulders fell. "Seriously?"

"He also got you a cab. It's out front. Paid for." The man's dark eyes roved over her outfit. "He don't talk to fans. Or anybody, really. You must have made an impression."

Not much of one if he'd stood her up. "Thanks, but I'll get my own ride."

The giant didn't budge. "Sorry, no can do."

"Excuse me?"

"I gotta get you in that cab. Falcon made that very clear."

What was it with men wanting to control her? She'd rather march away and hoof it home, use the long walk to clear her mind, but this Goliath wasn't having it. "Fine," she said. "But only because my feet hurt."

He shrugged and fanned a hand for her to go ahead.

Once in the cab, she brooded. Falcon had been the one to call her on stage. He'd kissed *her*, after grinding against her body. She still felt the imprint of his fingers digging into her hips and spine. Not the behavior of a guy who'd ghost her. Maybe his face was disfigured and he was shy about it. Or he had a girlfriend and had freaked out. Or he was in witness protection for saving puppies from a crazed drug lord who used them for smuggling, and seeing her would put her and those sweet puppies in harm's way.

Her phone buzzed. She rolled her eyes at Duncan's name, but the message put her at ease.

Duncan: **Thanks for tonight, and don't feel bad about the Falcon thing. I'm cool with us just being friends.**

Finally, the guy took the hint.

Annie: **Friends sounds good.**

Duncan: **And if you ever want to add benefits to that title, call me. I'm not into anything serious.**

He certainly got points for being candid.

Annie: **Noted. And if you don't mind, please don't tell Wes about the date or the DJing stuff. I can't deal with his meddling.**

Duncan: **Only if you promise to talk with him about work.**

Annie: **Deal. I'll keep you posted.**

She'd tell Wes about her piano lessons and DJing once she'd achieved a measure of success, when he wouldn't call her Squirrel and tell her she was wasting her time. Until then she'd take a breather from him before checking on his work stress. Force all naughty Wes thoughts from her mind. She'd focus on her DJ lessons and try to figure out why Falcon had left her in the lurch. She'd do her best to forget Leo's July 27th anniversary was just five days away.

9

WESTON STOOD OUTSIDE IMOGEN'S, his hands shoved into his pants pockets. The bar's exterior was as shabby as the day he'd dropped Annie off for her first shift. A homeless man was asleep down the alley; drunk girls sang as they stumbled across the street, elbows linked. In his dress shirt and slacks, he probably looked as out of place as a tin man in the Sahara.

He checked his watch again. Only six minutes had passed. Annie's Monday shifts usually ended at midnight. Twenty minutes from now.

He shouldn't be anywhere near her, not since that kiss five days ago. He'd heard from her twice since that night. Two succinct texts. One to say she'd dropped Felix off with his secretary, and one to tell him she was working and couldn't hang out as they usually did on July 27th. She hadn't admitted she'd neglected her rabbit-sitting duties. No mentioned of her date or Falcon, the club, any of it. He'd played dumb while remembering every flick of her tongue, the tight press of her body against his. He'd avoided communication after that. A self-imposed restraining order.

Until today.

He'd texted her several times, had left voice messages. She hadn't replied once. So here he was. The last place he should be. He had no choice on the anniversary of Leo's death.

Pushing thoughts of that kiss from his mind, he snuck a bill into the homeless man's cup, a habit he'd picked up from Annie. People living on the street made him picture her and Leo like this, just kids, dirty and begging for food. It had made him realize the homeless were real people with real lives and real problems, who'd been knocked on their asses one too many times.

And look where Annie was today.

Inhaling that hit of pride, he walked into the bar. It was busy for a Monday. Not too packed to spot Annie. She wasn't wearing those insane red thigh-high boots or a sequined top, but she looked breathtaking in skinny jeans, heels, and a slim turquoise striped tank. She was a chameleon these days, creative and playful with her daytime vintage clothes, dressing seductively at work and clubs. His body stirred, the remembered feel of her hips against his flooding his veins. He fisted his hands.

She laughed at something a customer said, then glanced over. Her smile faltered.

They both knew why he was there.

She waved at him and grinned widely. Typical Annie, putting on a brave front. He always let her do it, didn't want to bring up upsetting subjects.

He met her by the bar. "Hey there, Squirrel."

"This is a surprise, Herbert." Another exaggerated grin. "You here for a drink?"

This close to her he saw a red mark on her cheek, a remnant of their kiss, and possessiveness washed through him, the desire to tell her who she'd kissed, have an encore performance. He cleared his throat. "No, thanks. I'm here for you."

She blushed, the sudden color unexpected. Like she felt the same intoxicating pull. "I might be a while," she said quickly. "This rush started late."

"I'll wait."

"Or we can chat another day."

"Or I can wait."

They stared at each other. She looked away first, mumbled, "Suit yourself."

An hour later Annie held up her finger, signaling she'd only be another minute. She disappeared through a staff door and reappeared with her purse. "Must be important if you waited this long."

He worked his jaw, debated how to play this. Avoiding the topic of Leo was how they rolled. He respected her privacy, and he had his own reasons for letting those memories lie. But they'd spent every July 27th together. They'd eat pizza or Chinese takeout. He'd watch a movie while she'd scrapbook. He'd tease her for quitting her Sudoku puzzles halfway through. They let each other grieve in their own ways.

Today she'd avoided him.

He stood from his stool. "There's a late-night dive a couple blocks down. Come for a drink with me."

She tucked her purse closer, chewed her lip. "Isn't it past your bedtime?"

"I have a second wind."

"If you're passing wind, I'll take a raincheck."

He barked out a laugh. God, she was funny. And he knew this Annie setting: sarcastic comedienne. He could work with this. "Come on, Anthea. Humor me."

She stared at him, then strutted ahead.

They walked side-by-side, enough space between them that

they didn't touch. The physical and emotional distance maddened him. He didn't understand why she'd been avoiding him, or why she hadn't mentioned her DJ interest. He used to be her sounding board. A job she hated, a new one she wanted, dreams of a West Coast road trip she'd laid out in a scrapbook —he'd heard it all. Now she was keeping secrets. Dating a player like Duncan.

Maybe his deceptions were to blame. His secret identity and DJ life. He'd left her standing in an alley, for God's sake, rather than come clean about being Falcon. He still hated himself for that cowardly act. He'd probably stonewalled her at other times, insensitive slips, pushing her away without realizing it, all in the name of his alter ego.

"What have you been up to lately?" he asked.

"This and that."

"Been going out at night?"

"Some, not much."

Talking to a brick wall was easier. "Did you happen to swap bodies with a moody thirteen-year-old?"

"That's rich coming from a control freak who still treats me like I *am* thirteen." She slammed to a stop, pressed her fingers to her lips. "God, Wes. I'm sorry. I didn't mean to yell at you." Her hand shook slightly.

His shoulders seemed to weigh a thousand pounds. "You don't ever have to apologize to me. Today's a rough day."

Her hazel eyes were all forest tonight. Dense, unreadable. "It's fine. I'm fine." She wrapped her arms around her middle.

He shoved his hands back into his pockets. It was either that or pull her into his chest. "Yeah, I'm fine, too."

He'd driven to the bar from work, had barely taken a break to eat today. Aside from running on his treadmill until his thighs cramped and his lungs screamed, the only non-work activity he'd done in the past five days was see Rosanna.

Since their deal, she'd made an effort to talk when they were out. They'd even laughed some. Yesterday had been their third public date. She'd regaled him with stories of her wild parties, the havoc she'd caused. She had no qualms talking to him about other men. He'd even told her about Annie. No details about his complex feelings for her, but he'd found himself telling stories, laughing, bringing her up often. But he'd never mentioned today's date and its significance.

"So," Annie said, awkwardness drifting between them. "I guess we're both fine."

"Seems that way." His old therapist would have had a field day with this level of denial. "But I think you're lying."

She snorted. "You're lying more than I'm lying."

It was a childish comeback, but she was right. He was lying about Falcon, about that kiss, about his secret DJ life. He was lying to the world about Rosanna, and he'd been lying to Annie about Leo's death for thirteen years.

"Liar or not, I could use that drink. You still in?" he asked.

Her attention drifted to his left, then dragged to her feet. A beat later, she nodded.

ANNIE WAS TIRED, emotionally, physically, and the patrons at Sticks and Stones sure put the dive into this bar. The first man she passed smelled like urine, the second like he'd slept in someone's gym bag, and her heels kept sticking to the floor. She had a sneaking suspicion the pretzels in those bowls had been swept up and reused.

"I knew there was a reason I've never walked in here." She scrunched her nose at a dark stain on the floor.

Wes settled into a booth bench. "Place seems fine to me."

She gave him a condescending smile. "Says the guy who

insists on having his towels laundered daily by his personal housekeeper, ensuring only the softest material touches his dainty hands."

He held up his hands. "These are not dainty."

No, they weren't. Wes's cuffs were rolled to his elbows. Muscles defined his masculine forearms, veins stretching along his hands. He had big hands. Strong hands. Very *non-dainty* hands. "Dainty is as dainty does," she said.

"Yet, I'm the one relaxed in this fine establishment." He placed his phone on the table and stretched his arm along the top of the booth, oblivious of the dirty napkin he was about to hit. The second his fingers brushed it, he snarled and snapped his hand back.

"Yeah, you seem really relaxed." She grabbed a fresh napkin, wiped ketchup off her bench seat, then slid in.

Wes picked up a beer list and flicked the paper's edge.

She tucked her hands under her thighs. "If you touch your mouth after touching that, you'll probably get gonorrhea."

Eyes bright, he laughed.

She used to make a game of it. The Make Weston Laugh game. Subtle jokes. Well-placed sarcasm. Coaxing a grin onto his stoic face had always given her a swell of pride. Tonight his laugh had a different effect. That strong chin, those sharp cheekbones and styled hair, his blue eyes and all that physique packed into tailored clothing—his level of handsome was giving her hot flashes, and his smile only upped his masculine appeal.

She'd tried to deny her recent growing interest in him, hide from it. Pretend it wasn't happening. This was Wes, after all. The guy who drove her extra-special batty. But there was no hiding from one startling fact: every time she relived her Falcon kiss, she ended up picturing Wes. She'd avoided him as best she could since. Tried her darndest to feel annoyance over attraction. But when she'd googled him this week, eager to cut his infuriatingly handsome face from a printout and create a new page in her Weston Aldrich scrapbook, she'd seen a picture of him with the stunning Rosanna Farzad, and her chest had ached.

A waitress came by to take their drink order.

"So," Wes said when she left, "you've been okay today?"

She'd have been better if they'd hung out as usual, silent about all things Leo, while still supporting each other. These new feelings complicated matters, especially since he'd been dating publicly, an anomaly for him. Wes bringing today's history up was also new. "Okay enough. It's always hard, but I think the lead up is worse."

"How do you mean?"

She was tired of rehashing things in her mind. She wanted to go to sleep and wake up tomorrow. Have this day, this week, this year be over. "I hate talking about it," she said.

"You and me both."

"I hate admitting he's gone." And showing her weakness. So why was she opening up now?

He nodded, the beer list forgotten. "I hate acknowledging what he's missed out on, even movies and TV shows he would have loved. I hate that I..." He glanced down and scratched his nose.

She pointed to his face. "Felix had that same twitchy look. I guess the whole 'owners look like their pets' thing is true. Except for the dainty hands. Felix has more masculine hands."

There was that smile again. "If I looked like an animal, it would be a jaguar, Squirrel."

"What the hell's a jaguar-squirrel? I told you to quit the animal experimentation."

This laugh was louder. So damn sexy with his neck stretched and head tipped back. "If anything, we should experiment on your brain. Figure out why you're obsessed with animal mutations. Is it a bestiality thing?"

She cringed. "You crossed a line, Herbert. And how's Felix, anyway? Back with his rightful owner?"

Wes tapped his thumb on the table. He scratched his nose again and mumbled something under his breath.

"Sorry, my bionic hearing's on the fritz. Please speak at human volume."

"I kept him."

Her hearing was definitely off. "You kept the emotionally stunted rabbit-squirrel?"

"I had no choice. He's happier at my place."

Her cackle had heads whipping their way. Wes had always held a hard line against owning pets or plants or anything that took long-term care. She had no clue what had prompted the bunny adoption, but she imagined doing a new scrapbook page, with him feeding Felix from a bottle. "I should throw you a bunny shower. You can register at bunny babies."

He glared. She grinned.

Making fun of Wes was way better than rehashing how she'd flipped through Leo's old Batman comics this week and had found herself crying. She'd alternated between reliving her fading memories and blaring music in her quiet apartment, noise to drown her sad thoughts. But she hadn't been lying to Wes, either. She was okay enough today. Happy the date was almost behind her. Pushing through hardships was her normal.

Looking at Wes across from her, imagining straddling his lap and ripping those designer buttons from his perfectly ironed shirt, was definitely not normal.

The waitress brought their drinks. Wes sipped his beer. She guzzled her wine.

Annie didn't know when her attraction to Wes had begun or why, but the one-sidedness of it—her temptation, his oblivion—emphasized their power imbalance. Wes had more money. He was older, bigger, stronger. He'd had goals and a life plan since pre-school. She was her usual impulsive self.

"Why'd you stick around?" she asked, suddenly edgy.

He squinted at her, head cocked. "I told you, I wanted to hang out tonight."

"I mean in general. After Leo, when I went into foster care —why'd you insist on staying in touch, taking care of me?" She didn't know why she was pushing. Sitting across from him was scrambling her brain.

"Because I promised Leo I would, and because I care." His voice lowered, intimate almost. "You have to know how much I care about you." His blue eyes shifted to her cheek, to the small scratch from Falcon's mask. He swallowed. His attention darted to her lips, then to a flashing Budweiser sign above the bar.

Her hackles rose. Wes fidgeted when he was lying, which meant her biggest fear was true. "I'm your charity case."

"My what?"

"Your charity case. Your philanthropic duty. A project to make you feel like you're bettering the world, like your mother would have wanted. I'm just..." She was nothing real to Weston Aldrich, and the sooner she remembered that, the sooner she'd quit wondering how his non-dainty hands would feel on her body. "You know what, forget it. I'm not good company. I think I'll head home."

She started shimmying out from her side of the booth, but Wes clamped his hand on her knee. He stared at her so long, her lungs seized. "You're not a charity case, Annie. Don't ever think that."

God, the vehemence in his eyes. She tried to reply, tell him it was okay. He'd been unbelievably generous with his help over the years. She'd never expected more from him, had no clue why she wanted more now. A lot more. Those lips on hers.

He had scrapbook lips, a perfect pucker you'd find on a Calvin Klein model. Broodtastic with a side of devil-may-care. Or just plain devil. She couldn't open her mouth to speak.

His thumb moved slightly, harder pressure on the inside of her knee. "You're the most important person in my life."

Her insides hummed, an involuntary reaction to the contact and the intimate drop in his voice, and he was breathing harder, like there was more he wanted to do or say. Could he be attracted to her, too? Had he been as confused as her lately?

His phone rang, and the name Rosanna flashed on the screen. *Oh my God.* Annie had officially lost her mind. One touch from Wes and she was imagining the two of them riding off into the sunset, his stupid rabbit-squirrel on her lap. The guy was dating a notorious socialite, for heaven's sake. The woman was stunning, with piles of shiny dark hair and flawless skin. Annie needed to get a grip. Wes would never see her as anything other than a pity sister, and Falcon had stood her up. She'd have better luck asking out the urine-smelling man at the bar.

Wes didn't move to answer his phone. She didn't care. She shoved his hand off her leg while shoving her Wes feelings into her internal lockbox, next to all things Leo.

"Word of advice," she said as she stood and brushed off her jeans. "Don't bring your girlfriend here. It smells."

She turned and left. Not before Wes winced, like her words had stung him.

The second she made it home and slammed her apartment door shut, she got ready for bed, but she wasn't tired. She powered up her computer and searched her various online chat groups. She needed distraction. From Wes. From thoughts of Leo. From her overtired rambling brain. Pegasus wasn't around the Punchies scrapbook page, so she chatted with Deaf Jam in her BOOMPop forum. They messaged about music and upcoming festivals. She raved about Falcon's DJ skills, leaving out details about his kissing skills. There was no mention about what this day meant to Annie or how things with her and Wes had veered from awkward to worrying.

Instead of feeling more relaxed, the random online chat had her feeling antsier, claustrophobic in the apartment that had always been her comfort zone. A shift in focus was needed. Something to funnel her anxiousness into action. Falcon was the answer. She'd made progress with him at his last show. He'd singled her out, brought her up on stage. And that kiss? He owed her answers for his seductions, but the man was practically a superhero, vanishing into the night.

This wouldn't be a repeat of her Sudoku books, though. She wouldn't walk away because things were getting harder. She'd double down her efforts. Stake out his next gig. Be ready to tail him so she could unveil her masked man.

10

APPARENTLY WHEN ANNIE put effort into a goal, she lost sight of boundaries. She'd somehow become a stalker. Or a private eye. Or just plain creepy. She was in a dingy alley, parked in a taxi, waiting for Falcon's show to end. This had been the first of his gigs she'd missed since Vivian had introduced her to the DJ. Annie hated being outside while clubbers could let loose and dance inside, but doubling down her efforts meant not letting the man escape.

Falcon had had a driver pick him up at his last handful of shows, so she planned to tail his car and corner him once he was out. Yell at him for the rude ditching, then beg him to teach her everything he knew.

There was no "or" about it. This was definitely stalker territory.

The cabbie texted on his phone. Her window was rolled down slightly, so she could hear the heavy bass pulsing through the club's walls. It was nearly two a.m.

She held her breath, waited for a change in music to signal the end of Falcon's set. He always downshifted when he finished, played a mellower dance tune and slipped out the back while his team went to work. It was quite the setup, really. Roadies to assemble and take down his equipment, a driver to pick him up. Always elusive.

He had kissed her, though. And she wanted to know why.

A siren wailed in the distance. A few "whoops" carried from the alley. She strained her ears as the tempo thumping from the club changed, then five people careened around the building and ran to the back exit.

"Get ready," she told the cab driver. "He'll be out soon."

"Whatever you say, lady."

Spending money on this taxi-car-chaser wasn't in her budget, but pinning Falcon down took precedence. When she was a serious DJ, she'd save for her future.

The fans chatted animatedly, and more people tore to the rear exit, wanting a glimpse of their mysterious idol. When the back door cracked open, everyone shouted for Falcon, but a massive man pushed outside. Thick neck. Boulders for shoulders. Bouncers were a different breed of human. He towered over the groupies and tried to usher them away. A black sedan with tinted windows pulled up on schedule, the whole scene something from a reality show, paparazzi lying in wait for an A-list celebrity.

It was tough to see through the gathering crowd, but people suddenly jumped and waved, their shouts carrying to her car.

I love you, Falcon.

Amazing set, man.

Sign my boobs!

Annie gave the crowd a death stare as the last shout registered. She'd like to sign something special on that woman's boobs. *Hands off. He's mine.* Two ridiculous thoughts, since the guy had stood her up and her sexual energy had been focused on a different male as of late. Still, there was no forgetting that kiss, how his raw passion had lit her up.

She glimpsed Falcon's masked face and wide shoulders before he slipped into the car.

She pointed to the sedan like a movie extra. "Follow that car, sir."

The cabbie shook his head, but he pulled out and followed Falcon. She gripped her seat belt and leaned forward. Another car wove between them.

"Can't you drive faster?"

"This ain't *The Fast and the Furious*."

"It isn't *The Longest Day*, either," she mumbled.

When a red light forced her to watch Falcon's car disappear ahead, she cursed. The light turned green. She bounced her heel and scanned the road, a shaky laugh releasing when she spotted the sedan at a distance. Falcon's driver wasn't taking weird side streets, worried about being followed. They hadn't counted on one super fan, who'd been kissed and dismissed, to become a secret spy.

The cabbie, doing a pretty darned good Fast and Furious impression after all, dodged cars to catch up and flicked his signal to follow Falcon down a side street, but when they turned the corner, the sedan was gone.

He braked and shrugged. "Looks like we lost 'em."

She squeezed her fists and groaned. They were in a residential area with old red brick homes. Most porches had warped steel awnings. Long staircases led up to front doors, and there wasn't a soul in sight. So much for doubling down her efforts and demanding answers from Falcon.

The cabbie looked in his rearview mirror at her. "Where to now?"

She closed her eyes, tried to slow her breaths. This wasn't the end. She wouldn't let her frustrations derail her efforts.

This drive to succeed made her want to sink her teeth into her life more fully, hunker down and see what she could accomplish. Sighing, she opened her eyes, and her spine snapped straight.

A man was walking on the opposite side of the street, toward the main intersection. She couldn't see his face, but he was dressed in black with a backpack hanging off one shoulder. When he passed under a streetlight, sparkles and colorful feathers caught the light—Falcon's mask sticking out of the bag.

She did a happy dance in her seat. "I'll get out here, sir. Thank you for the top-notch driving."

Money shoved at him, she hurried out and followed Falcon at a distance. She should have worn a black unitard, not the flowery dress she'd scored at a secondhand shop, but the mid-thigh cut looked cute with her ankle boots, and she wanted Falcon to like what he saw. Another kiss might help get Wes off her mind.

She stuck to the shadows as much as possible, keeping back, biding her time. The man hiked up his bag, and the mask poked farther out. There was no mistaking his build or those beautiful feathers. She still couldn't see his face, but her skin tingled, curiosity and excitement buzzing. When she gathered her courage, she'd call his name. Confront him about his disappearing act. She'd see the man below the mask and demand he teach her his ways.

The best part? Dude had no clue his cover was about to be blown.

WESTON INHALED until his lungs ached, then exhaled through his nose as his shoes echoed off the sidewalk, a backbeat to the rhythmic whooshing in his ears. He should have let his driver take him home tonight. It would have left him time to reorganize his intro for his next show. Play with the video footage, since tonight's venue hadn't had space for his new setup.

He should have done a lot of things, but he'd needed air. To just walk. Breathe. Try to get his head right.

Tonight's set had gone well. His mixes had been seamless, the new songs he'd chosen hitting perfectly. The crowd had been amped up, moving as one, a writhing beast feeding off his music. He was sometimes twitchy after shows, too wired to sleep, adrenaline pumping. This restlessness was more frustrated than euphoric, though. And he knew why.

Annie hadn't been there.

He'd been nervous before his set, wondering if she'd show, dreading it. He was tired of fighting his feelings for her, wished everything could go back to how it had been before. But there was no undoing that kiss, or untangling his growing attraction to her from their years of friendship. He'd been sure her absence at his shows would free his mind from this relentless confusion. It had only increased his distraction.

His phone rang. He swung his backpack around and fished out his cell. At the sight of Rosanna's name, he answered. "If you sank another yacht, I don't want to know about it."

She laughed. "I've been good, Daddy. Promise. But I need to cancel tomorrow's date."

He shook his head at the night sky. "That's twice in a row. I thought we had a deal."

Last time she'd called to ditch him, Annie had seen Rosanna's name flash on his phone. Annie had shut down instantly, leaving him in that nasty dive bar staring after her, unsure why everything in him ached. Tonight's disappointment at her absence made it all worse.

Mumbling registered in his ear, as though Rosanna was

talking to someone with her hand over the phone, and footfalls sounded behind him. He turned and squinted down the street, but nothing was there.

"Sorry," Rosanna said clearly. "Yeah, we still have a deal, but remember that guy I told you about?"

He resumed walking, dropped his voice lower in case someone was nearby. "The indie musician with the pierced face?"

"No, the motorcycle guy. He's leaving for a cross-country ride. It's my last chance to see him before he goes."

The concept of monogamy was so foreign to her she couldn't even fake date properly. "That's all well and good, but we need to be seen together. If your father realizes you're still playing the field, or that we're lying to him, my deal could fall apart, and your *children's* children will be paying for that yacht stunt."

"You worry too much, Weston. I've told dear old Dad we're taking things slow. He seems pleased about that. Thinks it's sweet we're being old-fashioned. You should take Annie out on the down-low. You certainly talk about her enough."

He thought about her even more. "She's just a friend. *You* and I will go out this week. Dinner somewhere romantic but visible. And you will not cancel."

"Has anyone ever told you you're bossy?"

Annie, about a million and one times. "Be safe with Motorcycle Guy."

"You're sweet, Weston," Rosanna said quietly. "Too bad you're not my type."

It was too bad. If he found Rosanna attractive beyond her visual appearance, he might not spend his waking minutes wishing Annie was in his kitchen, or his living room, his private Falcon Cave, his bedroom, nestled into him, under him, around him, anywhere near him. He couldn't quit thinking about Leo, either, lately: Weston's idiotic choices the night he died, never confessing the truth to Annie. The closer he felt to her, the worse the lie seemed. If he liked Rosanna, he wouldn't be worried about hurting the best person he knew.

He put his phone away, rubbed his eyes. Rosanna would always be a wild card. He needed a backup plan, another way to secure this merger if their fake dating failed.

"Falcon!"

Weston froze. He didn't turn. Had someone followed his car? Had his driver taken a bribe, told a fan where he was? Hard to believe he'd take the risk when Weston paid him a grand a night for the drive. He contemplated reaching for his mask, putting the stupid thing on. If it got out that Weston Aldrich moonlighted as Falcon, Rosanna derailing the merger would be the least of his problems. Running from this fan was smarter.

But a hand latched onto his arm before he could bolt. He tensed, yanking free of the woman's grip.

"No, no way. You don't get to ditch me again."

Every bone in Weston's body seized. He knew that voice, but that voice shouldn't know Falcon. It shouldn't be anywhere near him. A stranger learning who he was would be trouble. Annie figuring it out? He may as well purchase a headstone now.

The woman—*please, God, don't be Annie*—took advantage of his stupor, grabbed his arm again, and spun him around. His stomach dropped.

Annie reared back. "Holy shit."

He tried to open his mouth, explain about the lies, the DJing, the late-night gigs, but like all Annie-related issues lately, he couldn't find the words. He was sick about the deception. Angry at being found out. This was worse than any of those grenades, though. In about ten seconds, once she'd recovered from the shock, she'd realize they'd kissed. That he'd kissed her, knowing exactly who she was.

Annie had become a statue. "Holy fucking shit."

He stayed mute, his heart punching his ribs so hard his hands throbbed.

Seven seconds and counting.

"Tell me I'm wrong. Tell me this isn't what I think it is."

He should say something, anything. Get ahead of the shit-storm about to unleash. Specifically, her inner pit bull. But Annie poked his face, pinched his cheek, and mumbled, "Not dreaming."

He laughed.

She curled her lip, shaking her head so hard she looked possessed. "No."

"No, what?"

"*No*, you don't get to laugh."

He had no clue why he was laughing. Annie always made him laugh, but nothing about this was funny. He focused on the pavement, her cute ankle boots facing his black sneakers. Another laugh squeaked out.

Three seconds.

"Seriously? I'm about to give you the verbal lashing of your life, and you're laughing? How could you not tell me you're—"

He looked up. Her eyes were wide, her fingers drifting up to touch her lips as a rosy blush pinked her cheeks. *Bingo.* She was probably picturing his lips on hers, his fingers tugging on her hair, their hips lined up, bodies primed. Or maybe that was just his depraved mind.

"You kissed me," she whispered.

"I'm..." He cleared the gravel from his throat. "I'm sorry, Anthea. I should have told you."

Her eyes darted around, her fingers still on her lips. "You knew it was me. You knew, and you kissed me."

She wasn't gesturing and yelling, berating him for the Falcon lies, the secret life he hadn't shared, his lack of respect with that kiss. Her lips were parted, her chest swelling deeper. Everything was changing between them. Because of the kiss? Before the kiss? He wasn't sure, but there was something in her vulnerable gaze, the speeding of her breaths.

Was she fighting her feelings for him, too?

His body tensed in reply, as though he wanted just that. Which would make him a dick. Except for his one disaster, Weston had never had a girlfriend. He had arrangements with a few likeminded women, who preferred no-string hookups. Random nights between the sheets, no drama, no sleepovers. His one attempt to date with an eye on the future, he'd freaked out.

Three months into that relationship, Lila had told him she loved him, and his lungs had backfired. His chest had felt like it was rupturing. He'd pictured getting closer with her, opening up to her, allowing himself to love her. Only to lose her, being left so alone—his early losses returned tenfold—that he'd torn out of there, barely an excuse given as he'd busted onto the street, never to speak with her again.

Now he had friends with benefits. They were sweet and lovely, and demanded nothing he couldn't give. He hadn't called any of them in a while. The thought had sickened him slightly these days. Not as much as the hurt emanating from the one person he was trying to protect.

"I had to get you away from Duncan," he said, grasping at straws. His best excuse for that kiss.

She flinched.

"He's not the man for you," he went on. "He uses women, sleeps with them and moves on. You should never have gone out with that guy." And he needed to learn when to shut up.

The lie had come out easily, as lies did when mixed with

truth. He *had* called her up on stage to get her away from Duncan, but he'd kissed her because he'd wanted to, and now she looked like someone had torched her scrapbook collection.

How would she look at him if she learned why Leo had really been shot?

"I'm sorry, Squirrel," he said, at a loss.

I'M SORRY, Squirrel. Sorry! After lying to her for months. Years, maybe. Sorry, after dragging her on the stage and kissing the daylights out of her. Sorry, after standing her up, then admitting the only reason the Kiss of the Century had happened was to control her and keep her away from Duncan.

And the "contrite" man was *sorry*?

Annie's right eye twitched, her whole body one spasm away from karate chopping Wes in the neck. "Don't ever call me Squirrel again, and maybe I was the one doing the using. Maybe I wanted to walk on the wild side and have fun with a guy as hot as Duncan."

Wes's nostrils flared. "Don't."

"Don't what?"

"Don't bait me, Anthea. You're just trying to get under my skin."

He was kind of right, but she wasn't about to admit it. "You don't know a thing about me. Not anymore. And I obviously don't know a thing about you."

"That's bullshit, and you know it."

"Do I?" She glanced around at the passing cars. Traffic lights flipped from red to green. The air was still. She felt wired and exhausted. "The Weston Aldrich I knew was the heir of Aldrich Pharma, not a late-night DJ who kissed women while wearing a mask. Do you do that often? I missed your early shows. Did you use your mysterious charm to lure women onstage and..." She gasped. She thought back to that night, the timing of it. "You kissed me when you had a girlfriend."

"I did not." His reply was sharp, vehement, but he looked a tad green around the gills. "We weren't exclusive."

She reviewed the timeline. She'd found pictures of him and that Rosanna beauty together before the performance in question. *Before* the kiss. They'd been holding hands in the online photo, on their way to a bar or dinner. Definitely a date. The image didn't mean they'd been exclusive, but everything about that kiss felt wrong: how into it she'd been, whimpering into his mouth, rocking against him. He'd had her panting for more, and it had been a setup. A ruse to get her away from Duncan. She hadn't even known who she was kissing, and she'd been willing to go home with him. Although the familiarity of his eyes sure made sense now.

Her throat closed. Saliva pooled in her mouth. However upset she'd been when Wes had basically admitted she was his charity case, this was miles worse. And here she was, reliving that kiss again. The heat. The wanting. The...

Whoa.

She looked Wes hard in the face, searched the ribbons of blue in his eyes.

More than their mouths had been involved in that kiss. If Wes had wanted her away from Duncan, he could have just given her the note. A chaste kiss would have sufficed. But he'd dug in and had kissed her with passion, his whole body worked up, evidence of his arousal hot and hard against her belly. *A distraction kiss, my ass.*

There was more going on with Wes than he was admitting. Not that it mattered. He'd said "weren't" not "aren't." *We weren't exclusive.* Past tense implied there'd been a change in his and

Rosanna's coupledom, and that kiss was the tip of this nonsensical iceberg. "Why didn't you tell me you were a DJ?"

"Why didn't you tell me you'd decided to do the same?"

She slapped her thigh and cackled, the sharp sound carrying into the night. She abruptly clamped her mouth shut. "Let's be clear about something, Herbert."

"Who's Herbert?"

"You are, old man. I'm doing the asking, and you're doing the answering. You owe me that and then some. *Capiche?*"

He twitched his nose, looking more like Felix the rabbit-squirrel every day. "Let's walk while we talk." He shrugged his backpack higher and started toward the city.

She gawked at his back. "You're not seriously planning to walk to your condo. Or do you have a Bat Cave nearby?"

He turned slowly, impatience in the exaggerated move. "I have a Falcon Cave, not a Bat Cave. It's in my condo. And I need air, which is why I asked my driver to let me out."

"Do you have a Falconmobile, too?"

He smirked. "Wouldn't work. I'd need a car designed for homogenization."

"Designed for milk? Would it shrink into a freeze-dried powder that gets mixed into drinks to make you so annoying people around you drop dead, because that would actually make sense as your superpower."

He laughed.

She glared. "What did I say about the laughing, Weston?"

He dragged his hand down his face and sighed. "*Homogenization.* Not homogenized milk. It would have to blend in. And I wasn't planning on walking all the way to my condo. I needed air. Figured I'd walk a bit then hop in a cab when I got tired."

"Then let's walk. I have an inquisition to unleash."

He scrubbed his shoe over the sidewalk. The sound grated

her ears. "I'm sure you have a thousand questions. I have a number of my own. But it's late, and neither of us is in the right headspace. Let's grab a cab. We'll both go home and get some sleep. We can meet tomorrow night for a proper interrogation."

How convenient for him. "I want answers now."

"I'm too tired to give them to you."

Her tongue prickled with the urge to lash out, but the skin under Wes's eyes looked bruised, sunken. It could be the darkness, the late hour. According to Duncan, there was another source. She and Duncan had texted periodically since their date. He was actually pretty funny, last week's bout of texting banter amusing enough to have her cackling.

Duncan: **Are you sure you don't want to add benefits to our friend status? All the cool kids are doing it.**

Annie: **I don't give into peer pressure.**

Duncan: **That must be a typo. You mean you want peer pleasure, right?**

She'd replied with laughing emojis, and he'd replied by asking about Wes, wondering if his boss and friend was okay. He'd mentioned that Wes had been exhausted at work, grumpier than usual. Instead of calling Wes and checking up on him, all Annie had done was avoid him while chasing Falcon. With tonight's revelation, it was clear Wes was burning the candle at both ends. Tonight, in this blue-gray light, he looked haggard.

"Fine," she said, her emotions warring. "Tomorrow it is, and you better not think about lying."

Weston was right to postpone this interrogation. She was confused about that kiss, his relationship status, upset he hadn't confided in her about his music. Not that she'd been much better lately. She hadn't told him about meeting that busker, the piano lessons, her DJ plans. And he was Falcon, the man, the myth, the musical genius! She'd been lusting after

Weston *and* his alter ego. The awareness ratcheted her spark of attraction into a full-blown fever.

She needed time to acclimatize, figure out how she felt under this mess of emotion. Get her haywire hormones in check. Then she'd attack him with a list of questions, none of which would be: *When do I get to kiss you again?*

11

"WHEN DID YOU START DJING?" Annie sat across from Weston, spine straight, her hands clasped together on his dining table.

The marble monstrosity sat twelve comfortably. The cool surface was clean and polished and did zero to douse the heat pulsing off her body. Anger heat. Defensive heat. Not *in-heat* heat. She meant business. She may have worn an off-the-shoulder maxi dress in shades of turquoise, exuding summer fun, instead of a blazer or pantsuit, but she had three pages of questions and a pen to cross off each one. She wanted to know why Wes had hidden his DJing. She was determined to have him teach her. She needed to understand why he'd devoured her that night and had lied about enjoying it.

No one was leaving this table until she was satisfied.

Weston removed his tie and folded it over the chair to his left. He undid the top two buttons of his dress shirt and rolled his cuffs, as though he had all the time in the world. Like he was the one in control. She gritted her teeth.

He matched her pose, non-dainty hands clasped, shoulders

squared. "I started playing in clubs three years ago, but I've been dabbling in music longer."

"How much longer?"

A small vein pulsed at his temple. "The year after my mother died."

Her heart squeezed. This confrontation was bound to unearth painful memories from both their pasts, but she'd been determined to maintain an emotional distance. There were reasons she'd kept secrets from him. He no doubt had his motivations, too. Yet here she was, one question in, already softening toward him. "Because you missed her?"

He unclasped his hands and ran a hand over his mouth. "Because I was angry. Violent at times. Marjory blackmailed my father by threatening to quit and forced me into therapy. It was suggested I find an outlet."

Wes's mother had died a year after Leo. Another devastating blow. Still, he'd maintained his weekly visits with Annie, had never failed to rag on her about homework, hobbies, friends. He'd show up random days to walk her home from school. He'd been serious, not angry. Intense, but not the type to lash out. "I don't get it. We hung out back then. You always seemed fine. I mean, fine for a guy who thought wearing loafers was dressing down."

He smirked, then swallowed. "I need a glass of Scotch with this conversation. I have that Chardonnay you like."

He didn't ask if she wanted a drink, just stood and moved through his kitchen methodically. He knew the wine she liked, expensive stuff she'd never buy at home. He stocked it for her, along with her favorite salt and vinegar chips and rocky road ice cream. He even had an *Architectural Digest* subscription because she used the magazines for scrapbooking. None of these details were new, but warmth spread through her chest.

This man who'd kissed her passionately knew her better than anyone. And he had a girlfriend.

Wes returned with their drinks and walked to her side. His hip brushed her arm as he set her glass down. They both froze. Her belly windmilled.

He returned to his seat and took a pull of his Scotch. "I was never out of control with you," he said, his attention on the glass in his hands. "Everything was always better with you."

It was a good thing he wasn't looking at her. Her cheeks felt like they were on fire, and the windmill situation upgraded to dizzying spins. She sipped her wine. The toasty notes clung to her tongue, settled her stomach. Her body loosened as she looked at Wes for what felt like the first time. "I wish I'd known you were struggling."

"I didn't want you to know."

"I'm strong on my own, Wes. I never needed you to be strong for me."

"It was never about that."

"Then why hide the music from me? The therapy? I told you when I had counseling. You were the one who said talking about tough stuff was important." He'd been the reason she'd stuck with those sessions. She'd despised them at first, had grown to accept them, and was thrilled when they'd been done. In hindsight, they had helped. Wes had helped her, but he'd never let her help him.

He ran his finger around the rim of his glass. "There were things about Leo's death I didn't want to talk about. It was all too hard at the time."

She pictured Wes's devastated face when he'd woken her at the shelter, his choppy words, his tears. Visions she didn't want to recall. They weren't here to rehash what they'd lost. This was about his secret identity, the changes in their relationship.

She consulted her question list. "You could have picked up guitar, drums, the triangle. How'd you end up DJing?"

"My man hands are too big for the triangle."

Smart ass, trying to distract her by being adorable. "Wrong answer."

He smiled. "Same reason you're into it."

Right. Leo. She took her pen and crossed off that obvious question. "How'd you come up with Falcon?"

"Same answer."

The Batman comics Leo had loved, which she should have realized, too. Another useless question. "Don't get too comfortable. I'm starting with the easy stuff."

Wes leaned forward. "When did you get bitten by the DJ bug? And why didn't you tell me about it?"

"This is my inquisition, not yours."

"Quid pro quo, Squirrel. If you want answers, you need to bend."

Fine. If he wanted answers, he'd get them. "Two months ago, and I didn't tell you because of that nickname."

His dark eyebrows drew together. "You didn't tell me because I call you Squirrel?"

"At least your hearing isn't failing in your old age."

"Explain yourself."

She opened her mouth to finally tell him how demoralizing his judgment could be, when she heard a soft *scritch*ing. She'd been in Wes's condo enough to recognize the hum of the air conditioner, the ringing echo of steps when walking on his hardwood floor. This sound was new.

Side-eyeing him, she pushed her chair back and snooped through the kitchen, scanned the loft condominium's open space. The fancy paintings and dramatic sculptures were still fancy and dramatic. The reclaimed brick walls still stretched up to the third story, making her feel small. Nothing was new or out of place, then she heard another *scritch, scritch, scritch.*

"What are you doing?" Wes asked from his chair.

"Investigating. I heard..." She walked toward his living area, made a wide circle around his leather sectional, and abruptly laughed.

Wes didn't ask what she'd found. Weirdo knew what had her grinning. "I completely forgot you kept the rabbit-squirrel. Does he sleep in your room with you or out here?"

"You didn't answer my last question."

"Because you have a real, live pet. But I'm confused. When I met you outside your building, you were coming from work. You weren't carrying the cage, and I'm pretty sure you didn't have Felix cradled against your stomach in a Rabbit Bjorn."

He looked up at the towering ceiling, his attention meandering to the massive widows. "His separation anxiety's gone."

"His anxiety's gone? Just like that?"

"At least your hearing isn't failing in your old age," he said, stealing her line.

Such a comedian. "How'd you cure him?"

"Living here has calmed him down."

She squinted at the rabbit, but he looked the same as when she'd first met him. "I still don't get why you kept him. You hate pets the way most people hate eating liver. What changed?"

"Felix is different."

"Oh, I know he's a rare rabbit-squirrel with a penchant for world domination, but you've always said..." She trailed off as she recalled his pet dismissals.

Over the years, she'd suggested he get a cat or fish or monkey, because the guy could afford one, to warm up his solitary life. Easy companionship. Wes's answers had always been the same: *It's too much commitment. I don't have time. Pets require care I'm not equipped to give. And they smell.*

She'd roll her eyes and tell him he was made of stone. He'd retaliate with a Squirrel joke. Annoying, but his vehement pet stance could be linked to the kiss conundrum. Aside from this Rosanna socialite, Wes had never had a long-term girlfriend. He would sometimes mention a night out with a woman, but as long as she'd known him, he'd been single. She'd never given his lifestyle much thought. There had been no physical attraction to prompt curiosity.

She was curious now.

Odor factor aside, commitment issues might be a more defining attribute of Wes than she'd realized. There was no way around the bond Annie and he already shared. Building upon that with intimacy was daunting for her. It was likely as scary for him. He might even have liked kissing Annie as much as she'd liked being kissed by him, but the depth of their relationship had sent him running to this other "safer" woman, one who didn't come with their emotional history.

She chewed on those possibilities while squatting next to Felix's cage, her knees fanning out the soft fabric of her dress. She poked her finger through the wire slats. Felix munched his hay. "I'm glad you have each other," she said loud enough for both pet and owner to hear. Wes's stylish condo felt more like a home with the silly rabbit.

"Back to the nickname," Wes said, ignoring the rabbit in the room. "What does that have to do with your DJ interest?"

She stayed facing Felix. It was easier talking to him. "When you call me Squirrel it reminds me you think I'm flighty and incompetent and never stick with anything worthwhile. I've always known I'd figure out my life eventually, and when I decided this was what I wanted to do, I didn't want your judgment to discourage me."

She'd never admitted that much to Wes, too worried about hurting him or their friendship. Even now, her pulse quickened, picking up speed until she felt shaky squatting next to the cage. She stood, straightened her dress, and faced him.

Wes's cheeks were slack, his brow crumpled. He stared at his glass as though crestfallen. "I'm so sorry," he said quietly.

Weston Aldrich didn't do heartfelt apologies. He ran a multi-billion dollar company with single-minded precision. He was a planner who'd led a secret life for years, never buckling, never showing weakness.

Abruptly, he pushed back his chair and stalked over to her. He gripped her upper arms. "You are smart, Annie. And creative and funny and talented. You're unbelievably capable, and I only ever wanted you to reach your potential. Consider that nickname banished."

His genuine distress weakened her limbs. Or maybe it was their proximity. The shoulders of her dress slipped lower, and his fingers bit into her bare skin.

He'd taken her to the Hamptons last summer. A work function which had included families and friends. Initially, she'd said no, always feeling like his charity case. He'd insisted she come. In the end, she'd loved the hot sun on her skin, how it had warmed her bones. She had loved watching Wes laugh with coworkers and then smile at her. He'd dragged her into the water, the two of them messing around and splashing each other until Weston was all she could see. She'd forgotten how in tune she'd been to him that day.

The same sensations assaulted her now.

She dragged her gaze up, past the chest hair peeking out of his open collar, the masculine knot of his Adam's apple, all the way to those scrapbook lips. She licked her lips, trying to remember how Wes had tasted after they'd been sweaty and dancing. She met his eyes and sucked in a rough breath. His pupils had dilated, darkened, eclipsing all that complex blue.

He released her with a jerk of his hands, turned around, and dropped his head forward. His shoulders were hitched high, the tightness of his shirt hinting at coiled frustration below. She wanted to go to him, knead those tense muscles, finally ask him if the merger was tough on him and find out how she could help. She wanted to kiss the sensitive spot at the back of his neck and wrap him in her arms, tell him his apology meant more than he could know.

Kissing him had meant more than *she'd* realized.

All their years together—the frustrating and funny, the good and the bad—had bound them irrevocably, but this relationship was the cornerstone of her life, and it was shifting. Quickly. The prospect suddenly terrified her. And he had a girlfriend.

Best to steer them in a safer direction. For now. Focus on their joint love of music and the fact that she was going to be his apprentice.

"TAKE ME TO YOUR FALCON CAVE," Annie said from behind him.

Weston continued counting his breaths, slowing his pulse. Being this close to Annie was testing his willpower, and he was furious with himself for letting her down. That stupid nickname had been a joke. Her defensive comebacks had been amusing. She'd jab at him with her usual wit. Tease him for being uptight and controlling and a general pain in her ass. More proof jokes were rooted in truth.

He *had* thought she'd been wasting her talents. He'd wanted her to be successful, self-reliant. If she'd told him about the DJing, he would have tried to steer her toward a steady job with a decent income and good benefits. A career with a future. For all the "nurturing" he'd done, he'd only managed to undermine her confidence.

There wasn't much he could do about the past. About Leo, any of it. But he could change the present. Make sure Annie knew how capable she was. As long as he did it from a distance.

Their drinks abandoned on his table, Weston led Annie down a side hallway, to the locked door at the end.

She hung back a few steps. "I thought this room held old financial records."

He inserted his key, glanced over his shoulder. "I lied."

"Shocker," she mumbled. "At least tell me you have a Falcon suit loaded with cool weapons developed in Aldrich Pharma's secret laboratory. And if there's one of those gadgets that shoots a wire between buildings so I can slide from skyscraper to skyscraper, consider it stolen."

"There's no suit or gadgets, Sq...*Annie*." Old habits died hard. "It's a boring sound room with DJ equipment." Except nothing about the space was boring to Weston. He'd never imagined sharing the space with anyone. The people he knew would find the equipment tedious, the soundproofed walls oppressive, and he was suddenly nervous about Annie seeing his sanctuary.

He opened the door and switched on the light. Annie gasped.

A breath later, she faced him. "Why didn't you tell me about the DJing?" Her hesitant voice sounded small. Pained.

He always managed to hurt her, no matter his intentions. "A bunch of reasons."

She waited, checked her watch, dug her finger into her ear as though clearing it.

He laughed. "Is that your subtle way of telling me you want the reasons?"

"I wasn't going for subtle."

One of the many things he adored about her. "You've always hated talking about Leo. Every anniversary of his death we'd hang out, but you'd never bring him up. So I didn't, either. His birthday, same thing. Music defined Leo, DJing in particular. I was worried mentioning it would upset you." Or that talking about Leo would lead to talking about the night he died. "And when I came up with my Falcon persona and decided to pursue live shows, I had to be careful."

"Because of work?"

"They can't know about this, Annie. If investors learn I'm part of the club scene, they'll get spooked, consider me a liability. You're the only person I've told." Not by choice, but he was glad she knew now. One more secret he didn't have to keep.

"People have hobbies," she said defensively. "Even stick-in-the-muds like you. Don't you think you're overreacting?"

Karim Farzad had set his daughter up with Weston to tame her wild ways, not to hook her up with a man who put the wild into parties. "I'm not overreacting."

She didn't question him again or thank him for his trust. She gave him a long look, then walked into his music room.

He stood near the door, letting her explore his equipment, each piece painstakingly chosen. He'd thought about Leo when designing every inch of this space. He'd imagined his friend's excitement over the wall's acoustic panels, the sound diffusers in the ceiling grid. Leo would have asked if he'd used the right number of bass traps to control low frequencies. He'd have checked if the acoustic panels were the best material to reduce reverb and echoes.

The leather couch, the wall of shelved records, and the Njideka Akunyili Crosby mixed-media painting were all Weston, but every time he walked in here, he felt Leo's presence.

With Annie in his inner sanctum, he felt things he'd rather not analyze.

Her sandals clicked over the hardwood floor, the fabric of her turquoise skirt swishing as she moved. The off-the-shoulder dress was lively. Completely Annie, and achingly alluring. The visible curves of her shoulders made his thighs flex. She ran her fingers over his collection of MIDI controllers, the turntables and mixers, the TV monitors stacked on the back wall, ending at his computer.

"It's as expensive and extravagant as I would have imagined." The softest smile graced her lips. "It's also beautiful."

He rubbed the back of his neck. "You think so?"

"I know so." Her gaze swept over his equipment. "My teacher has good stuff, but basic. Even Felix could make music in here."

"I doubt it."

"Guys with money always underestimate animal intelligence, then genetically-engineered dinosaurs take over the world."

He laughed again, the simple act so easy around Annie. She was witty. Funny. One-of-a-kind. "Having better equipment makes the sound cleaner, helps with better fades and transitions, but art is still art."

"It is." She walked her fingertips over the electric keyboard on her right. "What's your favorite piece in here?"

Easiest question he'd had in days. "The Roland-Jupiter 4 synth. It belonged to The Cure. Passed through other bands, but I found it at an auction. There's a memory modification in the system. Not sure when it was tweaked, but it has thirty-two memory banks instead of eight. Stability can be a bit sketchy, but the filter is killer and the sound is pristine."

He hadn't meant to bore Annie with those details, but he

never talked tech with anyone in person, never had the chance to boast about his personal equipment. He glanced at her, expecting a glazed look in her eyes, like when he talked to her about savings accounts and retirement plans, but she was nodding slightly, a slight fidget to her stance.

"Do you have to pee?" he asked.

"This is my contained-yet-excited dance." She unleashed a small squeal. "Do you know how jealous I am right now? I can't believe how cool this space is. Scrapbooking-heaven cool, but with state-of-the-art DJ equipment, which probably makes it DJ-heaven cool, but I digress. You need to brush off those artistic fingers of yours and show me some magic."

He should usher her out. Make an excuse and send her home. Being in the same room, inhaling her intoxicating scent, boomeranged his mind back to their kiss, how good she'd tasted, how much more he'd wanted. Thoughts he needed to shut down. Once this interrogation was over, he'd focus on Rosanna and the merger. He'd ask Annie to quit attending his shows. She could e-mail him snippets of her mixes. He'd return them with critiques and let her use the studio when he was out. Anything, as long as it didn't involve them making music together.

He shouldn't indulge her whims now, but he regretted all those "Squirrel" jokes. The last thing he wanted was to discourage her again, and her contained-yet-excited dance had him smiling, that sparkle in her eyes too hard to resist. It was special to see her so passionate about something. One short session together couldn't hurt.

———

DANCING AT A CLUB while Falcon-slash-Weston played music was a special kind of high. Watching him in his studio had

Annie feeling nuclear. He stood while he worked, barely glancing at his fingers as they flew over knobs and levers. He'd picked an unfamiliar funk record from his shelves, used an old-fashioned turntable to scratch out a percussive beat.

Boom-ch-de-lat-boom-chit-chat

His body moved to the music, small jerks of his shoulders, his chest, his head as the beats moved through him. She was moving, too. Dancing, energized, smiling at Wes, who was dressed to the nines with his cuffs rolled and slacks ironed, funking out to the tunes.

He pointed to a lever on his mixer. "I've lined up the next song. Fade it in for me."

Was this a test? A pass or fail where he'd decide if she was worthy of his teaching? She still struggled with phrasing, matching the beats when introducing a new song. The pressure to prove she could do this had her nearing hyperventilation.

"Close your eyes," he said.

"So you can lick your finger and stick it in my ear?" A gross stunt Leo had taught him.

"It would be fun, but no. Close your eyes. Listen for the beats until you feel them more than hear them."

She dialed down her dancing, closed her eyes, and listened. She counted the phrasing in her head. It wasn't a typical eight-bar chorus, making it hard to track. She squeezed her eyes tighter, but dizziness rocked her. A warm weight pressed against her back—Wes's hand steadying her equilibrium. He was usually the calm to her chaos. The caution to her impulsivity. But the heat from his hand seeped through her dress. Hamptons sunshine warm. And she suddenly wanted more chaos than calm. To lean into him, feel his sunlight in her bones, live wildly without worrying about consequences.

Unfortunately, he seemed keen to forget their kiss, and

there was the minor problem of his girlfriend. Plus this was a test of sorts. One she had no intention of failing.

She held her breath, listened, listened, *listened* so hard.

"Feel it," he murmured in her ear.

How was she supposed to feel anything besides his proximity? His persistent blasts of bone-melting heat? She felt cheated, having kissed Wes without realizing it had been him. If she'd known, she would have...what? Mauled him on stage? Bitten his lip for his lies then licked it better like some depraved vampire? No. She would have panicked. She'd been fighting her attraction to him then. She wasn't fighting it now, but she was nervous around him, and the distraction was messing with her concentration.

She took deeper breaths, relaxed her tense body, and moved to the beat again. Wes matched her rhythm, his fingers spreading wider on her back. The contact pebbled her skin, and a small sigh escaped her lips.

Focus, Annie.

She quit counting the beats, let the bass control her movements instead, listened with her body instead of her ears. Moved more freely.

There. After the chorus. Two extra bars, then a drop.

She opened her eyes. Her finger itched to press the fader. She controlled her impulse, waited for the next chorus, no longer dizzy or uncertain. She was conscious of Wes's hand still on her back, but she was more focused on the music. The tempo changed. Her heart raced as she pressed the lever. When the beats lined up, she jumped, and Wes laughed.

She swiveled and hugged him, instantly realizing her error. Their proximity short-wired her already haywire hormones, made everything inside her glow warmer. Hot sun. Everywhere.

Wes latched his arm around her, both of them breathing hard. Something in his pants also felt hard. And did he just inhale her hair? "You did good, Squirrel...shit. *Annie.* You did good, *Annie.*"

He pulled back at his fumble, moved behind a console, hiding his crotch from view. It could be wishful thinking, but she was pretty sure their hug had affected him. This whole evening had affected *her.*

"I don't mind." She readjusted the shoulders on her dress and slowed her breaths. "Like this, the name's kind of sweet."

He didn't budge from behind the console. "No. It's not. I'll shake the habit eventually."

She suddenly wasn't sure she wanted him to. She may have imagined his reaction to her just now, but he'd said the nickname with pride, a private name only he used. It made her feel special. Admitting as much was sharing too much of her feelings, and it wasn't fair to berate him for the label one minute, then go all squishy at the endearment the next.

She wiped her palms down her skirt and surveyed her new classroom. "You'll have lots of practice not calling me Squirrel during our lessons. I can do three or four times a week. Five if you can swing it. And I can help with your shows, setting up or—"

"No."

She paused. Maybe he'd misheard her. "I know we haven't talked about you officially teaching me, but I'm committed to this. I'll work around your schedule. And three times is fine."

He seemed to grow ten inches taller as he crossed his arms, his expression suddenly as impenetrable as his father's. "You can use the space when I'm not here, send me tracks to critique. I don't have time to do more."

His eyes were still slightly sunken, bruised underneath. Balancing two lives, when one of those was heading Aldrich Pharma, was taking its toll. She should finally ask him about that, but he would use the topic change to his advantage. "You make time for your own music, right? You don't show up to your sets and wing it."

His fingers looked like they were crushing his biceps. "Your point?"

"If you don't have time for instruction, let me sit in. I'll be quieter than Felix. You'll barely notice I'm here."

His gaze darted to her cheek, then to her lips. It was the same fidgetiness he'd exhibited in the dive bar, before she'd known about his dual identities. Interesting. Her cheek had still been chafed from his mask that night. It could have been a reminder of their kiss to him. Attraction he didn't want to face.

"Answer's still no," he said curtly, not meeting her eyes.

Weston always made eye contact. He'd lectured her on the importance of strong handshakes, eye contact, and listening when networking with people or potential employers. She'd give him a limp shake to annoy him, but she'd listened to his advice, and she was attuned to his behavior now. His uncharacteristic awkwardness suggested she hadn't imagined his body's response to her. Maybe her Rosanna theory was also on point and Wes had feelings for Annie, but he couldn't handle all they entailed.

The prospect of dating him certainly scared her, but what if he was the reason she'd never fallen in love? What if her heart had known all along where it belonged?

She'd have to do some sleuthing on his relationship status, maybe ask Vivian's girlfriend for private-eye tips. First she had to lock down Wes the DJ. "You sure that's your final answer?" she asked. "Because an anonymous call to your father or Biotrell—that's the company you're wooing into a merger, right?" When his jaw looked ready to break, she grinned. "Like I said, a quick call about a certain executive's extracurricular activities wouldn't look too good for you, would it?"

Anger practically wafted off of him. "You wouldn't."

Of course she wouldn't. But the threat hit on target. "Maybe I would, maybe I wouldn't. Is it worth testing me?"

He jabbed a hand through his dark hair and slashed a look at the exit as though he might bolt. Instead he leveled her with a baleful stare. "You have yourself a deal. But you won't talk while you're here. You won't ask questions. I won't even know you're in the room. Don't think I'll bend the rules and go easy on you."

She was done with easy. She was ready to learn the extent of her perseverance.

Which now included learning if Weston Aldrich had feelings for her.

12

"SAY THAT AGAIN." Weston was having déjà vu. It was the only explanation as to why he was in his office, staring at his father, once again at a loss for words.

His father's face was pinched. "Saanvi gave her notice. She's leaving."

The blow was as harsh the second time around. "She's our best researcher. She's one of the reasons we're Karim's top choice for the Biotrell merger. And she signed a non-competition clause. She's not going anywhere. We'll offer her more money. Better perks. Whatever it takes to keep her on board."

"You don't think I pulled out all the stops to convince her? And she's not taking a job with our competition."

"Then why the hell would she leave so suddenly?"

"She said she needs a break." His father's left cheek twitched.

As a kid, that small muscle spasm would send Weston searching for shelter: a door to slip through, a menu to lift in front of his face, a nearby escape hatch. When he got older, the twitch meant threats were on the horizon.

The day Weston had blown off a summer work meeting, still reeling from his mother's death, Victor S. Aldrich had sat Weston down, his cheek twitching, face splotchy as he'd listed his son's faults. "You're out of control. It makes you weak. It's an embarrassment to me, to the Aldrich name. You want respect in life? Earn it. You want to be successful? Don't welch on commitments. Everyone has hardships. Another stunt like this and you can find another job."

It hadn't been an empty threat. After his wife's death, Victor had fired his longtime chauffeur for picking him up late. Once. Even as a kid, Weston had overheard the man cut off his own parents, whom Weston had been forbidden from speaking with. Years later they'd been refused attendance at their daughter-in-law's funeral, because they'd once asked to borrow money for a gambling debt. A taint on the family name, Victor had declared. He hadn't yelled or cursed at them. The man was vicious in his quiet decisiveness, but he could ooze venom.

He was also brilliant and savvy. And incredibly sad.

No one else would know it to see it, but Weston knew. He saw. He'd seen Victor blow into the house with flowers and gifts, whisking his wife away on last minute trips. He'd catch them dancing in the living room, no music playing, secret smiles on their faces. Victor hadn't been a natural father, but he had loved his wife. And they'd had family dinners back then. Between Victor's bouts of domineering temper, there had been moments of affection as he'd ask Weston about his day and praise his school efforts. Birthdays and holidays had held laughter and joy.

The man now spent holidays at the office and his secretary purchase and deliver birthday gifts. The only affection he showed Weston was a nod for work well done. Their relationship would never be functional, but Weston didn't have the heart to tell the man where to shove his briskness. Cutting him off would tarnish his mother's memory.

At least with business, they had something in common. "How do we get Saanvi back?" Weston asked.

"We don't."

"Since when do you give up?"

"Since I have it on good authority DLP has leverage on Saanvi."

"Blackmail?"

His father cocked his head. "Does this surprise you?"

No. Not when it came to DLP. Rumors had circled them for years, the worst story revolving around a woman's death. The company had never been convicted of hiring a thug to dig up dirt on the woman's husband—a ploy to sink their competition —but Joseph Anderson claimed someone had been tailing them. Their erratic driving had caused his car to crash, killing his wife instantly. No charges had been laid against DLP, but everything about them reeked of deceit.

Now Saanvi was likely caught in their crosshairs. She'd always behaved above board, as far as Weston knew, diligent in her work, appreciated by the staff. Could be her family had skeletons that needed protecting. Regardless, the loss was another merger obstacle. Saanvi was their head Alzheimer's researcher. Karim had hoped her input would push Biotrell's clinical trials to the next phase. It would be a hefty blow.

"As much as that loss pains me," Victor said, already heading for the door, "you're the one dating Karim's daughter. No bribes can alter *that* leverage. As long as you keep her happy, we have nothing to worry about."

Such a crock of shit. "So my work doesn't matter? The months and years I've spent lining up this deal mean nothing if I don't put a ring on Rosanna's finger?" The last thing either of them wanted.

His father's left cheek twitched again. This time Weston eyed his desk. At thirty-three he still wanted to dive under it.

"One sign of weakness—"

"And you become obsolete," Weston finished.

The saying had been his father's version of a bedtime story, along with *the Aldrich men don't fail* and *there's no empathy in business.* To Victor S. Aldrich, reputation trumped compassion.

His father puffed out a rough grunt. "Get your head out of your ass, son. You've always been too emotional. This is business, and every choice has implications. If this merger falls apart, our stocks drop. Investors will get nervous. Jobs will be lost. Yours might be one of them. There's more at stake than losing a deal you hoped would secure your personal footing with shareholders. Stop lamenting the hours you've worked. And for the love of God, get some sleep. You look like hell."

He marched out of the office as though his words hadn't stung.

Too emotional. Jobs will be lost. Yours might be one of them. There was no nepotism at Aldrich Pharma. Weston was Chief Operating Officer because he'd worked more than he'd slept since high school. He was smart. He was damned good at his job. The sacrifices had helped him cope when dealing with his personal losses. DJing helped, too.

But music was his weak spot. As was Rosanna's unpredictability.

DLP had proven adept at digging up dirt on adversaries. Dangerously so. Weston had become more diligent since Annie had discovered his secret identity. His driver kept his eyes peeled for tails. Walks home after shows were no longer an option. He slipped in and out of his gigs without so much as a nod at backstage fans. Falcon had zero digital footprint. The only person who could blow his cover was Annie, and he was ninety-nine percent sure she wouldn't rat him out. Rosanna, however, could undermine him with one misjudged selfie.

Marjory knocked on his open door. "Your ten o'clock with marketing tomorrow has been moved up to nine. I need the compiled Alera files before then if you want them couriered on time, and your lunch with the Warner Group will be trickier than planned. Their head bulldog will be attending. He wants to curb investment dollars. And Annie called."

Weston nodded while replaying his dates with Rosanna, his nights DJing, wondering if unsavory sorts had managed to tail him. "Did Annie leave a message?"

"I just told you the message. You weren't listening."

Story of his life these days. He'd barely digested tomorrow's headache of a day let alone listened to all Marjory had said. "Sorry. What did she say?"

"Do I get paid extra for telling you the same thing twice?"

Marjory's eighties shoulder pads matched the width of her curly red hair. Her sarcasm filled the doorway, too. "Do I get to deduct the hours you spend gossiping instead of working?"

"Do you want the message or not?"

He wasn't sure. The past four weeks Annie had sat in on his mixing sessions, not saying a word as promised, just bringing him a plate of cut up vegetables and hummus before he'd realized he was hungry, or a glass of Scotch, or homemade cookies, or a notepad when his was full. Intuitive, thoughtful gestures that made him inexplicably angry.

When he'd cancelled a session because of a dinner or posh gallery opening with Rosanna, or a weekend at Karim's country home, Annie had gotten distant and curt, and acid had burned Weston's gut. He'd even lied to Annie and invented a couple of dates so he could have some peace. Those nights had been the most frustrating of all.

He was spending more time with Annie than he had in ages, but he felt further from her than ever before.

"Yes," he told Marjory. "I want the message."

She clasped her hands and smiled indulgently. "Annie said *she would be late tonight.*" She raised her voice and talked slowly, as though English were his second language. "She said you can *let yourself into her apartment if you get there first.*"

He should cancel their plans. Annie had asked him to come over and see the DJing equipment she'd purchased, help her set it up. Nothing that couldn't wait, and he had a million things to do. His focus was already abysmal. But he pictured her chaotic apartment, that awful purple carpet and floral couch, the mess of magazines and scrapbooking decorations scattered in the small space, and a deep yearning took root. A craving for that familiarity. A moment to catch his breath.

Maybe he was putting too much pressure on himself. Pulling himself in too many directions. He could quit DJing. Walk away. Forget about his plans to use his platform for change. He'd mostly only done it for Leo and his mother, as it stood. Or he could walk away from Aldrich Pharma, quit fake-dating Rosanna and developing an ulcer every time the merger hit a snag. No more deals buckling, patents failing, stressing over competition taking a bite out of his market share. Pursue music with more determination and hope Aldrich Pharma thrived under someone else's lead.

The base of his neck twinged. A cramp gripped his chest.

Unable to clear his head, he left work earlier than he should have. Way earlier than he'd originally planned to meet Annie. He drove to her apartment, impatient to get there. He practically ran up the steps in the musty hallway, fumbled with his key to get inside. He couldn't think straight. Didn't understand this desperate need to be here, in this space, even with Annie gone. The second he pushed inside and saw the colorful anarchy that was all Annie, he could suddenly breathe.

The space smelled like her. Of sage and honey and... chicken noodle soup? He dragged the back of his hand along his forehead, fingers shaking slightly. Leading two lives was getting to him.

He exhaled heavily and noticed a piano. Annie hadn't mentioned a piano. Only DJ equipment purchased secondhand. Was she planning to use the old piano for her mixes? Try for a more classical sound like in his intros? They hadn't discussed her DJ plans. Every time she came over, he expended all his energy into keeping his emotions contained and her at a distance. But he thought about her all the time, relived their kiss when he closed his eyes.

The last thing he wanted was for his control to snap, to feed his depraved thoughts by actually pressing her against the wall, kissing her senseless, feeling that first hot push of his body inside hers—sweet agony—then freak out and lose her for good.

He loosened his tie and yanked it off as he dodged a purse lying on the floor, then a stack of magazines. He slipped on a random sock and almost nailed his shin on the coffee table, before making it to her couch. With his ass finally planted on her soft cushion, he sighed and rested his head on the back. His eyelids felt like lead weights. His neck still hurt. He'd rest for a minute, then he'd pull out his phone and text human resources, start the ball rolling on replacing Saanvi. He'd call Rosanna, plan their next date. He'd get back to the promoter who'd been messaging Falcon for a gig, then he'd work on the Alera files, have them on Marjory's desk before the sun was up.

He'd just keep his eyes closed for a few breaths.

SOMEONE WAS SAWING a log in Annie's apartment. Or robbing her while wielding a chainsaw. Or Wes had fallen asleep as he sometimes did and was doing his best impression of a vicious warthog.

She opened her unlocked door, and lo and behold the warthog impersonator was comatose. His head was tipped back, his heavy thighs splayed apart. One of his hands clung to his removed tie, and his other was flung to his left. The heinous sound escaping his lips made her wince. And was that drool on his cheek? Nothing about this scene should be attractive, but Wes looked so vulnerable, younger and disheveled, and in a need of a cuddle.

Her heart gave a soft whump.

It wasn't a maternal whump, much to her chagrin. It was an *I-want-to-care-for-that-man-because-that-man-is-mine* whump. She hated that pathetic whump.

The undeniable force had grown exponentially this past month, and God knew why. Wes had been short with her more than kind. He'd been gallivanting around town with his girlfriend. He'd even lied to her a few times, claiming he'd had a date with Rosanna, when social media photos later showed Rosanna, solo, partying with friends. Intel Annie did *not* know because she'd stalked the couple online. She did *not* spend her free hours mooning over a man who wanted nothing to do with her. That would be sad. Pathetic.

Another soft whump confirmed her sad patheticness.

She schlepped her sad self into her kitchen and poured a glass of wine. Cheap stuff that made Wes's lip curl. His snoring stuttered a few times, then roared loud enough to wake a giant. She laughed as she sipped. At least Rosanna had to deal with this freight train at night. Which implied they slept together, probably naked.

Annie opened a cupboard door and slammed it shut.

Wes gasped, shooting upright.

"Sorry," she said sweetly. "Did I wake you?"

He blinked and scrubbed his hands down his face. "What time is it?"

"Time for you to see a doctor about that heinous sound coming from your mouth. That noise could be used to torture prisoners."

A sleepy smile pulled at his lips, and everything inside her clenched. His sleepy smiles were sexier than his regular smiles. The gravel in his groggy voice was a whole other level of alluring. She chugged a mouthful of wine.

Wes propped his elbows on his knees. "What time is it?" he asked again.

"Just after nine. Vivian had a last-minute appointment, so I worked a few hours for her. And I'm starving. Have you eaten? We should order food."

"After nine?" He scanned her apartment like he'd forgotten where he was. "I slept three hours?"

Three hours implied he'd been there since six. Unless he had a meeting or business dinner, Wes never left work that early. She wasn't sure he took bathroom breaks. They'd been so careful around each other since his Falcon revelation and their kiss revelation that they hadn't talked about anything of substance. Duncan still texted, asking if she'd spoken with Wes yet, worried about his boss's focus, inserting his usual jokes in the mix. Annie would banter back, putting off his concerns, instead of confronting Wes and getting answers.

She had been a bad friend.

"Don't move," she said as she went into her room to change. Sweatpants and a T-shirt were needed for this conversation. And more wine.

Wes nodded vaguely, a faraway look on his face she'd never seen. Definitely more wine.

Ten minutes later, they each had a glass of Chardonnay in hand. Wes was still leaning forward, elbows on his knees. Annie sat cross-legged facing him, inches apart on her not-very-large couch. "You're burning yourself out," she said.

He ran his tongue over his teeth. "It'll pass. When the merger goes through, things will calm down."

"That could be months."

"I'll manage."

"You didn't hear yourself snoring like a man who hadn't slept in a year. You're not managing."

He sipped his wine and grimaced. "This tastes like it smells."

"Cheap and cheerful?"

"Like rancid vinegar. I'll send over wine for you to store."

She should rip him a new one for insulting her affordable wine, but the infuriating man was going for a diversion. "I don't want your fancy wine. I want you to talk to me before your juggling act lands you in intensive care."

"Unless you've suddenly earned your PHD and can jump in to head up one of our R&D divisions, you can't help with this."

"I can help by listening."

He took another sip of wine, grimaced again, then swallowed. "I'll be fine. I just needed a break. Time to myself. A little peace."

And he'd sought that here. At her apartment. The same way sitting quietly in his recording studio made her content. It didn't matter Wes ignored her when he worked. She learned by watching, felt part of his creative energy even as she'd get sidetracked studying his profile. He scratched his nose when he was stumped. He bounced his left heel when he was excited, on the cusp of a great mix. She loved reading his body language and being around him.

But she disliked the odd moments she'd catch him staring

at her while she scribbled in her notebook, a look of longing on his face. That forlorn look confused her. She despised her jealousy when he had his Rosanna dates.

She really, really hated seeing him distraught now.

"If a break is what you need, I have a suggestion."

"I'm not letting you dye my hair pink."

"As fun as that Halloween was, I have something more therapeutic in mind." She held up a magazine and flapped it in the air. "We're going to scrapbook."

"I don't scrapbook, Squ..." He grunted. "You know I don't get along with glue and sparkles."

"You also used to hate pets and now you're a proud owner of the world's most terrifying rabbit-squirrel. It's never too late to change!"

He found a spare inch on her coffee table and deposited his wineglass. "I thought you needed me to set-up your DJ equipment. And when did you get a piano?"

She could have set up her gear herself, but asking Wes for help had been a moment of weakness. In his condo, she'd promised to give him space, not interrupt his music sessions with chatter or add to his stress. She'd been good at keeping quiet, but she missed his teasing. Her quips. Their fun banter. She missed when he called her Squirrel.

She'd hoped having him in her apartment would return the fun to their friendship, even if friends were all they'd ever be. Wes clearly needed fun.

"The equipment can wait," she said. "Scrapbooking wins every time." It always helped her decompress. "If you order dinner, I'll get you a fresh book of your own. There are menus on the coffee table, under the basket of pens. Order whatever you want, except that spicy Indian food or the Greek fish that smells up my place."

Without waiting for him to rant or complain, she hopped

off the couch and hurried into her room. She reached for the stack of empty albums on her closet shelf, pushed up to her tiptoes and nudged the top one closer. A bang and crash had her freezing, but she hadn't caused the noise. A curse came from her living room.

Then she heard, "What the *fuck*?"

Mildly concerned, she nudged the album down and inched toward her bedroom door.

Where she screamed.

Wes was kneeling on the floor, pens scattered everywhere, bent over the last thing she wanted him to find. She debated running for cover. Pulling the hall fire alarm? He stayed bent over her secret Weston Aldrich scrapbook, mercilessly flipping the pages. He had never looked so livid.

When he reached the worst page, she covered her face.

"I can still see you, Squirrel. You better start explaining what the hell this is."

The page in question had been crafted the day she'd gotten her driver's license. Weston had given her a car. She should never have accepted the top-safety-rated Volkswagen Golf. The gift had been another example of his need to control Annie and feel like he was doing "good" in the world. Eighteen-year-olds, however, were pleasure seekers.

She had snatched the keys after hugging the stuffing out of him, and had announced she was going for a drive on her own, to explore her newfound freedom. Wes had asked her to check in when she got home. A simple request. He hadn't accounted for Annie having way too much fun driving five hours to the Ausable Chasm Bridge, music blasting as she'd sung along. She hadn't been able to resist staying for sunset photos. She'd chosen to sleep in her fancy new car instead of driving home past dark. Her phone's dead battery had made a call to Wes impossible.

Upon her return, a furious Weston had stolen her car keys and rescinded his gift. She'd then created a collage by stuffing cutout dog poop into his two-dimensional mouth. Artistic expression that had made her feel vindicated.

The book had been safely hidden under her couch for years. He was never supposed to see it. She hadn't accounted for spilled pens and Wes crawling around on her floor.

"That's private," she said. "You don't have permission to look through it."

"You don't have permission to defile my pictures."

"I don't need your permission, Weston."

"I think you do, *Anthea*."

He'd called her Squirrel a moment ago, Anthea now. Names she should still hate, but she found her horror subsiding. "I do not need your permission, and I'm actually glad you found the album. It's the perfect example of why you're going to start your first scrapbook."

"It's the perfect example of why we're never going to speak again." He flipped several pages, found one of him with a rabbit attached to his front in a Baby Bjorn sling. An almost-smile threatened to crack his fury.

She joined him on the floor and forced the book closed. They were both kneeling, surrounded by a rainbow of scattered pens, like kids in a playroom. "I started this book when I was young and frustrated. If I was annoyed with you, turning that angst into art was a way for me to let go and move on."

A line sank between his brows, deep and troubled. "When I'd call you Squirrel?"

"Sometimes."

He glanced at the closed album. "And now? Why do you still deface pictures of me?"

He looked up and searched her eyes, the open curiosity so unguarded she debated telling him the truth. *Because I have feelings for you. Because every picture of you and Rosanna cuts like a knife. Because when I go to sleep at night, I imagine how your skin would feel sliding against mine.*

"Because things are changing between us," she said.

She couldn't read his reaction to her confession. She had no clue if he sensed her deeper desires. His chest expanded, his upper body tilting slightly forward. An eternity later, he said, "I feel it, too. I hate it."

The distance between them? Or living with this unquenched desire? "So what do we do about it?"

His gaze strayed, dropped to her lips for a beat. Pulsing heat overtook her body as he reached forward and brushed her hair over her ear. "We order takeout. Then we scrapbook and maybe watch a movie. We talk and hang out and work through whatever this is."

She knew what this was for her. She just wasn't sure what this was for him.

If he weren't dating Rosanna she'd ask. She'd put herself out there and demand to know if he'd been turned on when they'd kissed because of the adrenaline rush of the stage or because of her, if their moment of intimacy in his sound room had been as discombobulating for him as she suspected. She'd ask and she'd force his answer. But he was dating another woman.

"Scrapbooking it is," she said.

13

"Pass me the scissors. And that Bahamas ad." Wes was on the floor, long legs stretched out under Annie's coffee table. He clenched a green marker in his fist as he glowered at his scrapbook page.

"If you keep making that face, it'll stay that way."

"Why does the glitter get everywhere?" He rubbed his eyes, defeated. "It was supposed to stay in the clouds."

"Because your man-hands are too big for delicate work."

He accepted the scissors and ripped magazine page, then shot his big mitts in the air. "So, you finally admit I have strong, masculine hands."

"I admit nothing." Including the fact that scrapbooking with Weston Aldrich was Tickle Me Elmo fun. "Your ego doesn't need the stroking."

He pointed at the wonky palm tree filling half his page, the jagged airplane he'd cut and pasted. "My drawing skills are up there with a three-year-old's, my scissor abilities aren't much better, and I have no clue how I got glue in my arm hair." Lip curled, he picked at his forearm.

This really was the best night ever. "It wouldn't be fair if you were a crazy smart executive, a crazy talented DJ, *and* a crazy amazing scrapbooker. Challenges keep you grounded."

"You said this would be fun and relaxing. What part of me looks happy and relaxed?" He brushed a stray thread off his cheek and wound up with green marker smudged on his skin.

Definitely the best night.

She smoothed down the ribbon on the corner of her piano page. The keys were made out of various materials, some soft, some silky, a few out of leather. She'd created a scrolling music sheet with buttons and string to indicate the notes, all glued next to a photo of her piano student Joyce. It wasn't as creative as some of her pages, but she loved bumping her fingers over the textures, reading the image like Braille. If only reading Wes were as easy.

"Fucking hell," he mumbled as he tried to shake a partially glued piece of paper from his thumb.

"You're trying too hard to make your page perfect. Let it be whatever it will be." She peeled the paper off his thumb and stuck it in their garbage pile. "But don't you dare touch that *Vogue* page. I dream of wearing that dress and will not have you destroy it."

He picked up the open magazine and scanned the image. Black scrunched lace was layered over a bold cherry printed maxi dress. Fun. Flirty. Classic Betsy Johnson. The model was posing for a perfume ad, but the dress was the real standout.

"I can see you in this," Wes said, sounding irritated. Because of the dress picture or his art project, she wasn't sure. His attention slid back to his scrapbook. "What's the point of doing something I'm bad at?"

She lifted one of her Sudoku books from the table. "Do you ever see me getting frustrated because I can't finish these pages?"

His gaze skipped to the other two books on the floor. "That habit of yours is maddening."

"Answer the question, Herbert."

He smirked. "The creatively brilliant Anthea Ward is carefree and happy in all things in life and never gets frustrated. She'd rather quit when puzzles get hard, than hurt her brain."

"You're a real comedian." She fanned her hand at his travel-inspired scrapbook page, which was as atrocious as he thought. "Stop thinking about the outcome. Just create."

His amusement swirled down some invisible drain. "You make carefree look easy."

"It's not easy. Not always, at least. I've started teaching piano and it's—"

"When did you start?"

She listened for annoyance in his abrupt question. Irritation that she hadn't shared her newest job/hobby. All she heard was curiosity. "A couple months ago, and it's hard. As much as I practice, I worry I'll never be good enough to teach beyond the beginner level. I've thought about giving up— which is shocking, *I know*." She nudged his calf with her foot under the table. A sad smile, too sad for a scrapbooking night, tilted his lips. "But someone in my life is always on me to stick with the tough stuff. You might know the guy. He irons his underwear and his socks."

Wes didn't laugh at her joke. He stared over her shoulder at her bookcase. The wood shelves were filled with more unfinished puzzle books, romance novels, mystery novels, historical novels. No rhyme or rhythm to her taste. "I don't think I'm fine," Wes murmured, as though to himself. Then louder, "When you asked about how I'm coping...I think I'm drowning a bit."

She closed her book, whisper-soft, worried too much noise would send Wes back into martyr mode. "At work?"

"Work, the merger, my music—biting off more than I can chew."

"Can you cut back on any of it?"

He brushed excess sparkles off his page, an absentminded movement. "There's too much on the line at work right now. And I'm on the cusp of something with the shows. A way to engage the crowd in social issues."

"The video feeds?"

His eyes snapped to hers, questioning. "I haven't put my finger on it yet, but yeah. I have this unique access to people. They're already in a space they love, attuned to me, listening to music that lifts them up. It's the perfect medium to say something meaningful, but it has to be the right message, and it has to be done right. I need more time to figure it out."

He hadn't mentioned the video recordings while she'd been around. With his no-questions rule, she hadn't asked him about his plans with the project, but the gimmick had so much potential. Leo would have loved it. He'd be ten steps ahead of them, thinking of ways to broaden their appeal, make them more than background beauty. Maybe the images could be a tribute to him, a way to remind people lax gun laws had consequences.

"I could help with that aspect," she offered. "Play with footage that might work." She wasn't sure Wes would like the gun-control angle. They'd only started talking about Leo. She could work on it before telling him, make sure it had merit before spilling the idea.

But the control freak said, "No." Didn't even blink.

"You don't think I'm good enough to help?"

He made a weird face and grunted, then pulled himself up

onto the couch. "You have enough on your plate. I won't add to your stress."

"You already are."

A rough laugh rushed out. "Now I feel worse. I should probably go, let you get some sleep."

He didn't move to leave, and he didn't understand what she was getting at, all stuck in his head as usual. "I'm glad you came, and I don't want you to go. But, yeah, seeing you stressed upsets me." That wasn't quite it, though. Seeing him struggling affected her on a visceral level. She took a breath and said quietly, "When you hurt, I hurt."

He closed his eyes, his elbows falling heavily on his knees. A familiar pose. Her lungs felt like shriveled husks. She had no clue where that admission had come from. It hadn't even been a thought in her lovesick head. Those hadn't been head words, though. Those had been heart words.

He didn't reply or accept her help or acknowledge the depths of what she'd admitted. He stretched out his fingers and picked at the glue stuck to his hand.

Glue she could focus on. Scrapbooking. Her late brother's best friend zapping her heart with static-electric bursts? Hard pass.

She fetched a warm washcloth from her bathroom, returned, and crawled between Wes and the edge of her coffee table. She knelt on the floor in the middle of his spread thighs. Probably a bad idea. "If you let me touch your manly hands, I'll rescue you from glue prison."

His hard jaw sharpened further, his cheeks becoming dark craters. An intimidating look from any other man. Not on Wes. She knew he slept with a nightlight on in his en-suite bathroom and drank warm milk when he couldn't sleep. Under his granite exterior and piles of money, he was just a man trying to get by.

After an awkward few seconds—her on her knees between his heavy thighs, him looking all Mike Tyson about to go ten rounds in the ring—he offered her his hand.

The second she touched his skin, she flinched. Or he did. Maybe they'd both flinched as their fingers softly brushed. That galloping heart was definitely hers, though. She should drop the cloth, let him de-glue himself on his own. Not risk him seeing how deeply he affected her.

Tibetan monks didn't have that level of willpower.

She splayed her palm out under his, letting the tips of her fingers press against his pulse point. Tingles spiked the fine hairs on her arm, more static-electric bursts scrambling her brain. If she felt his pulse correctly, hers wasn't the only heart rate accelerating.

Keep calm. Quit reading into things that aren't there.

She ran the wash cloth along his thumb, softened the stuck glue enough to pick it off, then rubbed the warm-damp fabric over the spot to soothe the inflamed skin. She found another spot, did the same. His back relaxed, hunching heavier over his bent knees. She worked the cloth over his fingers, taking her time on his knuckles, traveling delicately along the dips in between, then pressing harder. His blueish veins stood out, the pads of his palm lightly callused from working out, but his nails were clean and trim. Strength and elegance rolled into one.

A classical song with a commanding backbeat.

Then the glue was gone. His hands were warm and clean, still held by hers, and she wasn't ready to lose this heady connection. She dug her thumb into the center of his palm, massaged in an outward motion. Wes's eyelids slid shut, and a purr rumbled from his thick chest. She didn't speak, too terrified to break this spell.

"I like piano for you," he said softly. "I'm glad you're playing again."

"It feels good, even though it's frustrating at times." Whispered words as their hands touched. "I love that you're DJing. I don't think I told you how talented you are. It's really something to behold. Leo would be so proud."

His fingers closed slightly over hers, his other hand shifting, moving slowly toward their joined hands. Contact. More static. He traced the outsides of her fingers as that electric energy sizzled through her body. "He'd be amazed by you," Wes murmured. "*I'm* amazed by you."

I love you. The thought filled her struggling lungs until they ballooned. So full. Too full. Too much air to hold as she digested this frightening revelation. She loved Weston Aldrich. It wasn't really a shock. It was the biggest shock of her life.

She loved his uptight designer clothes and fascination with modern art. She loved his silly rabbit and his resting brood face, and how his laugh made her feel unbuttoned. She loved that he worried after her, cared for her, showed her his soft underbelly while being everyone else's kingpin. She loved his scrapbook-worthy lips and tidal-wave eyes that never failed to pull her under and how she was the best version of herself around him. Funnier. Challenging, because he challenged her.

She loved Weston Aldrich, but he was in a relationship. Unattainable. Unless, *maybe*, her pathetic hope had been true and he was dating Rosanna because he was scared of this intense connection.

He released her hand, rubbed his palms down his thighs. Rubbed her hope away.

She bit down on her cheek. She should know better by now. Tonight was about them returning to their normal, not unrequited love. She could do normal. She *would* do normal. She would not lose his friendship to her infatuation.

"I think we've scrapbooked enough tonight. Movie time?" God, her voice sounded strained.

She extricated herself from the small space between his knees and the coffee table. He nodded while tracking her movements, his piercing gaze following as she stood. She rubbed the soreness from her knees and tossed him a practiced grin. "I have it on good authority you love watching things blow up. That new movie with The Rock should fit the bill. I can stare at him while you get your testosterone fix."

He didn't crack a smile or joke back. He watched her intently, then dipped his chin and looked at his scrapbook page. "Explosions sound good."

At way-too-early in the morning, Annie woke as twisted a contortionist. Her mouth tasted like stale wine. She winced as her lower back torqued. She didn't remember the movie ending or falling asleep on her couch...or resting her head on Weston's lap.

A very awake lap.

Its owner was passed out, but he shifted slightly. Everything about Wes was solid and masculine: the thick expanse of his thighs, corded forearms, broad chest, shoulders meant for lugging heavy things or just looking super strong. From her angle, his angular jaw was downright brutish. Her gaze flitted back down to the male power stretching the fly of his pants.

She sighed. He stirred.

Life wasn't fair.

The soft wool of his slacks rubbed along her cheek as his legs spread wider. *Danger, Will Robinson.* One large hand moved to her neck, dragged up, up, into her hair. And her body bloomed, a painful ache spreading lower. Wes murmured, too low to make sense, but he seemed in the throes of a dream, eyes still closed, body loose. All but his straining erection.

She seriously needed to move. Bolt upright and quit picturing sliding his zipper down, freeing him, touching him, running her tongue around that thick girth.

She steeled her willpower, took one last look at all she couldn't have.

Then Wes said, "Annie. Oh fuck, *Annie.*" His sleep-fueled voice was gravelly. Erotic.

His fingers gripped her hair tighter.

She tensed, stole a glance up. He'd said *Annie.* Not Rosanna.

His eyes were still closed, his lips parted as his hips did a seductive roll. Was he dreaming about her? Did the thought of them together, skin against skin, turn him liquid, too?

His fingers dug into her scalp, pressed her face closer to his erection. The ache between her thighs flared into a bonfire. She was anchored against the couch, awkward, her hot breath brushing his fly. She wriggled to get some kind of friction between her legs, a bit of relief.

Wake him up, the rational side of her brain urged. She pressed her lips to the hard ridge of his penis instead, hummed in satisfaction at the daring move, couldn't believe how hot and hard he was. God, she was depraved. Sick. Twisted. Taking advantage of a sleeping man, who had a stunning girlfriend, but he was dreaming of *Annie*, rolling his hips for her.

He groaned. "Fuck, Annie. *Fuck.*"

His fingers jammed harder into her hair. His hips bucked. Then he jumped to his feet, sending her flying. Her shoulder smacked the coffee table as she hit the floor.

"Shit, Annie. You okay?"

He knelt down and tried to help her up. The effort involved her knee hitting the table again and both of them twisting uncomfortably. By the time they stood, he was panting. She bit her lip, and he stared at her mouth. A feral quality in his aqua eyes made them look more raging sea than calm waters, but he turned abruptly and adjusted himself in his pants.

"You were dreaming about me," she blurted. Whatever his relationship status, she couldn't ignore this. Wouldn't. That moment of abandon, however subconscious, proved she wasn't alone in her feelings.

"No, I wasn't." Still with his back to her.

"You said my name."

"You must have heard wrong."

She swallowed a growl. Going along with his denial would be the easy path. The expected Annie path. She was done with easy. "Interesting theory, but I specifically remember hearing you say, *Annie. Oh, fuck, Annie,* as you tried to hump my cheek. So I'd say you're the one who's having memory gaps."

He swore, dropped his head forward. His turmoil was potent. She wanted to help, not hurt. She wanted answers more.

She pressed her hand to his straining back muscles, felt them tense then release. "I'm not sure what's going on with Rosanna, how serious things are, but I know you've lied to me a couple times. Told me you were seeing her, then I'd see pictures of her out on her own those nights." Stalker alert, but she was past the point of caring. "I think you're trying to keep your distance from me."

Her hand rose with his deep inhale, but it didn't lower. He was holding his breath and his words. The guy was whip-smart when heading Aldrich Pharma, a genius who could schmooze a pack of wolves. With her, these days, he was all broody silence.

She'd have to be the brave one. The honest one. The one willing to put it all on the line and possibly lose. She hoped she wasn't about to lose. "I'm taking a major plank-walk here, but...I think about you all the time. It started before I knew you were the one who kissed me, and it obviously skyrocketed after that. And the angsty scrapbooking? My recent efforts have been out of jealousy. Seeing you with Rosanna has been crazy hard. And I can't even believe I'm saying this stuff out loud, but I'm tired of pretending I don't have feelings for you. Real feelings. Not just lusty thoughts, which are totally there, too."

Seriously? Lusty thoughts? She needed a cure for her foot-in-mouth syndrome. "What I'm saying is this is scary and confusing for me, but also kind of exciting. We know each other so well, all the good and bad, and our love of music is special. We could rock a stage together, which isn't the point here. I know we fight like cats and dogs, or in our case rabbit-squirrels and mutant jaguar-squirrels, but if you give this—*give us*—a chance, I think we could be epic."

His back was still turned. She tried to catch her erratic breath, kind of wished she could shove that deluge back into her mouth as she waited and waited, wobbly on her unsteady legs, her heart beating in her throat. He remained mute. Deathly still. Like he'd fallen asleep on his feet. Had she misread him? A dream was only a dream, after all. Not real. He wasn't facing her, claiming her, telling her Rosanna had been a distraction to keep him from what he truly wanted.

His silence should be answer enough, but she was tired of hoping. One hard punch was better than a thousand slaps. "Tell me you want Rosanna, not me, and I won't bring it up again. We'll get back to our normal, whatever that is. Tell me you haven't spent your nights reliving our kiss, and I'll find a way to let this go."

She pressed her hand to his back again, tried to feel his heartbeat through the tense muscles, learn his truth. He leaned into her touch, just a millimeter. Enough that hope gave her a little leap of joy, then he turned and grabbed her wrist.

"I'm not dating Rosanna." His eyes were wicked hard. She flinched. "It was a request on behalf of her father to secure our business merger, which no one can know about. She's still dating on her own, and I'm free to do what I want with whoever I want. And I..." He locked eyes with her, didn't blink. "I don't want you, Anthea. Not like that. That kiss was the adrenaline of performing. This morning's dream meant nothing. I'm a guy and guys get hard in the morning, especially when a woman's lying on his lap. I don't want to hurt you, but I don't feel the same and I need to get to work."

She stood motionless as he snatched his tie from the couch and scraped his hand through his messy hair. He glanced around, like he had more he should take with him, the slightest bow to his posture. There was glue on his navy slacks, sparkles on his ear. His cheek was creased from her couch, and it still had that green smudge. He was disheveled and lovely and he would never be hers.

He looked at a photo of Leo on her wall, then at her. Something—*regret?*—flickered across his face. Then it was gone. Another emotion she'd obviously misread. He turned and stalked out, his new scrapbook left behind, splayed on her floor next to her splintered heart.

14

—————

"IF YOU'RE THINKING about jumping, word to the wise: the glass is shatterproof." Duncan moved into Weston's line of vision and raised a stack of folders. "The revised Alera files. Numbers aren't ideal, but they're better. Today's meeting should go smoothly."

Weston nodded distractedly, keeping his focus on the steel skyline. A dense fog wove through the jutting skyscrapers. Humidity clung to the windows. "We still have to find more funding, which means the team needs to improve clinical trials. And I spoke with marketing. There are issues with the Seprivan launch."

Duncan replied, saying something about the competitor undermining their push to market, but Weston's mind was as murky as the view. He'd felt physically ill since scrapbooking at Annie's last week. A persistent nausea that had his body aching. He'd been too fatigued to use his home gym. He walked through his days half asleep, while barely sleeping at night. His mind felt like a sieve at work.

He kept remembering Annie's voice, hopeful yet tentative,

as she'd spilled her heart to him. *I think about you all the time. I'm tired of pretending I don't have feelings for you.*

Her devastation at his harsh rejection.

"I'm going on a limb here," Duncan said, breaking through Weston's morose thoughts, "but you seem a tad distracted. Is everything okay?"

Weston slipped his hands into his pants pockets. The Italian wool felt scratchy. "Not really, no."

Duncan dropped the files on Weston's desk and resumed his position at the window, both men watching the hovering fog. "Care to talk about it?"

What he wanted was to erase his past. Bring Leo back. Change the decisions he'd made that fateful night, and the lies he'd told Annie since. He wanted to believe he could date Annie without eventually hurting her by freaking out. "Thanks for asking, but I'll be fine."

"You don't have to be an island, Wes. I know this merger's stressful, but there are people around you who can help. *I* can help, if you'll let me."

The merger should be the only thing occupying his mind, but he was back to remembering dating Lila, her calls after he'd run out on her, all of them tear-filled and confused. Then one final angry message: *You're an asshole, Weston. I don't know what broke you, but I hope you're honest with the next woman you date before you break her heart.*

"I'll be fine," he repeated as he swallowed the sourness in his mouth. Pushing Annie away had been the right choice. The responsible choice. He massaged his neck. "Thanks for the files."

Duncan lingered a second longer, then nodded and left.

Weston picked up his phone and called Rosanna. "Let's go out tomorrow night. Get some visibility. I'll take you to Angelonia. It was written up this week."

"Hello to you, too, Weston. How nice of you to call."

He tried to smile at her sarcasm. His face felt like it had been injected with iron. "I'll pick you up at eight."

"What makes you think I'm free?"

"Because we made a deal, and I expect you to uphold your end of it."

"What's up with you? This isn't your usual level of grouchiness."

"Nothing's up." Unless the atrophying of his organs counted.

"Does your therapist believe that bullshit?"

He hadn't seen a therapist in years, but there was no doubt his inability to voice his troubles would have infuriated her. He rested his hip on his desk and eyed his bucking bull sculpture on his coffee table. "I hurt Annie last week," he finally admitted, words he hadn't been able to force out with Duncan. Something about Rosanna made her an easier sounding board.

"Is this the Annie you talk about nonstop but swear there's nothing going on?"

"There isn't anything going on." Which was precisely the problem. And the solution.

"Let me rephrase: is this the Annie you won't admit to being infatuated with?"

He opened his mouth to deny her claim. Nothing came out.

"Are you not attracted to her?"

Annie was stunning and sexy and had starred in one too many of Weston's recent erotic dreams. Attraction wasn't the problem. Neither was compatibility. She was perfectly messy and ridiculous and everything he could want in a woman, but if he confessed that truth to her, things would be set in motion he couldn't undo. "Annie's my kind of perfect, but I'm not the right man for her. There are things I've kept from her. Unforgiveable things. And I have a bad track record with women. So I distanced myself by hurting her."

"That's pretty heartless, Wes."

"Is that supposed to make me feel better?"

"No, but this might: you're probably wrong. I don't know what you haven't told her, but worrying you'll hurt her because you've hurt other women is nonsense. From the tidbits you've shared, it sounds like she's different to you. More important. But you've built up this nasty version of yourself in your head and you think you're destined to walk through a snake-infested jungle no matter which path you follow. I say start forging not following. Get a machete and hack that shit up."

Easier said than done when straying into this unknown could mean losing Annie in the end. He still believed this tension-filled blip would pass. They'd resume their friendship in time. Their easy bickering. So why did staying away from her make him feel like he was dying inside?

"I'll pick you up at eight tomorrow," he told Rosanna. Taking her to Angelonia was what he needed. A break from his quiet condo. A night of laughing at her wild stories. Eventually, his infatuation with Annie would end.

ANNIE THREADED her fingers through the fringed threads hanging off the end of her throw pillow as she studied the water stains on her ceiling. The gray smudges looked like a jellyfish battle, or a Rastafarian with super cool hair. She blinked, her eyes blurring as she stared harder, deciding on jellyfish at war. By the time she glanced down at her computer, there were two messages from Deaf Jam. According to the time, the last one had been there ten minutes.

Deaf Jam: **Did you develop a case of instantaneous blindness or am I boring you?**

More like she'd developed a severe case of the mopes. She'd been miserable this week, sad and listless. Barely eating. Not even cramming her face with chips and chocolate. Her self-confidence was at an all-time low. Falling in love with Wes was the worst thing she'd ever done.

Heaving herself to sitting, she replied as her Harley Quinn alias.

Harley Quinn: **Sorry for the silent treatment. I'm a bit of a sad sack these days.**

She'd tried to stay positive since Wes had walked out her door. Between waitressing shifts, she'd made halfhearted attempts to practice DJing. She'd gone for walks outside, had logged on to her Punchies page, chatted with Pegasus and a couple of other women. Some online friends' genders were a mystery. Others had been sussed out through their chats. Deaf Jam was (supposedly) a married man in his late twenties who worked at the post office and loved talking music through the BOOMPop site. Their conversations usually invigorated Annie. Tonight warring jellyfish on her ceiling were more her speed.

Deaf Jam: **Something happen?**

Annie's instinct was to brush him off. Discussing personal problems wasn't part of their usual chats, but her sad-sack state was becoming tedious. She chewed her lip, debating how honest of a reply to give.

Harley Quinn: **I'm in love with a guy, but he blatantly told me he's not interested.**

Blunt and succinct for the win.

Deaf Jam: **That's harsh.**

Harley Quinn: **Lepers feel more attractive than I do right now.**

Deaf Jam: **Better he was honest than lead you on.**

Harley Quinn: **In theory sure. In practice it sucks.**

It felt like someone had stuck her heart in a blender.

Deaf Jam: **If this dude told you he's not interested, no point mooning over him. He doesn't deserve you. Go out. Find some guy to have fun with.**

Again, easier said than done. Annie had never been a once-and-done girl. She liked romance, dating. Getting to know a man.

Harley Quinn: **Casual hookups aren't usually my thing.**

Deaf Jam: **Nothing wrong with blowing off steam by blowing...**

Harley Quinn: **Why do guys always fall back on blow job jokes?**

Deaf Jam: **We're the more primitive of our species.**

Harley Quinn: **Agreed, and one-night stands feel skeezy to me.**

But she remembered Duncan's forward suggestions to add benefits to their "friend" status. Hooking up with him wouldn't be as nerve-racking as taking a stranger home. Based on his continued jokes on the subject, he'd probably agree to a no-strings romp between the sheets. The thought still made her squeamish.

Deaf Jam: **If this guy made you feel shitty, a casual fling could help you get your mojo back.**

Or it could make her feel worse.

Annie thanked him for the advice and dropped her head back onto her couch cushion. Deaf Jam was right about her mojo: it was obliterated. Nonexistent. She was edgy and sad, and she felt incredibly unattractive. A man telling you a kiss was adrenaline, not lust, was up there with getting laughed at naked. She eyed her phone. Maybe calling Duncan wasn't the worst idea. He was free with his compliments, quick to make a woman feel desirable. But she wasn't overly attracted to him.

Their occasional texts were always light and fun, with Duncan eventually prodding about Wes, worried about his friend and boss, but she couldn't imagine kissing him.

Still, a *friendly* night out with a guy could be just what she needed.

She grabbed her phone and texted Duncan one word: *Hey.*

When he didn't reply, she resumed analyzing the water stains on the ceiling. Not a particularly fun activity, she sat at her piano instead and played. Choppy at first, then she closed her eyes, pictured Leo beside her, moving her fingers to the right keys. She relaxed slightly, let the notes tumble from her fingers, but they sounded thoughtless and angry, a strike of chords to excise her frustrations.

She hadn't spoken with Wes since his epic brushoff. There had been no friendly chatter, no talk of more DJ lessons. Her only remote connection to him had been working on the video feed, without him knowing. Another activity to busy her mind. She'd searched through endless clips, all portraying the effects of gun violence, sorrow and devastation in violent images, hope and artistic portrayals in others: objects that looked like guns dissolved into a blur of butterflies, graveyards of rifles and revolvers and semi-automatics covered with dirt, blooming into flowers and new growth above.

The possibility of change. But first, the violence.

When she'd learned Vivian had video editing skills, Annie had offered free piano lessons in exchange for her help. She hadn't explained how deeply the gun violence images affected her, why the topic was so personal, but they'd created something bold and moving. A flowing montage Wes could enhance with his beats.

But she hadn't breathed a word about her work to Wes. Her humiliation and pride kept her quiet. Wes hadn't opened the lines of communication, either. He must be utterly embarrassed for her.

She practiced a jazz rhythm next, harmonizing the melody, a weave of notes from delicate to robust, along with a few flat clunkers that hurt her ears. She slowed her breaths, rocked her body to feel the sound and melody. *Feel don't listen*, Wes had said. She played until she was nothing but breath and movement, no drama punching holes in her heart.

Music was freedom. It was escape. The only way to unlock that privilege was to first master the rules. Build then break. Create then dismantle.

Drown the sad with glory.

She hadn't quite reached glory, but this rhythm was doing it for her. It would be cool to use the piece in her DJ set. Add some soul funk to the jazzy beats.

She snuck a glance at her phone. The screen was lit, and her fingers hit an off note.

She hated how uneasy she felt, anxious and jumpy. She wasn't sure asking Duncan out was the smart move, even as friends, but this quiver in her stomach wasn't all hesitation. This clammy sinkhole was rejection and longing, topped with a dollop of grief. On top of Wes's sexual brush-off, she might have lost her best friend.

She walked over to her phone and checked the message.

Duncan: **I was thinking about you this morning. Wondered if you'd had a chance to chat with Wes yet. He's looking worse for wear.**

She stared at the text until her eyes burned. Was Wes haggard because he regretted his abrupt rudeness? Was he having second thoughts? Just as quickly she squeezed her eyes shut. She was so done with her pathetic pining. Instead of texting Duncan back, she dialed his number.

"Is something wrong?" Duncan asked in a hushed tone. "Did you speak to him?"

"This actually isn't about Wes. I have a question."

"Oh."

His flat reply shouldn't hurt, but she was a giant bruise, the slightest hint of rebuff poking her insecurity. "Did you want to go out sometime? Not as a date. Like, there will be no benefits, to be clear. Zero *peer pleasure*. I just thought it would be nice to hang out as friends. Grab dinner or something. We'd split the bill, of course. Because no benefits will be happening. And if you're busy that's cool, because I'm thinking I'm babbling and we should hang up and pretend I never called." She rolled her eyes, horrified with herself.

Duncan laughed. "You're cute when you're nervous."

Cute wasn't the word she'd choose. "It's been a rough week. But you're easy to be around, and I need a night out with no heavy topics. I promise I'm not always this weird."

"Weird works for me, and I've noted the benefit clause. But I choose the restaurant and insist on paying for dinner."

She slumped, relieved at his willingness to go out as friends. "I'd usually argue, but I'm desperate. What are you thinking?"

"I actually read a great write-up about Angelonia—trendy French fusion place. How's tonight?"

"I'm working tonight, but I'm free tomorrow."

"Tomorrow it is. And Annie?"

She bounced an agitated knee. "Yeah?"

"If you change your mind on the benefits, you won't get an argument from me."

15

DUNCAN PICKED Annie up right on time, his bright smile still blinding. His cologne still made her nose itch, and he was still dressed to attend a board meeting, but his first words to her were: "You look ravishing."

Her crushed ego gave its first feeble signs of life. "You look pretty handsome, too. For a friend's night out," she added.

A pleasant drive later, he led her into a boisterous restaurant. "It's not an all-night rave, but the food's supposed to be outstanding."

The red brick walls reminded her of Wes's condo, as did the minimalist art, but laughter and noise lifted with the jazz tunes, warming up the space. Tables were spread out, lining the long room. "It's perfect. And I like the music." The chefs in the open kitchen moved like a choreographed dance troupe. Bartenders dressed in black popped ice cubes and shook drinks. "Classy but cool. Excellent choice."

Duncan blushed, the modesty surprising but cute. "Only the best for my *no-benefit* friend."

He placed his hand on her lower back as they were led to their table. Not quite a friend move, but the attention was nice.

Once they were settled, Duncan clasped his hands on the table and fiddled with his college ring. "How's the DJ thing going? Is that Falcon guy teaching you like you hoped?"

She appreciated the personal question, but she appreciated their waitress arriving at the table even more. Duncan ordered a martini. She ordered a negroni, while figuring out how to side-step that landmine. Duncan didn't know his boss was Falcon. He could never know.

Once the waitress left, Annie forced an honest-ish reply. "I worked with Falcon for a bit, but he's too busy to keep it up." Too afraid of her lusty advances. "I'm practicing solo now and might take more lessons from this guy Julio, who's also pretty killer. Still figuring out my style and how to approach it all."

"But you love it? The music, the club scene, being onstage —that's your dream?"

She wasn't sure if she'd ever be as amazing as Wes, but she wouldn't let their drama thwart her plans. "I don't know about dream, but the bug bit me and now I'm hooked. I'll make it work, one way or another. What about you? Is working for Aldrich Pharma your dream job?"

His gaze cut to his ring. He spun it slowly. "Weston took a chance promoting me when he did. There was another candidate more qualified, but when he called me in to give me the news, he said, 'You have less experience, but there's more hunger in your eyes. The job's yours, as long as you promise not to let me down.'"

"That's a great vote of confidence, but you didn't answer my question."

He sipped his water, placed the glass down, and kept his gaze trained on the table. "It's an amazing job, rewarding and challenging. Everyone's on their A-game, especially when the shit hits the fan. There's a real team feeling there."

There was tension in his voice, though. Discomfort in his body language. And he was still evading. "I know firsthand how obstinate Wes can be. He must be an impossible boss to please."

She pictured her head on Wes's lap, how badly she'd wanted to please him, *please herself* with a filthy lick of her tongue. She sipped her water and crunched an ice cube.

Duncan straightened and slung an arm over the back of his chair, discomfort gone, expensive grin returned. "I can please anyone, anytime. It's a skill, and Weston's a great boss. Demanding, but the good ones always are. They push you to be better."

Something flickered in his eyes. Disappointment? "So why do you look like he's about to fire you?"

A waiter brushed close to his chair, and Duncan shifted forward. "Like I told you, I'm worried about him. As many times as I've tried to get him to talk, he refuses. He sticks to himself, and I feel responsible in some ways. Like I'm not doing my job well enough. If I knew what was eating at him, I could figure out how to delegate better, ease his burden. You've still had no luck getting him to open up?"

Wes had opened up to her plenty, not all truths she'd wanted to learn, but his work admissions in her apartment proved Duncan's concerns were warranted. Annie still worried after Wes, regardless of their issues. Aside from his stressful work and secret-identity drama, fake dating a woman for a business merger must be exhausting. As nice as it was to feel less jealous of Rosanna, none of it changed Wes's brutal dismissal of Annie, or that Annie could still help him with his video montage, *if* she shook off a fraction of his painful rejection.

Maybe that was what she needed to do. Tell him about the video she'd created to help them recover from this downswing. Force them to interact again.

An effort that would entail pretending she wasn't in love with him.

"He confided in you, didn't he?" Duncan's intuitiveness caught her off guard. Her turmoil must be tattooed on her forehead.

"Sort of."

"About the merger? Is he struggling with anything specific?"

Wooing Rosanna for a deal was pretty specific, as was his double life, but no one could know about those arrangements. Duncan smelled her secrets, though. He was literally on the edge of his seat, wanting to help the man who'd taken a chance on him.

"Honestly, Annie, I know the ins and outs of that merger like the back of my hand. I've worked with him on the financing, the fine print. The guy's drowning at work and his father's taken notice. The last thing Weston needs is more pressure from Victor. Anything Weston said might help."

Victor S. Aldrich was a walking gavel, judge and jury over his perceived domain.

After Leo's death, when her first foster parents had gotten pregnant and told her they'd decided to quit fostering, she'd stayed at Weston's mansion for the night, stressed and sleepless over her future. She'd told Wes it was cool. She'd be fine wherever she was. Deep down, she'd been a roiling mess. Clementine had been at that foster home. The pigtailed, freckled foster girl that had been so quiet and scared. She'd only just started to smile, and she'd asked Annie if they could stay together always. Annie had stupidly said yes.

Unable to sleep, Annie had tiptoed down to the kitchen in Wes's mansion and walked by the study or library or whatever it was those extra rooms were called, where she'd heard angry voices. Wes and his dad.

"Why can't she live here? God knows we have the room and money."

"Her mother died with a needle in her arm. Her father's some miscreant who disappeared. Her brother got shot in a seedy club. You've clearly lost your mind, son."

"You're worried what people will think?"

"What people think defines who you are. Have I taught you nothing?"

"Think of it as charity work. The country club crowd loves a hero."

An angry grunt. "I can't keep you from visiting her, but you shouldn't have brought her here tonight, and you will never bring her here again. She's not welcome in this house."

Annie had been disgusted with Victor that night, but she'd also been angry with Wes. Living on the streets had taught her to rely on herself, not others. Wes taking over, trying to make decisions for her, had made her feel weak. Incapable of taking care of herself. His father's disdain had rubbed salt on that wounded pride.

She'd snuck out of the mansion afterward, returned to the foster home she'd soon lose, where she'd helplessly watched Clementine sob quietly into her pillow. Wes never mentioned the conversation with his father or asked why she'd left. Annie's anger had dissipated over time. She became thankful for that encounter. A reminder that if she was going to make it, she had to rely on herself. She also eventually saw Wes's kindness for what it had been: concern for her.

Wes had returned to college and became a more permanent fixture in her life: more overbearing, more watchful, more involved. To this day, she was politely reserved with his father.

She wasn't sure how Wes coped with that man's disapproving wrath.

Duncan waited on her now, patient but not quite, tapping his thumb on the table. She wanted to tell him about Rosanna and Falcon. She was concerned about Wes, just like Wes had always been concerned about her, but they weren't her secrets to share.

"Speak of the devil," Duncan said in a tone she couldn't decipher. His attention was locked on the entrance.

When Annie realized who he was staring at, her stomach bottomed out. Wes swept into the room with Rosanna on his arm, and everyone in the restaurant seemed to hold a collective breath. The socialite was even more exquisite in person. Her bronze skin looked airbrushed, her thick, shiny hair fresh from a shampoo commercial. Wes whispered in her ear as they neared. Rosanna whispered back. Wes laughed heartily.

Annie tried to shrink in her seat.

Duncan stood and blocked the couple's path. "So you *do* actually get fresh air. I thought you'd built an underground tunnel between work and home."

Annie focused on her plate. She adjusted the spaghetti straps of her white lace dress. It was floor length, sewn with layers of intricate lace, the V dipping down her cleavage nearly transparent. The cut hadn't allowed for a bra. She'd felt sexy and feminine when she'd put it on. Going out with Duncan may have been platonic, but dressing nice had been part of the appeal of their night out. A chance to feel pretty. With Wes here, she felt like she was playing dress-up. A lonely woman on a "friend" date, who couldn't forget about the man she truly wanted.

"Hello, Anthea." There was a bite to Wes's formality, challenge in his clipped tone.

Disapproval that she was out with Duncan?

Wes wouldn't know there was nothing romantic about their night, and she was glad for it. The guy had some nerve, judging her when he'd discarded her advances with the care of a back-alley surgeon. She had half a mind to cause a scene, upend their table and tell the world Weston Aldrich was emotionally challenged and couldn't date a real woman, but theatrics would involve talking to him. She didn't want to look up and see him this close with Rosanna.

Except...screw that.

She wasn't about to spend her life creeping around on the subway to avoid a confrontation with them. He wasn't interested in Annie. He'd made himself abundantly clear. She was allowed to dine here with Duncan or any other man.

She ticked up her chin, forced a placid expression. "Weston, pleasure as always. This must be your girlfriend. You two make quite the dashing couple."

Wes flinched. Rosanna beamed. Annie brushed her long hair over her shoulders, putting her braless dress on display, and smiled at Duncan. "Sit so we can chat more. Let the two lovebirds be." To Rosanna she said, "It was lovely to finally meet you."

Kill those suckers with kindness.

Duncan obliged. Weston's jaw looked tight enough to chip a tooth. The jerk could afford dental care, so he could gnash those ivories all he wanted.

Wes took a step away, cheek still bunching from his gnashing teeth, but Rosanna held her ground. "Anthea? I don't think Wes has mentioned you."

Of course he hadn't. She was nothing but charity work to him. It shouldn't still sting, but it did.

He cut a caustic look at Annie's lacy dress, like the day he'd driven her to work and had judged her outfit. "She's Annie," he said, curt. "Anthea is her full name."

Rosanna's stunning dark eyes widened. "Oh, wow. *The* Annie. I take that back. Weston's told me a lot about you."

Hopefully he'd left out the part where she'd offered her body and soul to the man. "Don't believe everything he says. If he said he sleeps with a nightlight on because he's worried about stubbing a toe, total fib. He still has boogie-man nightmares."

Rosanna laughed and nudged Wes's arm. "I like her."

"You two have a good night." Wes nodded sharply and dragged his date off, not before Rosanna cast another long look at Annie.

Duncan resumed his seat, and Annie tried to will her haywire pulse into submission. Their drinks arrived. They talked. They ordered food. All normal behavior, but Weston's appearance had dashed her hopes of forgetting him with a fun night out. Careless with her feelings, or not, she was still hopelessly in love with him. She cut and ate her rack of lamb, each piece of chewed meat barely making it down her throat. When she felt too overheated and frustrated to continue making small talk with Duncan, she excused herself to the bathroom, where her cell phone promptly buzzed with a text.

Wes: **Are you out with him to get back at me?**

He was a real piece of work, assuming her choices revolved around him. But she *was* out with Duncan to distract herself from thinking about Wes. Pesky details.

Annie: **What I do is none of your business.**

Wes: **Everything you do is my business.**

Whoa there, cowboy. Man was getting too big for his designer britches.

Annie: **You had your chance at everything and you walked away. You may be fake-dating, but I'm not. I like Duncan and he likes me.**

The lie was petty. She should regret it, but she didn't. Dots bounced as he replied. They appeared and disappeared. Annoyed, she sat on the lounge chair in the bathroom's alcove and stared at those dots like she was about to be told winning lottery numbers. She should shut her phone down, swipe on some lipstick, and get back to Duncan. Resuscitate their fun banter. Quit letting Wes pull her emotional strings.

Then Wes's reply came.

Wes: I lied at your apartment. You're all I think about. Get rid of Duncan as early as possible. I'm coming over to your place tonight.

A toilet flushed. A faucet ran. She clutched her phone so tightly it pinched her skin as she read the message again, the words slowly sinking in.

He lied. He couldn't stop thinking about her.

Did he actually want to *be* with her?

A woman walked in and smiled at Annie. Annie's answering grin probably looked clownish, exaggerated and shocked. *Weston wants to be with me.* He might be reacting to Duncan, assuming his controlling persona, feeling possessive. But, no. That didn't jive with all his signals and signs the past months. That kiss. His body's reaction. That dream. And Rosanna had said he'd spoken about her...

Wes wanted Annie as much as she wanted him.

She stood and pressed her hand to the wall, tried to clear the giddy fuzz from her head.

A woman applying lipstick at the mirror frowned. "You all right?"

Annie touched her breastbone, felt the proclamation of her pounding heart. "I think I'm perfect."

She'd have to end her night with Duncan early. Assuming he'd been honest about their friend status, he wouldn't be offended, and she wouldn't have to explain why. She wouldn't do it right away, though. Not before Weston Aldrich experienced a fraction of the hurt and dejection he'd caused her the past week. If he understood that pain, he might think twice before four-wheeling over her heart again. She wouldn't be able to hold out for long. That much was obvious. Even for a few hours, it was her turn to be in charge.

"IF YOU KEEP IGNORING me and staring at Annie, people will think our fake relationship is on the rocks. And quit looking at your phone."

"That's rich coming from you, considering our first date."

Rosanna nudged Weston's foot under the table. "I didn't like you then."

"I didn't like you much, either." He was equally as frustrated with her tonight. This texting disaster was all Rosanna's fault. He watched Annie as she tilted her head and sipped her wine, her neck elongating, all that soft hair falling behind her shoulders. He swallowed a groan.

"You told me to be honest with her," he said, terse. "I was honest. Why hasn't she replied to my text?"

"Give me your phone."

He shoved it at her, agitated. Annie hadn't glanced at him once since returning from the bathroom. She'd looked at Duncan plenty, though. She'd leaned forward on her elbows, giving him a nice view of that slinky dress, her breasts practically visible through the elaborate lace, while he was stuck here, hands tied, on an infuriating fake date.

He shouldn't have told Annie how he felt. He shouldn't have confided the depths of those feelings to Rosanna, either. She'd been relentless since they'd sat down, all up in his face about Annie. *She's beautiful. Like really beautiful. She definitely likes you. She was jealous of me. You need to ask her out.*

A more detailed confession later about the scrapbooking disaster and his wretchedness this week, Rosanna had been coaching him, infecting his mind, making him think he could be with Annie and not fuck everything up. Fear of loving and losing had done a number on him, and if the gradual caving of his chest the past week had taught him anything, it was that he already loved Annie. As a friend. A confidant. An integral person in his life. Missing her had flattened him. Seeing her with Duncan had sucked the air from his lungs.

If she and Weston added lovers to their relationship, losing her would be the dirt on his stone-cold grave. And he couldn't do any of it without telling her the truth about Leo.

Rosanna read the message and made a face. "I said be honest about your feelings. Not boss her around."

"I wasn't bossy."

Rosanna cleared her throat and deepened her voice. "*Get rid of Duncan as early as possible. I'm coming over to your place tonight.* You may as well have added *woman* at the end of that, all caveman style."

"That was direct, which is the same as being honest. Now she's ignoring me."

"Are you this dense in your business dealings?"

Weston felt a growl rumble in his gut. He glanced at Annie again. She was smiling and laughing with Duncan, happy with a careless player, probably to piss him off.

"You encouraged this," he said, the muscles in his neck straining. "So you need to help me fix it."

Rosanna passed him back the phone and patted his hand. "It's simple. You hurt her and didn't apologize."

"I told her I lied."

"Does that sound like a groveling apology to you?"

He reread his message, his heart sinking with each word. "Shit."

"However you feel now, she's been feeling ten times worse the past week. Not only do you owe her a heartfelt apology, but you owe her some control. That's what she's reclaiming right now."

Wes took a swallow of his wine, had to force it past the regret lodged in his throat. He'd hurt Annie. Badly. He'd hurt himself in the process, but he'd understood the why of it. He'd had the comfort of her truth with him, the feelings she'd admitted. He'd known he could fix things if he'd wanted to. All she'd had was his rejection and silence. "What if you're wrong and I only hurt her more?"

"Again, are you this dense in your business meetings? If you are, I should counsel my father to kibosh this merger."

"Dating a woman isn't a business meeting." Rosanna raised a dark eyebrow and gestured between them. Point taken. "You know what I mean."

"I do, but if you backed down from every 'what-if' in business, you'd be peddling knock-off purses on the street corner. You're a risk taker, Weston. That's why Aldrich Pharma is the behemoth it is. That's why my father wants to be under your umbrella. Annie isn't a merger in those terms, but she's a risk. If your desire for the end result outweighs your fear of failure, it's a risk worth taking. So that's your question: how badly do you want her?"

He'd missed Annie hovering at his back in his studio this week, making up ridiculous stories about Felix. He couldn't close his eyes without seeing the shocked devastation on her face when he'd left her apartment. He couldn't blink without reliving their kiss. He wanted her badly, regardless of the risk. And Leo had asked him to protect Annie, make sure she was happy. Maybe being with her was the answer to everything. Together, she'd always be safe. He'd be the best version of himself.

If she could forgive him for her brother's death.

He sure as shit wanted to be the one sitting across from her now, making her laugh, holding her hand, whispering how gorgeous she looked in that dress.

He ran his thumb over his phone's screen, thought of the best way to grovel. He settled on following Rosanna's advice again.

Weston: **I'm sorry. I won't come over. It's up to you how this moves forward. I'll be up at home if you want to stop by later.**

He hit Send and watched Annie. She glanced at her purse but continued talking to Duncan. She kept looking at her purse intermittently, never reaching inside. Sweat gathered at the back of Weston's shirt, and he felt like punching something. Himself, mainly. When she finally pulled out her phone and read his message, the smallest smile lifted her lips.

His forehead nearly hit the table in relief.

"I told you I give the best advice," Rosanna said.

He massaged his chest and faced her, still surprised by their growing friendship. "For a woman who hates relationships, your female intel isn't half bad."

"For a stuck-up suit, you're a real softy."

He wasn't sure about that. He wasn't sure he was ready to open himself up to Annie, but he knew he'd pull an all-nighter on his couch, watching his front door for a sign that the most important person in his life was willing to trust him again.

16

Annie paced in front of Wes's front door, her movements stiff and jerky. She was freaking out, unable to knock on his door or use her key to sneak in.

Since tonight's dinner, she'd reread his messages twenty-one times. Not twenty or twenty-two. Exactly twenty-one times to make sure she hadn't misunderstood his intentions. She read them again now. Time twenty-two. Just to be sure.

I lied at your apartment. You're all I think about. Get rid of Duncan as early as possible. I'm coming over to your place tonight.

I'm sorry. I won't come over. It's up to you how this moves forward. I'll be up at home if you want to stop by later.

Why couldn't she knock on his stupid door?

Drawing dinner out while waiting for Wes and Rosanna to leave first had been a challenge. Not because Duncan had been a bore. They'd had fun in the end, as she'd expected, and he'd been cool with them parting ways from the restaurant. Not before he'd said, "FYI: friends with benefits are more fun than battery operated toys," which had made her laugh.

The Beat Match 181

She'd felt giddy hailing a cab, excited to get gone and meet Wes, but the ride to his condo had felt too short. Once there, she'd stared at his building, unable to go inside or take a full breath. For reasons she hadn't fully understood, she'd chosen to walk around the neighborhood instead, stopping periodically to reread his texts, stalling when what she really wanted was to dive into Weston's bed, find out what it would be like to kiss him with her eyes open, knowing he was the man gripping her body, turned on, their tongues tangling with intent.

But, no. She'd read his words one more time, had walked around the block one more time. She'd delayed so long he was probably asleep and snoring. And she was overheated, like she was having hot flashes at the tender age of twenty-seven. A rare case of early-onset menopause. Or Wes-o-pause. That must be her current affliction: she was desperately grappling to hit pause.

She loved Wes. He obviously had feelings for her. Once she stepped through that door, for better or for worse, everything would change. Bigger changes. No *returning to their "normal"* changes. This was their final frontier and blasting into outer space seemed less daunting than opening Weston's door.

Hand trembling, she fitted her key into his lock. She took a massive breath, which did zero to assuage her nerves, then turned the key while trying to keep quiet. She didn't want to wake Wes or Felix, or find out Wes had acted out of rash jealousy and had changed his mind about this invitation.

She eased the door open. The lights were still on in the kitchen, but darkness weighted the rest of the condo. Her armpits and forehead felt damp.

"Took you long enough," a rough voice said.

She yelped and dropped the key. Wes was on the leather couch by the windows, heavy thighs sprawled, hands clenched into fists. The dim lighting slashed shadows across his face as he sat. Not for long. He stood and stalked toward her, resolute, single-minded, like he was going to grab her, devour her, kiss the Wes-o-pause out of her.

She abruptly said, "Bathroom," and skittered in her heels across the hardwood floor, away from all the erotic maleness gunning for her. She closed the door and locked it. She wasn't sure if he'd followed her. She couldn't hear much besides the loud thud of her heart. She had no clue why she was running from the one man she wanted.

She did have to pee, though. Walking and stalling hadn't done her bladder any favors. It must be why she'd dodged the sexual animal in the other room, but she didn't leave after flushing the toilet and washing her hands. She grabbed two luxurious hand towels and pressed them under her armpits to absorb her sweat. "Get it together," she whispered to herself.

A knock sounded. "Everything okay in there?"

She was far from okay. "That's a pretty rude question to ask a woman in a bathroom."

"You're not just any woman."

"And you're not just any man." He was *the* man. The bar. A previously unreachable level. "I'm not decent."

"As in undressed?"

"As in gross and unattractive."

"You're stunning, tonight and always. And you forget I've seen you at your worst: drooling when you sleep, snot hanging out of your nose on that cold sailing trip through the harbor, hungover and stuffing your face with salt and vinegar chips. I've seen it all, Annie."

Not even close. But...*stunning*. She looked in the mirror, tried to see beyond her hysteria. Although her dress was still lovely, white towels protruded from under her arms, her neck was splotchy, the hairs at her temple had frizzed slightly, and her hazel eyes were wide. Wary. More brown than green. This wasn't how she'd imagined their night beginning.

"You should go to bed," she said. "I'll let myself out. We can meet up tomorrow, talk about whatever this is."

"Not happening."

"But—"

"You are *not* leaving, Annie."

God, his tone. Rough. Adamant, with a hint of desperation. This still wasn't at all what she'd imagined. "Weston..."

"*Anthea...*"

She groaned. "I'm standing here with your perfectly plush towels stuck under my arms, drowning in stress sweat because the idea of what might happen between us, which is exactly what I *want* to happen, might *actually* happen and it's turning me into a human fountain. STRESS SWEAT, Wes. I'm practically dripping this nonsense all over your marble floor. Trust me, you haven't seen it all."

A pause. It lengthened painfully. Maybe she should've held back a morsel of truth.

"Open the door, Anthea."

She didn't reply.

"Open it or I'm picking the lock."

"You know how to pick a lock?"

"Leo taught me a few tricks."

She huffed out a watery laugh. She loved that visual, those two as teens, huddling over a lock, thinking themselves master criminals. She loved Wes, and if he was truly interested in her, he wouldn't care that she was blotchy and frizzy and a general mess. Steeling her frazzled self, she forced her feet toward the door and turned the lock.

WESTON PUSHED the door open slowly, revealing the woman he'd once only seen as a child, his best friend's little sister, annoying and cute. Then just annoying. Then strong and resilient and the most astounding person he'd ever known, even if she never finished her Sudoku puzzles and refused to tidy her apartment. Now she was this. *Mine.*

He didn't reach for her like his body demanded. This was all too new and difficult for them both. He still had to confess about Leo, explain about his relationship issues.

He flexed his fingers, forced them loose at his sides. He hated that he wasn't kissing her, that she'd ever kissed any man but him. This visceral possessiveness felt unfamiliar, but maybe it wasn't. He'd always felt protective of her. He'd just never let himself look hard enough to analyze why and see the feminine allure glowing under her skin, through those soft curves, her rainforest eyes, the plump bow of her bottom lip.

She really did have his towels stuck under her arms. Her eyes were glassy, as though she'd been crying, or she was about to cry. The skin around her neck, up to her ears, looked red and irritated. All he could think was: *love.* I love this woman.

A solid punch straight to his heart.

"Nothing will happen between us until you're ready," he said. Until they were both ready. "I just want to talk tonight, or just sleep. I need to give you a full apology and better explanation of...things, but we can go to sleep and deal with this in the morning, when we're fresh."

She squeezed her arms tighter to her sides, those ridiculous towels poking out. "Like sleep, as in together?"

"If it's up to me, yes. I..." Why the hell was his throat closing up?

Seeing Annie out with Duncan had twisted something inside of him. Rosanna's advice to be truthful and apologetic had given him the push he'd needed to reach out. But it had been this week's utter loneliness that had knocked his head straight. He hadn't known heartbreak until he'd hurt Annie with his petty lies and had a taste of how painful it was not talking to her.

"I've been messed up since that scrapbooking night," he said, forcing the words out. "I'm tired of denying how I feel about you, to myself and to you. So, yes—I want you next to me tonight. But if you're more comfortable in the guestroom, that's fine. As long as you promise not to leave without talking to me in the morning."

"I'm scared," she whispered. "I just...feel so much, and I'm suddenly terrified this will backfire. I can't lose you, Wes."

Exactly why he'd been a spineless jellyfish. He understood her better than she realized. "We're both scared because we know how huge this is."

Her eyes dropped to his crotch. "I mean, it looks big, but not *that* big."

He laughed. Tossed his head back and let go until his cheeks ached from smiling. Yeah, he understood her. Losing Annie wasn't an option, which meant he had to prove his worth. Offer her complete honesty and, if she actually forgave him, try not to let his past ruin his future. Make himself into the prince she deserved.

He grabbed the towels under her arms and tugged them free.

She relaxed and mumbled, "So gross."

He laughed again. "The grossest. Now get over here."

When she didn't move, he closed the distance between them and pulled her against his chest. He wrapped one arm around her back, dragged his other hand through her hair until she melted into him. His body stirred. There was no controlling this pulsing need. He still wouldn't touch her until they'd talked. "My bed or the guestroom?"

She purred lightly, brushed her nose and lips against his neck. "Your bed, as long as we only sleep. I need to take this slower than I realized, and I need to shower first."

He wasn't sure how he'd manage knowing she was naked in his shower, water sluicing over her breasts, between her legs. He was barely containing himself now, which Annie no doubt felt. Her breath caught. She shifted her hips. "Jesus. Where do you buy underwear for that thing?"

Chuckling, he stepped back and jerked his chin toward his bedroom. "Get in there, get showered, and get into bed. I'll make sure this *thing* keeps to his side of the bed."

Annie glanced at his crotch again, his erection straining the fine wool of his Armani suit. He hadn't bothered changing since dinner. He hadn't done much besides stare at his front door, waiting for Annie. Now she was here, staring at his clothed body like the sight of him had hypnotized her.

She blinked, swayed slightly. "I, um..."

He smirked. "You were going to shower."

She looked up, a slow grin curving her lips. "Right. Shower. Then we have a slumber party on the respective sides of your emperor-sized bed." With a sultry look, she turned, hips swaying as she sashayed toward his room. Rosanna was right to question his business savvy and mental prowess. He should never have suggested they sleep in the same bed, but he wanted her as close as possible. Once they talked, he could lose her for good.

A cold shower of his own later, he walked down from his upper level, turning off lights as he neared his bedroom. Hopefully Annie had had enough time to calibrate, relax and settle. Accept that she wasn't running from him, and he wasn't running from her. They would finally face the intensity between them.

He knocked on the door. A loud snore erupted, fake and

obnoxious and all Annie. He pressed the door open and leaned on the frame. "Careful, or you'll wake Felix."

Annie was in one of his V-neck T-shirts, the front dipping low, all of it too large on her. Her blond hair looked darker, wet and loose around her shoulders. Her skin was clean and fresh. A vision on his crisp, white sheets.

She eyed him, nose to toes, and frowned. "Please tell me you don't sleep in that."

He glanced down at his T-shirt and linen pants. "It's better than my usual sleep attire."

"You look like you're going yachting. All you're missing is a dollop of caviar and a glass of expensive Scotch. How is this better?"

"I sleep naked."

She took an eyeful of him, cheeks blushing, like he *was* naked and she was starved. Exactly how he wanted her. Hungry. Ready for him. When he finally got his hands on her, slow wouldn't be an option.

"I bet the women you've had love that," she said, a slight break in her voice.

Was she jealous of his past? Not that he was much better, considering his vicious jealousy tonight. Even when younger, the boyfriends she'd talked about had irked him. He'd assumed his reactions had been of a protective nature, a big brother looking out for his little sister. How blind he'd been.

"I've never slept with a woman," he said.

She raised a skeptical brow.

He pushed off the door frame and stalked toward the bed. "Let me rephrase—I've never slept with a woman overnight. I sleep alone, and I sleep naked."

She watched him approach, tracked his every move. She was sitting up, his shirt on her revealing a swell of beautiful breast, the sheets gathered up to her waist. He flipped off the main light and slid into his side, resting his head on his palm. He looked up at her from his lower position. Giving her height, power, control—Rosanna's advice still in his mind. He waited for her to speak.

"If you don't sleep with women, why'd you ask me to sleep over?"

He wasn't sure. Even with Lila, during their three month relationship that had ended with him ghosting on her, they had never slept together overnight. He liked to run early, work late. Easy excuses. The night she'd whispered *I love you*, she'd been grasping at straws, unsure why he wouldn't stay over, thinking the declaration would be a turning point for them. It had only emphasized how messed up Weston was.

That was then. This was now. This was Annie, looking down at him with big vulnerable eyes. He wished he could see their color better—untrusting brown or vibrant green, or a swirl of both as she tried to figure him out. "I want you to sleep over because it feels right," he said. "I want this because I've never had it with anyone and can't imagine sleeping next to anyone but you."

True closeness. The thing that scared him most. The thing he might lose.

"Wow. That was...*wow*."

She might not think so shortly. "Do you want to talk now or in the morning?"

She scraped her teeth over her bottom lip. "Morning?"

Relief had his breath rushing out. He did want this night, a simple sleepover, something he'd never shared with anyone. The vulnerability of waking up, unguarded and pliable, next to a woman he loved. A test to see if he'd panic in the morning. No sex on the table, just intimacy.

She scooted lower, pulled the sheets up to her neck. "So you're really sleeping in linen pants?"

"Absolutely." He wouldn't survive tonight if Annie accidentally brushed against him.

"We need to get you flannels."

"I don't wear flannel."

"You won't become a lumberjack. Or a hipster."

"I'd become hideously unstylish."

She mock shuddered. "The horror."

He shifted closer to her. "Would you like me in flannel?"

She reached over and traced his eyebrows, the length of his nose. "I like you all formal and buttoned up, knowing there's a secret DJ under all that expensive wool."

He plucked her hand from his face, kissed her palm, and pressed her hand against his sternum. They linked fingers, and she sighed. They didn't talk again. He watched her eyes get heavy, her limbs sinking heavier into his mattress. Her breath slowed and deepened until her lips parted slightly. Heat flared in his chest, so hot and fierce his bones ached. *Mine.* Every inch of this woman was his. Until he shattered her image of him.

17

ANNIE WOKE WITH A START. It took a moment to remember she was in Wes's sumptuous bed, her head resting on his cloud-soft pillow. His cozy duvet was draped over her lower body, the thing likely stuffed with swan feathers and unicorn hair. A heavy arm was latched over her waist.

A handsome arm. Wes's arm.

Nothing had ever felt so right.

His hand was locked around her ribs, the tips of his fingers brushing the underside of her breast. The way her shirt was twisted around her waist, all that separated her from the man of her dreams was her underwear and his ridiculous linen pants. *I sleep naked. I've never slept with a woman before. I can't imagine sleeping next to anyone but you.*

She shifted slightly, fluttery tingles slipping through her body, traveling lower, tugging on her belly and every sensitive nerve. Wes groaned softly, tightened his grip on her until she felt him against her backside, crazy hard and ready for her. She wasn't far behind, wetness gathering. She had no choice but to move. She pushed back slightly and wriggled.

His hot breath rushed against her ear. "Don't do that again."

She did exactly that again.

"Annie." Wes's body turned to stone, his arm a vise around her. "If you rub against me again, I'm not sure I'll be able to remain a gentleman."

"Who said I wanted a gentleman?" True, she'd been a hesitant mess last night, but sleeping next to Wes, hearing his confession, seeing the sincerity in his eyes as he'd admitted a fraction of his fears had both calmed and aroused her. "I want you, Wes. I'm done waiting and second-guessing everything."

She swiveled her hips again, tried to turn in his arms, see his face. All she managed was to twist her head. Wes's cheeks were flushed, his striking bone structure sharper than ever, but his eyes had a dazed look, his eyelids still heavy with sleep.

"We haven't talked yet," he said, as though each word pained him.

"Maybe I don't want to talk. I just want to feel for once. Forget our tangled past and where this is going, enjoy each other before we weigh everything down with our worries. Unless..." She paused, suddenly unsure, feeding off his hesitation. "Unless you don't feel the same."

He dropped his gaze, loosened his hold enough to turn her toward him. Deep lines puckered his brow. "Trust me, I feel the same. I want to be next to you, over you, around you, moving inside of you so badly I can't think straight. I am consumed by you, Annie." His eyes lifted, catching her in waves of uncertainty. "But I'm damaged and scared I'll hurt you if we do this before you know what you're getting into. There are things I haven't told you."

She feathered her fingers over the strong bones of his face. A sculpture of raw intensity. "I know you, Wes. You think I don't, but I do."

"You don't know this."

"It doesn't matter."

"It matters to me."

She wasn't exactly sure what had him holding back, but she had a guess: his commitment issues. Wes had remained single through adulthood for a reason. Losing Leo and his mother had likely done a number on him, making him leery of reopening himself up for that kind of hurt. She understood the hesitation, but living in a bubble wasn't truly living.

She traced his frown lines. "I know we have things to discuss, and we both have morning breath, which is usually a hard limit for me, but after all we've been through, don't you think we deserve to just feel *good*? Shake off the past, forget the future for a minute. Any talk you want to have can wait. Let your mind relax for once and quit planning ten steps ahead."

His legs shifted, a restless slide beneath the sheets as his breathing picked up. "I don't want to hurt you," he said again.

"Like I said last night, it looks big, but not *that* big." He laughed. Mission accomplished. She kissed his mouth gently. "You can't hurt me, Wes. Not when I know exactly what I'm doing. I want this, and if you think denying me is smart, remember I have a key to your home and can fill your shampoo bottles with hair remover. I also have half a mind to kidnap Felix and set him loose with the other rabbit-squirrels before the breed goes extinct."

Another sleep-roughed laugh rumbled from him. "Your brain fascinates me."

She reached down and cupped the hard ridge of him through his linen pants. "This fascinates me."

Air hissed through his teeth as a myriad of emotions crested his face—hesitation, worry, anger? Then he surged, his powerful body rotating on top of her, no longer playing nice, the gentleman replaced with the rake. He notched his hips between hers, kept her controlled under his bulk as he lowered his head and captured her lips. She moaned and opened for him. She was rewarded with a harsh grunt. They moved together, wet and deep, his lips bruising in their demand. She may have kissed him once before, oblivious to the man he'd been, but this was different. It made her feel miles more vulnerable, yet powerful. Weak and strong at once. And, God, he was between her thighs, rubbing right where she ached.

"Open your eyes." He licked the beauty mark beside her lips, a playful move that had her smiling.

She did as she was told, gasped when he rolled his hips.

He groaned. "I'm not Falcon. I'm not some guy you forget by dating someone else. When we're together, I want your eyes open so you remember who it was that rocked your world." Another hip thrust. She cried out. "We clear?"

"You're even bossy in bed. And rock my world? You really are old, Herbert. Maybe I should have rethought this."

"Wicked woman," he murmured and kissed her roughly.

She latched her legs around his waist, ground against him so thoroughly she almost came. He was insanely hard, a steel rod sliding over her, rubbing as he palmed her breasts through the shirt she'd borrowed. He kissed her mouth, nipped her lower lip, moved to her throat, her jaw, her ear—every erogenous zone in the Northern hemisphere.

She pawed at his T-shirt. "Off."

He pushed up to his knees, grabbed his shirt by the back of his neck and yanked it over his head. Her body burned up. She'd seen him shirtless before, swimming in the Hamptons, but never like this, between her spread thighs, his erection tenting those linen pants. His breaths came fast and shallow. She touched his pecs, slid her thumbs over his nipples, delighting in his answering groan and the smattering of chest hair trailing downward. "You're so hot."

"I'm burning up because I'm about to strip you."

"You better work fast."

The V-neck she wore landed in a heap on the floor, her underwear flung next to it. He was back on his knees, looking down at her with such unmitigated desire she could only lie there and pant. "Wes?"

He paused. One word from her and he tipped his head to the side, searched her face. "Yeah?"

"I can't believe this is happening."

"In a good way?"

"In the best way."

His well-kissed lips quirked up. "If you could see what I see, you'd know it's better than the best." He leaned over her and delicately palmed her breast, held the weight of her, followed by a soft squeeze. His neck muscles strained as his eyes slid shut. "You're as perfect as I imagined."

"I'm not perfect."

"You're my kind of perfect."

No man had ever told her she was his kind of perfect. No one had ever touched her like she was a work of art.

She reached for the button on his pants, needed to touch him, feel him slide into her so deeply there was no beginning or end to either of them. He moved out of reach, dipped down to take her nipple into his mouth. Tongue, teeth, a wet lick that had her bowing off the mattress. He moved purposefully, his fingers scraping her ribs, the swells of her hips, each grope and caress commanding but not strong enough. She wanted red marks like the one his mask had left on her cheek, a visual reminder of how good he felt, all that honed muscle sliding against her soft skin. "I need you, Wes. Inside me. Please."

He didn't relent, exploring every inch of her, moving lower then returning to her belly, back to her breasts, between her legs again, never touching her where she ached, only blowing a hot stream of air over her sensitive flesh, so surprising she gripped his hair and cried out. "Stop teasing."

"This isn't teasing. This is how it'll always be with us. Pleasure so good it hurts."

"Then make me hurt. Make me scream."

He glanced up from between her legs, a devilish spark lighting his face. "Patience, Squirrel."

His use of her nickname had tears burning her eyes. She bit the insides of her cheek, refused to let the tears fall. She'd missed that name. She'd missed him so much the past weeks. Months, really. It had been so long since things had been easy between them.

He licked her then, a long slide that had her bucking. She plunged her fingers into his thick hair, held him in place as his fingers and tongue worked her into oblivion, building her up then teasing her, controlling her body the way he controlled her heart. Her legs tensed, pleasure a hot grip that yanked her under as she screamed Wes's name, eventually crumpling into a pile of boneless bliss.

He looked up at her, his lips shiny from what they'd done, ferocity in his eyes. "No one gets to see you like this but me."

A statement. Wes, controlling as ever. Their new normal.

"Only you. Now get those pants off."

He stood from the bed, flicked the button on his linen pants —so ridiculous—his eyes never leaving her. Her body was satiated, loose and pliable, but the second he dropped his pants, no briefs caging all that male perfection, her insides clenched. "You're spectacular."

He turned serious, stared hard into her eyes. "We're spectacular."

How was this even happening?

He turned toward his closet, the view of his toned behind and strong back mind-bending, but she said, "Stop."

He spun around. "Are you okay?"

Again, one word from her, and he hit pause. So much care for her. He was *consumed* by her, or so he'd said. That made her next words all the more important. "Have you been tested recently?"

His eyes got more intense, if that was even possible. "Yes. I'm clean, and I've always worn condoms."

"Always?"

"Always."

"So I'll be your first bare?"

His length jerked. He gripped the base, gave it a rough squeeze. "The first of many things, apparently. You're covered?"

She nodded. "No condom needed. I'm on the pill, and I'm clean."

His lips moved, a quiet mumble she couldn't hear, then he was on the bed, over her, kissing her while pressing their bodies together—her breasts to his chest, their hips aligning, his length nestled against her belly. God, he felt amazing. So hard and smooth. She secured her legs around him and rolled so she was on top, his erection trapped between them. Not in her, just rubbing, that huge body under her control. Not that either of them were in control here. This was them out of control, risking their hearts, forgetting about the future and living in the moment.

Wes gripped her hips, steadied her from below as he rolled against her, not pushing in, just maddening thrusts that blurred her vision. She moved in time, watched his biceps flex, his pecs and abdomen harden, every muscle defined as they rocked. She never wanted to leave this bed. She didn't want to discuss why Wes thought he was damaged or how they were going to be a couple when he was fake-dating a woman to secure a merger. She didn't want to pretend she didn't love him so deeply one wrong move could ruin her.

WESTON'S BODY was on fire. He was so close to slipping into Annie, and she was drenched, ready for him. He wasn't sure he was ready for this. Watching her fall apart before had wrecked him. The way her head had tipped back, her full breasts pushed up as she'd called his name in ecstasy, he'd never known satisfaction like that. A crush of possessiveness.

Having sex bare would shatter any remaining composure, but he was beyond sense. Past caring about the *how* or *when* or *if* of their future. He was an asshole for letting this happen before they talked, but he couldn't make himself stop.

He squeezed her breasts, ate up her body with his hungry eyes, tugged her down for another rough kiss, loved feeling her soft breasts pressed to his hard chest. She was the humor to his seriousness. The light to his dark. Ridiculous and infuriating at times, but she *was* his kind of perfect. If he messed this up, he'd never forgive himself.

He manhandled her, flipped them back over, needing some semblance of control. The illusion of it, at least. Her hair was wild from sleeping with it wet. Her lips were shiny and plump, her neck and breasts red from where he'd sucked too hard—his late best friend's little sister transformed into a sexual goddess. Into the most integral person in his life.

How would he manage if he lost her?

"You okay?" She touched his cheek, worry in her slanted browns.

"I'm perfect." Because of her. With her.

A punch of desperation flooded his veins.

He positioned himself at her entrance, couldn't believe he was about to sink into Annie. She canted her hips, tried to coax him in. He held her steady, mesmerized, watching his length disappear into her, one inch, another. So hot, wet. All Annie. A pause as he twitched and she gasped.

"More," she demanded.

"I wish you could see what I see," he murmured. He pushed in farther, a slow slide until they were flush. Then he moved. *They* moved together, pulling at each other as their bodies merged, a give and take as they went deeper, farther, deeper still, but the close wasn't close enough. The far made him angry. He pumped harder, needing more. He could barely swallow through the roughness crowding his throat.

"Annie. Fuck, you're..." Everything. At what point in his life had she become everything?

He pressed lower, caged her between his forearms, never letting her look away. Her hazel eyes shone—springtime green, glistening with possibility. He snapped his hips, ground against her, kissed her so hard their teeth clashed. Not his smoothest move, but it didn't matter. The future didn't matter. Together, like this, Annie was all that mattered.

"God, Wes. I'm close." She knocked her head back, squeezed him so hard lust blasted up his thighs. Too soon. He lifted slightly, reached between them, desperate to make this unforgettable for her. The second his thumb brushed her, she clenched and cried out. The sharp tug on him stole his breath. She shook, incoherent as she let go, and he was right behind her, a blinding rush roaring up his spine. He cursed. He called her name.

All he could feel and see and smell was Annie Ward.

He kissed her eyes, her nose, the birthmark beside her mouth. "You okay?"

She stroked his back and nodded. "I don't ever want you to move."

He couldn't agree more. Moving meant reality. Reality

meant talking. Talking meant things could get shaky. "I might never go into work again." Or leave this room.

Annie circled her hips, just enough to make him growl. And fire him up.

Then his cell rang.

He bit her collarbone, licked it gently, determined to ignore the world a while longer. "I'll throw my phone out the window."

She raked her fingers up his back and over his shoulders. "What if it's work?"

"It's definitely work." Another meltdown. More stress.

"You should get it."

"I should debauch you again."

She laughed softly. "Or that."

He kissed her until the ringing stopped, refused to give up this slice of perfection. He still couldn't believe he was bare in Annie, his release seeping out, something so erotic about that hot slide coating them.

Another goddamn ring. He hung his head and cursed.

There was no avoiding fate when it was gunning for you.

18

Annie watched Wes warily as he glared out his massive windows, his phone clutched in his hand. His tone was direct and curt. He paced a steady line. This was the third call since they'd woken up and the blissed out, affectionate man from the bedroom had officially vacated the premises. This was business Wes. Pulled-in-a-million-directions Wes.

She loved him more than ever.

He hung up and dragged a hand through his hair. He was already showered, shaved, and suited up. Tie. Button-down shirt. Slacks. She was back in her sexy lace dress, the only clothes she had at his place.

She picked up his coffee mug and joined him by the window. "Is work always this insane?"

He glanced at the offered mug, but his gaze roved to her legs, up her thighs to the low neckline of her dress. His eyelids fell heavy. "Are you always this sexy?"

He pressed a kiss to her neck.

She almost dropped their mugs.

He took his coffee, eyes now locked on her face. "It's not unusual, but the merger has taken the intensity to a new level."

"Is it worth it?"

"Without a doubt. If the merger falls apart, we'll lose market share. It'll affect our bottom line, our growth. Jobs would be cut."

All a huge deal, but that wasn't what she'd meant. "Is it worth it to *you*? I've only ever seen your work life at a distance and didn't realize it was this intrusive. Is it what you want to do, or did you get into the family business because it was expected? Do you love building a pharmaceutical empire as much as you love DJing?"

He took a slow sip of his coffee. "My father may have steered me toward Aldrich Pharma, but I couldn't imagine not working there. My name's on that company, and engineering pharmaceuticals makes a difference in the world. It's a legacy of sorts. The DJing is a rush, but not like the accomplishment I feel at work. When life has been rough, work has been my escape. Problem solving, so many moving parts under my control. If you're not in it and focused, everything falls apart. It's a different kind of gratification, but no less important."

"So you love it? Even with all this stress?" That kind of pressure would have flattened her. She flipped the page when a Sudoku puzzle got too hard, quit jobs when they became tedious.

"Aldrich Pharma is part of who I am. It makes me happy in an exhausting and thrilling way, and our breakthroughs change lives. If I lost it or left, it would be like losing a piece of myself. So, yes, the stress is worth it. The hours are worth it. But thank you."

"For what?"

"For asking. No one has ever cared enough to ask how I feel."

The coffee mug was toasty in her hands. Weston's sincerity made the rest of her warm and sated. "It's okay if you need to go. I know we said we'd talk, but you're busy and I don't want to add to your stress. And I haven't mentioned it, because we were doing that whole ignoring-each-other thing the past week, but I worked on your video feed. I took it in a different direction, which you might hate, but it's pretty good, if I do say so myself. Vivian helped splice it together, but it needs your genius beats to bring it to life." His blue eyes were intense. Unreadable. The white-blue of an immovable iceberg. "If you don't end up liking it, that's cool. I won't be offended. I can try something else or do nothing and let you create whatever it was you envisioned because I've clearly overstepped."

He plucked her coffee cup from her clutches, placed it next to his on the glass end table, then he was everywhere, one hand in her hair, the other pressed against her back, fingers digging into her spine. His mouth moved against hers in a seductive rhythm that short-circuited her brain. He tasted like coffee and untempered desire.

"I can't wait to see the video feed," he said, his voice deliciously rough. "And I want to work on the music with you, have you in my studio when I'm there. Teach you the way I should have taught you when you blackmailed me. I want you with me as much as possible, sleeping over every night." His request was desperate almost, like he thought she'd say no.

Had he lost his marbles?

"Count me in for it all. And blackmail is still on the table. I'm sure I can come up with a few things to entice you to perform your best." She raised what she hoped was a seductive eyebrow.

He smiled, but his expression looked strained.

He must be worried about their impending talk. Their

precarious future. All surface nonsense, as far as she was concerned. Nothing he could say would change how she felt.

She flattened her hands on his chest, reveled in his masculine firmness. "I love that you called me Squirrel again. It's weird, but I missed that." A vulnerable confession. An olive branch she wanted him to grasp: *no matter what happens, we won't lose each other.*

"I'll call you whatever you want. For as long as you let me." He sounded downright unsure now, slightly pained.

She kissed his jaw. "Whatever talk we need to have changes nothing, so please don't worry. And you're going to be late. You should get going."

He flinched, a small move, but her hands were on his chest. There was no mistaking that slight jolt. Something was going on with him, and it felt like a lot more than a talk about his commitment issues. His nervous energy seeped into her, a gradual churn that had her stomach hollowing out.

He released his hold on her. "We should talk now. Before I go."

"Okay..." His body was all hard lines and angles, impossibly tense. "Should I sit down for this?"

He gave his head a small shake. "I've only dated one woman seriously. You might remember Lila?"

"I do." Annie hadn't been jealous of the beautiful redhead, per se. She hadn't even realized they'd dated seriously, but she'd been catty about her, judging her clothes and voice and perfect skin the way envious girls lashed out.

"I cared about her," he said, eyes on Annie, never looking away. "I wanted things to work with us, but when she got serious, I panicked. I ghosted on her and never called again. I cut her off, avoided her calls. I hurt her deeply because I'm a disaster when it comes to personal relationships."

"And you're worried you'll do the same to me?"

He nodded, still holding eye contact. He wanted to show her how real this was, the possibility of him pulling another runner, like he had the scrapbooking night. A disappearing act. The way Leo had disappeared on them both. His mother, too. Her parents. Death wasn't a choice, but leaving was leaving just the same. "You're afraid to love and lose." The worry she'd guessed at before they'd made love.

He gave another tight nod.

Did he not see they were already neck deep in this? That she had just as much to lose?

"Even if we'd never slept together, I wouldn't be able to handle losing you, Wes. There's no erasing our years together, or how much I care about you. And I think you feel the same. Adding sex—which was awesome, by the way." He smiled, small but perfect. "Adding sex heightens this thing between us, but there's still no way to protect ourselves. Best friends or lovers, we're already attached where it counts. Like your job, in a way. But bigger. Losing each other would be like losing a piece of ourselves."

He pushed his hands into his pockets, licked his lips. "You're right. I know you're right. It's just taken me longer to realize there's no fighting us. Keeping you at a distance has only made me feel...empty. Not as bad as if I actually lost you, but this week without you, knowing how you felt and fighting what I wanted, was beyond painful. I just can't predict how I'll react as we get closer."

If he freaked and ditched her, she'd have a massive hole in her heart. How she'd felt the past week, but miles worse. None of it mattered. "There's no going back from here. You said you're consumed by me, and I feel the same. Being with you this morning was more intense than I ever expected. And it wasn't enough."

"I'm all in, Annie. I want to be inside you again, now. Every second. I want to be your everything more than I want to take my next breath." But he was still reserved, holding back from her.

"Then let's do what we want." In her mind, they only had one option.

He was still so tense, his wide shoulders hitched high. Seducing him could help. A reminder of how great they were together. Kiss that frown off his face, let him know she'd be here if he panicked. She sauntered toward him, an extra sway in her step, and reached for him, but he gripped her wrists.

"I lied," he said.

She tried to meet his flitting eyes. "When?"

"About Leo's death." He looked up, his devastation plain, and she flinched.

She jerked her wrists out of his hold. "I don't understand."

Wes swallowed convulsively and started to pace. "That night, at the club, Leo and I separated and were supposed to meet at a certain time, leave before the last couple of songs. He didn't want to get back to the shelter too late. He was always like that, making sure he got back to you at a reasonable time. And I knew what time it was, knew when he wanted to leave. But I was having fun and chose not to go."

Wes quit pacing and his arms fell limp by his sides. There was so much defeat in his slumped posture, so much contained agony. Part of her wanted to reach for him again, be his rock. A larger part couldn't speak. She was frozen. She didn't want to hear the end of this story, learn new grisly facts she'd have to accept.

"I was selfish," he said quietly. "I didn't care what Leo wanted. I liked that I was on the wrong side of town. Being there was a middle finger to my father's controlling ways. I wanted to be out past curfew, ruffle his perfectly groomed feathers. So I didn't meet Leo and he came looking for me. That was when the shots rang out. He was hit when he stepped in front of me. He took the bullet for me, even though we shouldn't even have been there. He died because I was a selfish bastard."

The plaintiveness in Weston's voice was undeniable, his remorse palpable, but Annie couldn't look at him. Leo, the bullets, blood, his riddled body blocking Wes's—that was all she could see. A new image she'd have to live with. And it felt so fresh. Like he was dying all over again, the brother who'd promised to look after her always.

Together, he'd said. *I'll always keep us together, no matter the cost.* He'd begged homeless men and women to pretend to be their parents in shelters. He'd helped her with homework so poor marks wouldn't flag teachers. He'd taught her piano to give her the gift of music when they had nothing but each other to get through each hungry day.

He'd broken that precious promise, and she'd spent many nights furious with him, angry to the point of punching herself in the thighs, tugging out small sections of her hair. She'd been so alone, so lost. Because he'd been too loyal and wouldn't have left Wes to fend for himself. In turn Leo had left *her* and now she had to relive his brutal murder because Wes had withheld the truth.

Tears burned, a hot stab that traveled to her throat. She couldn't breathe, couldn't see through her blur of tears.

"Annie, I'm so sorry. I should have told you. I was ashamed, too much of a coward to admit what I'd done."

She clutched her throat, tried to swallow through a sob.

"Annie, baby. I'm here. I'll help you through this. Please let me help you." Wes enveloped her in his strong arms. Arms that had felt like heaven not so long ago.

They were suffocating now.

She wrenched away, dashed at her cheeks, despising that

Wes was seeing her like this. She didn't acknowledge him or his confession. She couldn't speak without falling apart. She needed time and space to process, to grieve and be angry. She needed a lot of things right then, and none of them were Weston Aldrich.

TIME HEALED ALL WOUNDS. The saying was a total cliché, but it had mostly held true for Annie. The days and months following Leo's death, she'd gradually compartmentalized her grief. She'd learned to breathe through the pain, focus on happier memories, shake off the bad and let in the good. She'd built relationships online. Friends who didn't get too personal and upset her carefully carved balance. Wes and she had never talked about Leo, either. Not outright. Not until recently. She had thought he'd sidestepped the subject out of respect for her. Now she knew the source of his avoidance: Wes had been consumed with guilt.

Annie flipped through an old scrapbook, one of the first she'd made, thanks to her first foster home.

June—her foster mom—had verged on being a hoarder. Precariously piled magazines and newspapers had filled the house's every nook and cranny. Annie's counselor had suggested art therapy as an outlet, but straight-up drawing had frustrated her. One rough day, when a magazine piano advertisement had reduced Annie to tears, she'd slashed up the page. She'd hated crying. She still did. But her hands had moved of their own accord after that, glue found, scissors unearthed, a hodge-podge assembled into a sloppy scrapbook page. At the center of her first artistic endeavor had been a photograph of Leo playing piano.

Creating became cathartic after that. An outlet. Time to do, not think. That page was the one and only she'd ever centered around her brother. She'd avoided all things Leo and piano and clubbing afterward, until happening upon that subway busker. A piano played. Her heart revived. The urge to be a DJ like he'd dreamed so clear and true she couldn't believe she'd wasted all those years trying not to think about him.

She didn't want to waste more years. She didn't want Wes to think she hated him because he'd been a stupid kid who'd made a stupid decision. He'd texted her nonstop after his confession, pleas to talk. Apologies. She hadn't replied because she hadn't known what to say. By day two he'd threatened to come over if she didn't respond. So she'd replied with a simple message: *I'm okay, but I need time. Please don't message again. I'll reach out when I'm ready.*

Five days later she'd been going about her life, working waitressing shifts, cooking, eating, sleeping, messing around with her DJ equipment. She missed Wes something fierce, but she hadn't done any reaching.

She put the scrapbook away and opened her laptop. Her BOOMPop homepage flickered to life. Deaf Jam's icon was lit. They hadn't chatted since he'd encouraged her to hook up with a guy to help find her mojo. Their discussion had been vague then. No details about Wes shared. She could unload on him with her sad story now, or see if Pegasus was on the Punchies site, talk through what she was feeling, a computer screen safely between her vulnerability and another living soul, but that would be her wasting more time. More minutes. More years pretending she didn't need real, live people close.

She ditched her laptop and called Vivian before she overthought the choice. The second Vivian answered, Annie said, "I'm having a rough day. Can you come over to chat?"

Three hours later, Vivian was on Annie's couch, legs folded under her, compassion softening her friend's face. "I can't imagine what you've been through, and I kind of hate this Wes guy for stirring it all up again."

Annie resented him for that as well, but she didn't hate him. She hadn't hated sharing her story with Vivian, either. Vivian had listened to her with a sympathetic ear, asking questions intermittently, prodding when needed. Annie spilled about her parents, living on the street, her mother's overdose, Leo's death. She didn't remember the last time she'd felt this immense relief, like a pressure valve had been released on her chest.

"Wes has been the mainstay in my life, the one constant that's helped me keep it together. And he's obviously never gotten over his guilt about the shooting, which is sad but makes sense. What I don't get is why the thought of talking to Wes now has me anxious. I love him. I miss him. And all this stuff with Leo is in the past, even if the story has changed slightly."

Vivian ran her hand up the back of her pixie hair. "Maybe it isn't as much in the past as you think. Maybe you haven't dealt with Leo's death. I mean, you've avoided talking about any of it with me until now. Who else do you lean on?"

The answer to that question was pitiful. "Only Wes, and we usually avoid hot-button topics. At least, we used to."

"Hence your vacation on Wallow Island." Vivian's pointed look was far from subtle. "I won't pretend I know how you feel. Your life makes mine seem like a *Leave It to Beaver* episode, and I had to come out to my very traditional parents, but I spent many nights moaning about my worries to anyone who'd listen. Some people go the therapy route. I'm good griping to friends. Either way, one of the keys to solid mental health is talking."

"I know," Annie said, properly chastised. She knew she dodged intimate friendships, just like Wes had actively abstained from romantic relationships. His fear of abandonment. Her fear of hurting. She should thank him for unearthing this fresh pain. Without it, she wouldn't be dipping her toes into deeper friendship waters with Vivian. "Does today count as talking?"

"It does. And I'm honored to be your sounding board."

"You realize this makes you my closest friend."

Vivian grinned. "If you'd told me we were besties before this went down, I'd have come over with my chocolate cheese dip."

Annie curled her lip. "Chocolate and cheese?"

"Best comfort food on the planet."

"Or the most revolting."

"So is living in this disaster you call an apartment. Do you ever clean up?"

Annie laughed. Wes had said as much and worse, about a hundred and one times. "It's tidier than you think. I know where everything is."

Vivian glanced around placidly. "If you say so. But back to our heart-to-heart and your current dilemma. Are you angry at Wes for what he did? Is that why you haven't called him?"

Annie replayed her last five days, including her worst moment huddled on her shower floor, crying onto her bent knees. "I don't blame Wes for what happened. He wasn't trying to hurt Leo. He couldn't have known what would happen. I blame lax gun laws and those assholes who used violence to settle a grudge."

"So what's holding you back from him?"

Annie had asked herself that question daily and had come up empty each time. Sitting here with a friend, her truth no longer bottled up, clarity slowly settled. "I think I needed time to grieve. I refused to cry as a kid. Aside from the night Wes told me Leo was gone, I kept my shit together. Come hell or high water, I was determined to survive, and I guess survival to me meant squashing my feelings, which is the exact opposite of what will happen with Wes. I'll probably break down again when we finally talk, which is exhausting, so there's that. But I also don't want him to think I'm weak. I'm always worried he thinks of me as a charity case."

"Weak? You're a freaking Amazonian Warrior."

Annie flexed her arm and poked at her pathetic biceps. "Hardly."

Vivian tossed an embroidered pillow at Annie's face. "Don't make me hurt you. Crying isn't weakness. Refusing to get help, which includes talking about your issues, is weakness. We're all human and fallible. Including your man. You need to talk to him, especially since you're the first person he's ever had a sleepover with. Those are not the actions of a man who thinks you're charity. My guess is he's going nuts with worry."

Annie's heart ached at the thought, and Vivian was right: crying in front of Wes would make her stronger, not weaker. Her concerns about him seeing her through pity goggles were her insecurities, not his. She'd been choosing safety over vulnerability, wasting more of her life when she should be living boldly, like Leo would have wanted.

She leaned forward and squeezed Vivian's hand. "Thanks for coming over...and putting up with my stonewalling since we met."

Vivian returned the affectionate squeeze. "Not a problem, especially since I need free DJ services for Sarah's upcoming birthday party."

"I don't think my skills are party ready yet, but my teacher, Julio, might be free."

They chatted about the prospective event and the regular customers at work who drove them batty, easy conversation that made Annie feel like a functioning human. Vivian hugged her tightly when she left, after making Annie promise she'd call Wes.

She was ready to face him now. Embrace everything about him, including the fact that real closeness meant letting him see her at her worst. But he deserved more than a phone call. She picked up her cell and dialed his secretary.

"Aldrich Pharma, this is Marjory."

"Hey, Marjory, it's Annie."

"Well, thank God for that. Please tell me you two have kissed and made up."

Annie chewed on her nail. "He told you about us?"

"That man keeps his personal life as secured as the Federal Reserve Bank, but he's loved you since you sprouted boobs. Any idiot can see it."

"Don't be ridiculous." Marjory had always been observant and candid, but the boob comment was pushing it.

"Someone around here has to be honest. And let me rephrase: he's been denying the fact that he's loved you since you sprouted boobs, especially to himself. And you've been just as blind. Which happens to the best of us, and I'd normally leave you both to your own devices. I was fine letting you get there in your own time, but I've never seen Weston like this. Whatever happened between the two of you, it's killing him."

Annie clutched her hand to her heart. "Is he there now?"

"He's been here every minute of every day, thinking he can work himself hard enough to forget you. He's here so much he brings his rabbit to the office. The rabbit, Annie. Do you hear what I'm saying?"

He was spiraling because of her. Because he believed his lies about Leo had ruined any chance at a future together. "I'm on my way," Annie said.

20

WESTON MASSAGED his temple as he analyzed the spreadsheet on his computer. Dollars going out. More funding needed. Investors with cold feet. A new project that required him to write a detailed business plan. All in a day's work, but wrangling his brain on target was a losing battle. Work was supposed to be the one place where he could shut out the world. Forget the bad. Bury it under numbers and spreadsheets until he looked up at the end of the day and couldn't remember what time it was or if he'd eaten dinner.

No longer.

He eyed the metal bull on his coffee table. The bronze sculpture was small and striking. The beast looked ready to buck, its muscles coiled, a braided rope flying from the animal's writhing neck. Annie had once said Weston made her feel like that bull, caged and controlled.

"But the bull's getting away," Weston had said, confused by the statement. "He broke the rope."

"Of course you'd think that," she'd said.

He had purchased the sculpture, seeing power in the piece,

the innate drive to break free and forge your own path. But maybe Annie had been right. Maybe the flying rope was only a tease of freedom, as though the beast was within grabbing distance of its master. Exactly how he felt these days, tied to the one person who'd tamed his inner beast, unable to reach her, too weak to pull away.

The numbers on his screen blurred slightly, merged into fuzzy lines. He looked at Leo's picture. A habit he'd been indulging in more since that horrid talk with Annie. "I fucked up, buddy." His computer's fan buzzed slightly. The air conditioner hummed. "My stupidity got you killed, and now I've devastated your sister. The one thing you asked of me, I messed up."

Take care of Annie. She has no one.

How could Weston have been so careless with her heart? He should have told her the truth from the start. Bucked up, been a man, admitted he was the reason Leo had died. She probably would have held it against him. They never would have gotten this close. He wouldn't feel like he was dying inside, and she wouldn't have buckled under his dreadful admission.

All this time, he'd been worried he'd hurt her by running when things got intense. All he wanted to do now was run toward her, regardless of the emotional noose tightening around his neck. Surely that meant he could handle a real relationship. He hoped, at least. But she'd asked him to stay away.

His phone buzzed. He rushed to check the screen, a pathetic junkie hoping for an Annie fix, but the text wasn't from Annie.

Rosanna: **We have a problem.**

Just what he needed.

Weston: **Did you sink another yacht?**

Rosanna: **Hilarious, but no. I was tagged on Instagram. Someone caught me out with Ricardo.**

He didn't remember which guy Ricardo was.

Weston: **Incriminating?**

Rosanna: **Sucking face. So, yeah.**

He wanted to be furious at her carelessness, but if Annie came back to him, he wouldn't risk her feelings by continuing this ruse. Maybe he should force Annie's hand now, show up at her apartment. Beg her to give him another chance he didn't deserve, or offer to just talk if that was what she needed. He rubbed his eyes and planted his elbows on his desk. If she gave him a second chance, he'd be whatever she needed.

As for this predicament, the business merger would have to stand on its own merit, and Rosanna would have to handle her wild ways with her father.

Weston: **We'll deal with it. Leak that we're having problems. Have a fake break up to end our fake relationship. I'll make sure the merger isn't affected.**

Because dating Karim's daughter should never have been part of the offer.

Rosanna: **I actually want to talk to you about the merger.**

His phone rang, Rosanna calling through. "Are you alone?"

A truer statement there never was. "Unfortunately."

"You sound pathetic. Are you on the outs with Annie?"

"What's going on with the merger?"

She made a disgusted noise. "You are such a dude, ignoring a personal question. But fine, we have more important things to discuss."

"I'm listening." Sort of. His focus was shot to shit these days.

"You said a while back DLP was shady, doing underhanded dealings."

That got his attention. He swiveled in his chair and stared out the window as he spoke. "Did something happen?"

"Not in so many words, but I'm worried about you. My father had a party recently, a work function hosted at a Greenwich restaurant. One of the higher ups at DLP popped by, and my father didn't give him the time of day. Dad seemed pissed he crashed the party. No big deal, but I went outside to make a call and saw the DLP guy down the block, yelling at someone on his phone. It was raining, so I hid under my umbrella and got close enough to eavesdrop. I only caught the end of the conversation, but—"

"Wes?"

Weston fumbled and dropped his phone, spinning in his chair as his eyes shot to Annie.

He hadn't heard her knock or walk in, but she was here, stunning in a whimsical dress, the thin fabric multicolored and lively, one thin strap slipping off her shoulder. He shoved his chair back and snatched the phone from his floor. "I'll call you later. Something's come up."

"No. Not later." Rosanna's voice took on a screechy high pitch. "Seriously, Weston—this is important."

"Not as important as Annie."

"I'm not kidding. I'm worr—"

He hung up on Rosanna. She'd live, and he'd apologize later. He'd been waiting on Annie for five days that felt like five years, and if he didn't touch her in five seconds he would combust. He rounded his desk, had her in his arms and against his chest before he took a full breath. "You're here," he murmured into her hair.

She clutched the back of his suit jacket and burrowed into him. "I am."

They stood like that so long he worried he was suffocating her. He kissed the top of her hair, breathed her in—sage, honey, sadness he wished she didn't feel. He pulled back to see her face. *Jesus.* "You're crying again. I've made you cry again."

She shook her head, not bothering to hide her tears the way she had at his apartment. "I'm just overwhelmed. Sad but also happy. And I..." Her voice cracked as more tears fell. "I've been trying to keep myself together for so long I've kept people, including you, at a distance. That's why I never talked about Leo with you, and why I couldn't call you this week. I'm not mad at you. I don't blame you for his death. I'm scared if I start crying I won't stop."

He didn't deserve her forgiveness. Not for that. He cupped her wet cheeks, his blood thundering at the simple touch. "I should have met Leo when he asked."

"Yes, you should have."

Blunt truth. Pain lanced through him. "It should have been me."

She shoved him, palms smacked hard against his chest. "Don't ever say that. God, you're an idiot. Don't you *ever* say that. It shouldn't have been either of you."

Now she looked like she wanted to hit him, a hard punch he could use. "They were my stupid choices. The consequences should have been mine."

"I know you were a stupid kid, Wes. That isn't breaking news. But I didn't know you were a stupid adult."

He tugged down his tie, unable to form a reply. Stupid was his motto these days.

She huffed out a breath. "We were all stupid back then. Leo left me home alone once, before our mother OD'd. He told me to make dinner, but I didn't cook the chicken through. I was eight. He never forgave himself for how sick I got. And I once thought I wanted to be a ninja. I started throwing knives at home and one landed in Leo's thigh. We all did stupid shit that could have gone sideways."

"None of that actually *did* go sideways. You didn't get someone killed."

"You didn't kill him!" He flinched at her shout. More tears tracked her cheeks. "I'm tired, Wes. I'm tired of not talking about Leo. I'm tired of keeping friends at arm's length when what I need is to scream and talk and smile about the good times with Leo. I also need to tell you that what you did sucked. It hurt to hear it, hurts to think about it, but you were a kid. And yeah, you should have told me the truth. But what's done is done. Life is unfair. Beating yourself up for mistakes that were out of your control doesn't help."

He felt like sagging to the floor, some of the guilt he'd lived with leaching out as he exhaled. Remorse over Leo would always sit heavy on his heart. No wise words from Annie or any therapist would erase that. But he was tired, too. Tired of hating himself for one reckless night. "I miss him so much."

She closed her eyes briefly, then looked at him, her chin ticked up. "So do I. But you know what else I'm tired of?"

He was tired of not kissing her. That much he knew. He wanted to lay her out on his desk, in front of his floor-to-ceiling windows, fall to his knees, taste her, grovel, supplicate, make her moan until she'd forgiven him his failings. Promise to try his hardest. Be worthy of her trust. "What are you tired of?" he murmured.

Her irises were a metallic green, shining with tears, a hard swirl of cedar setting off their vibrancy. "I'm tired of pretending I'm not in love with you, even though admitting as much might send you running. And this is the real me, messy and blotchy with a runny nose and mascara dripping down my face, which I should never have put on, but I missed you and wanted to look pretty even though it totally backfired. At least I don't have towels sticking out from under my arms, so there's that, but I'm not always strong, and I might need to lean on you sometimes. So like I said, this is the real me, and I'm hoping it's enough for you."

"Are you done talking?" He hadn't heard much after *in love with you.*

She sniffled and nodded.

He crushed his lips against hers, kissed her so hard and gathered her so tightly he lifted her off the ground. She wrapped her legs around his waist. He grunted into her open mouth.

"I'm sorry," he said between kisses. "I've never... With you—it feels like I've wanted you forever."

"Since I sprouted boobs?"

He laughed hoarsely, nearly dropping her on the floor. "Probably, but that makes me feel like a dirty old man."

"You can thank Marjory for that visual. And I'm sorry, too."

"For what?" He kissed her again, softer this time, unable to say what he truly felt. *Be patient with me. Help me if I fuck up. I love you.* He couldn't force out the words. He secured his grip on her instead, groaned at the hot press of their bodies.

She sighed. "I'm sorry it took me so long to talk to you, but I see your new best friend has kept you company." She hooked her legs tighter around his waist and pointed at Felix.

He'd forgotten the bunny was in his office. He blinked and saw his phone on his desk. His call with Rosanna felt like hours ago. He'd have to connect with her later, find out what DLP antics had her worried. For now he couldn't think about much besides how good it felt to have Annie in his arms, wrapped around him again, joking with him.

"Felix has been a good listener," Wes said into Annie's neck, "but he's a poor substitute for you. And don't apologize for needing time to figure things out or for needing support. I hate seeing you upset, but it means you trust me enough to let go. I want you messy, Squirrel."

"I want you always."

"Good, because you're stuck with me."

Wes had her on the desk, the skirt of her dress hitched around her waist as he worked his hand into her underwear. She gasped. "Are we really doing this in your office?"

"We will be doing this anywhere and everywhere I have you alone. Get used to it."

He curled and twisted his fingers. Her inner muscles clenched. She saw stars and bit her tongue to keep from crying out as he dropped to his knees, spread her wide, and gave her a long lick. Her head dropped back. She braced her sandaled feet on his powerful shoulders, couldn't believe she was in Wes's office, spread on his desk, his face between her thighs. She dissolved in seconds, then tugged him up by his hair, kissed him, loving the taste of herself on his tongue.

More. She wanted more, all of him in her mouth, hard against the back of her throat.

She pushed him to the floor, forced him onto his back and unzipped his fly. She swore at the velvet-hard feel of him.

"Jesus, Annie." His hips jerked. He pushed up to his elbows, his eyes darker and slitted with lust. "We don't finish this way. I want to be inside you when I come."

A plan she could get behind. For now she explored his length, used the wet glide of her tongue and mouth to make Wes moan. He spread his muscular thighs, his expensive slacks bunched under his knees. She pushed up his dress shirt, rubbed one hand over his contracting abs, felt each pulse as he fought his release.

"Stop." He gripped her hair. Not too rough, but the tug sent tingles down her spine. He got to his feet, stumbling slightly as he manhandled her back onto his desk. Then he was inside her, one smooth stroke that made them both cry out.

"This," he said, ferocity in the one sharp word. "This is us. Always. You and me."

She surged to meet him, her butt half off the desk and half on. A buzzing sound rang out. They ignored it. He gripped her tightly, kept her secure, sliding in and out so thoroughly she felt it in her toes. "I love you."

He looked slightly stunned, but he kept moving, one smooth thrust as he pushed deeper. He didn't say the words back. It stung briefly, but Wes bent down, kissed her hard, cradled her back so it didn't rub too roughly against his desk as they crashed together. *This.* He was right about *this.* Joy so full to bursting it hurt as they tipped into oblivion together, clutching each other and murmuring incoherent words.

They hung on to each other afterward, a deep contentment making her bones heavy. He slipped out of her slowly, used some tissues to clean them up, then fixed his clothes while she did the same, both of them sneaking tender glances at each other. His phone buzzed, the same noise she'd heard while defiling his desk.

"Someone wants to get ahold of you."

They were standing by his coffee table, but he didn't glance at his desk. He gathered her in his arms and kissed her again. Pressed small kisses all over her face. "Does it look like I care?"

"If people start calling me Yoko Ono because you can't focus on work and Aldrich Pharma goes to hell in handbasket, I'll be pissed. Answer it."

He pushed her hair to the side, rubbed his nose along her neck. "Come over tonight. Show me the video feed. Let's make music together."

God, she loved the sound of that. "I have to work tonight."

"Come over after."

More buzzing from his desk. "Weston, please check your phone."

He nosed her neck again, then straightened. "Only when you agree to tonight."

Was he worried she'd change her mind? Fall out of love with him if given more time to think? "Wes?"

He tipped his head, watched her intently.

"We're good. I might still get frustrated and sad about Leo. I might need space occasionally while I deal with everything, but nothing changes this." She gestured between them. "Nothing comes between us. Unless you're worried about Rosanna and the fake-dating thing."

He dragged his hand through his sex-mussed hair. "The Rosanna angle went bust today, but even if it hadn't, I would've put a stop to it. Whatever happens from here on out, we're together, publicly and privately. There will be no other women but you, and I'll do my best not to panic about my...issues. And *you* won't be going on any more dates with Duncan. I don't even like you talking to the guy."

"You can't dictate who I talk to."

"No, I can't." He focused on the floor for a beat. "But I get irrationally jealous when I see you with him."

She rubbed her sternum, surprised by her racing heart. "That night at Angelonia, Duncan and I were only out as friends. He's nice and I like him, and I plan to *stay* friends with him, but I promise you I'm not interested in anything more with him. And thank you for ending the ruse with Rosanna. I was pretty jealous over her, too. But what about your father?"

His glanced up sharply. "What does my father have to do with us?"

Their eavesdropped conversation the night she'd told Wes she had to switch foster homes seemed like forever ago, but she'd never forget Victor S. Aldrich's harsh words. *Her mother died with a needle in her arm. Her father is some miscreant who disappeared. Her brother got shot in a seedy club. She's not welcome in this house.* "Your father's not my biggest fan. He won't be happy we're dating." Something she hadn't considered while pining for Wes.

"My father doesn't get a say in this."

"Your father's a coldhearted man who only cares what people think."

Wes's nostrils flared. "Don't give him another thought. All that matters is us." He brushed her hair back tenderly. "Anything you need from me, you ask. It's yours."

She wished Weston's father didn't still unnerve her, but the man was as warm and fuzzy as an ice cube. She'd have to trust Wes in this. "I need you to take care of work so we can have fun tonight. I'll try not to be too late."

"I'll be waiting for you."

She pressed a quick kiss to his lips. He tried to tug her closer, but she shoved him back. "Don't make me hurt you."

"Don't tease me with dirty promises."

She gave him a wink and headed for the door but glanced back. She wanted to say those words one more time, even if he couldn't say them back yet or didn't feel the same: *I love you. I love you so much it hurts. I can't wait to kiss you again.* But Wes had his phone in his hand, a vicious frown marring his face.

His head flew up. "How did you get here?"

"I took the subway...why?"

"I'll have a driver take you home. He'll bring you to work and drive you to my place after. If you have to go out before then, let him know."

She pulled her fallen strap up her shoulder and folded her arms around her middle. "I thought we were done with you bossing me around."

"Bossy is in my DNA." When she didn't reply, he said, "Let

me do this. I'll be worried about you otherwise."

"I'm pretty handy with my subway card and Uber app. I'm adept at taking care of myself."

"It's not about your independence. It's about my...issues." His gaze kept flitting to his phone, that vicious frown returning.

"Is something wrong?" Or was he suddenly *that* concerned something would happen to her? His fear of loving and losing.

He shook his head slightly. "Just work stuff I need to deal with." He lifted his phone as though that was proof he wasn't acting strange. "A car will meet you downstairs. I can't wait to see you tonight."

Going with his odd flow, she blew him a kiss and left his office.

Marjory took one look at her and laughed. "Do I need to disinfect that room?"

Cheeks burning, Annie checked that her dress was on straight. She forced her eyes on Marjory. "I don't know what you mean."

"Likely story. Do we get happy-yet-broody Weston back now?"

Annie glanced at his closed office door, stymied by his reaction to whatever had been on his phone. He hadn't cared about driving her around until he'd checked his texts. His request could have been a delayed reaction, but it didn't sit right. "Is there something weird going on at work?"

Marjory rolled her chair back. "Weird how?"

"Wes got a text and seemed really bothered by it."

"Sounds like an ordinary day to me."

Possibly, but something felt off and she'd had all the drama she could handle. She'd drop it for now. Give Wes the benefit of the doubt and let his driver shuttle her around. Mollify the anxiety that had him scared he'd lose her. As long as his need for control didn't get *out of* control.

21

JOYCE'S last piano notes vibrated in the air, the entire phrase perfectly played.

Annie whooped. "You're a virtuoso," she said, beaming.

"I told you, dear, I don't pay you to lie."

"You're paying me to teach you piano while boosting your confidence with my exuberant personality."

Joyce clutched her wrinkled hands on her lap. "A job well done, on both accounts. When I set out on this piano mission, I expected a dowdy teacher and dull days. You've made Thursday my favorite day of the week."

I will not cry. I will not cry. Annie had become embarrassingly emotional these days, the dam she'd burst with Vivian and Wes infecting her life. She'd just never expected teaching others would move her this much. "I love Thursdays, too. You've become my favorite student."

"I'm your only student."

"That's where you're wrong. I signed someone up last week, and I've had two more inquiries." Thanks to Annie's scrapbooking skills, she'd created fun flyers that she'd posted around public transit and at several bars. She wasn't taking on advanced pupils yet, but if this kept up, she'd be able to cut back on waitressing shifts eventually. "I'll be turning people away before I know it, but you'll always be my favorite."

Joyce gripped the piano edge and used the leverage to stand. "You should spend some of those earnings cleaning up this place. Hire yourself a maid."

"You should use that smart mouth to do stand-up comedy. Start a Golden Girls revival."

Joyce coughed while laughing. "You're definitely my favorite, dear. See you next Tuesday."

"We meet on Thursdays, Joyce."

She grinned. "I know."

Annie frowned while making sure Joyce took the stairs okay, then she snickered. C U Next Tuesday. Joyce had just lovingly called Annie a C U N T.

She smiled while piling the piano music sheets. She stacked them next to a shipment of Sudoku books that had magically appeared last week. Below them was a mysterious bag of buttons she'd found tucked in her purse. Scissors that could cut through steel had materialized on her coffee table after a waitressing shift.

Whenever she asked Wes if he'd sent her the secret gifts, he'd shrug and say, "I have no clue what you're talking about."

Total liar.

If there was a boyfriend contest judged by attentiveness, thoughtfulness, and bedroom prowess, Wes would win gold with his hands tied behind his back, or her hands, as was the case that one time. He and Annie had been incredibly in sync the past few weeks, sleeping together every night, splitting their time between her tiny apartment and his massive loft. He didn't seem to mind staying over. He said her place felt like a real home, but when they made time to work on music, his loft was the go-to.

He had somehow mollified Rosanna's father, their merger still full-steam ahead, and he'd loved the video montage she'd created. Eyes glazed and voice thick, Wes had thanked her for focusing on gun control and making Leo part of the project. They had tweaked a few sections, played with different classical music fragments to heighten the emotional impact. He was planning to unveil it at his next big show, and she was really doing this DJ thing. Thanks to a push from Wes and more nudging from Vivian, she'd finally agreed to DJ Sarah's birthday party next month.

A deadline to focus on. Her first real gig.

Everything was absolutely, positively perfect...and she was absolutely, positively terrified.

If truthfulness were part of the boyfriend contest, Wes would fail epically. The control freak had become a domineering vigilante. He had his driver pick her up and drop her off everywhere. He kept tabs on her constantly, asking her to check in, messaging her at all hours. Every time she asked him what was up with the obsessive worrying, he'd play to her heart, and say, "Because you're the most important person in my life."

She'd get all moony and accept his lame excuse, then later, when she'd catch him sneaking off to talk angrily on his phone, she'd worry this slice of paradise was too good to last.

Her doorbell rang. She finished organizing the sheet music and answered the door.

A woman held out a large box. "This is for you, Annie."

She regarded her visitor warily. "Do I know you?"

"No, but I was told you were tall and beautiful, with hazel

eyes that changed with your mood and a sexy birthmark by the corner of your lips." She smiled. "The description fits."

Her Secret Santa must be at it again, and Annie reverted to moony status. She took the flat red box. The woman bowed slightly, then disappeared down the stairs while Annie tried to fight her giddiness. Wes's gifts were constant and unnecessary, but she loved that he was always thinking of her. He chose perfect presents, as though he could read her mind, because he knew her at her core. It was his way of saying "I love you" without speaking the words. At least, she hoped it was.

The card on the box read: *Meet me at eight.*

Below was an address to a swanky restaurant, and her pulse tremored. They hadn't been out in public yet. The Rosanna break-up had been front and center in gossip rags. He hadn't wanted to put Annie through that kind of scrutiny. She'd been happy keeping Weston Aldrich to herself. But this felt right. An excuse to flaunt the man of her dreams.

She undid the silky ribbon, set it aside for a future scrapbooking project, then lifted the lid and gasped.

She knew this dress, but it couldn't be here, in this box, in her shabby apartment. This was a Met Gala dress. A show-stopping stunner. She'd gone gaga over it when flipping through a *Vogue* issue. But how could Wes have known she'd coveted the fun, flirty fabric and pictured herself wearing the bold, cherry printed maxi dress, all that scrunched black lace funking up the style? Classic Betsy Johnson. Lightyears beyond her measly budget.

Then she remembered. The night she'd forced him to scrapbook. She'd told him not to use that page, that she loved the dress in the ad. Just one mention, off the cuff.

Now the dress was in her hands.

She pulled it out gingerly, danced around the room like she

was Cinderella and this was her coming-out ball. She found her phone and dialed.

"I was thinking about you." Wes always answered his phone like that these days.

She hugged the stunning dress to her body. "How'd you find it?"

"I don't know what you're talking about."

"It's too much."

"Still in the dark."

"How'd you even remember?"

Silence for a beat, then, "I remember everything about you, Squirrel."

God, this man. "It really is too much. I can't accept it."

"I have to work late, so I'll meet you at the restaurant. My driver will pick you up."

"Weston Aldrich, you're ignoring me."

"I'm doing no such thing."

She sighed, caressing the fabric in her hands. "How am I supposed to compete with this? I can't afford to buy you things."

"I don't need anything but you."

Those blasted tears returned.

Several hours later she walked into the restaurant feeling like a Disney princess. Her dress slinked around her body, her hair twisted into a low chignon, a few loose strands framing her face. Wes was at the bar along the wall, sipping what looked like Scotch. His charcoal suit was impeccable as always, the expensive fabric accommodating his broad shoulders and powerful thighs. He was intent on his phone, a familiar scowl making him look slightly vicious. She knew that look. It was the one she'd seen sporadically since they had made up in his office.

The second he saw her, the scowl fell. He scanned her from

head to toe, a lecherous grin spreading. He placed his glass down and walked over as though she were the only person in the boisterous room. One arm latched around her back, he pulled her close and kissed her brazenly, not a care to their audience.

"You look good enough to eat," he murmured in her ear.

"If you ruin a stitch on this dress, I'll torch your closet. Every last designer piece."

He laughed. "Noted."

She used her thumb to wipe her lipstick off his lips. "Were you waiting long?"

"You really do look beautiful, Annie."

"You have a habit of ignoring my questions."

He shrugged and nodded to the hostess, who led them to their table. Eyes followed them as they walked. She wasn't sure if it was the dress, Wes's commanding presence, or his recent Rosanna-related celebrity, but she felt like a bug under a microscope, albeit a nicely dressed bug. "Is it always like this when you're out?"

They settled at their table. His Scotch appeared by his plate. "Like what?"

"Like you're royalty. Everyone's watching us."

"They're watching you."

She rolled her eyes. "I'm not the one who dated a wild socialite."

"No. You dated a player who uses women and can't be trusted."

Low blow. "I told you, the second date was just as friends, and he's your executive assistant. If he can't be trusted, why'd you hire him?"

"I need strong people on my team. A hint of ruthlessness goes far in business. His personal life doesn't impact work."

"So you're saying I'm a bad judge of character?"

He opened his mouth and closed it. Instead of replying, he laid his palm face up on the table. "Can we start this conversation over? You've got that pit bull look about you."

"Now you're saying I look like a dog?"

One corner of his lips tipped up, cocksure and handsome. "I'm saying you're feisty and slightly savage when you're annoyed. It's sexy."

The compliment mollified her. She liked him thinking of her as strong and feisty, but she was tired of Wes evading her questions, specifically why he felt she suddenly needed a twenty-four hour guard. If he continued his close-lipped nonsense, she'd have no choice but to seek answers elsewhere. Speak with Duncan, even though Wes had a bee in his bonnet about the guy.

Tonight, however, wasn't the time or place. "I love this, by the way."

Wes stretched out his legs until they touched hers. He traced circles on the back of her hand. "Love what?"

You, she wanted to say. She hadn't been brave enough to speak the words again. She thought he felt the same as her, but it was hard to tell and harder to be so vulnerable in that uncertainty. "I love that we're still us. We still fight and bicker. We're us but better."

"Bickering with benefits." His free hand joined his other, stroking her hand and wrist.

The joke reminded her of Duncan's antics. Wes really had that guy wrong. "So many benefits."

He kissed her knuckles. "Tell me about your day. Has Joyce surpassed her piano teacher yet?"

Annie snickered, remembering how she'd left. "Sweet, old Joyce called me a cunt."

They talked and joked and squabbled, legs brushing under the table, fingers touching between sips of wine and bites of food. Annie forgot about the people casting glances their way. She quit worrying about Wes's work stress and intensive vigilance with her. They were an ordinary couple, dining in New York City, the infectious whir of chatter and music adding to their bubble of happiness.

At Wes's apartment, her stunning dress didn't stay on long. The public flirting had exacerbated their sexual tension, pushing them both to their limits. Wes devoured her body. She left bite marks on his chest and shoulders. They made love hard and deep, leaving them both sated and sweaty on top of his sheets.

"Let's make music," he said gruffly.

She grinned. "Count me in."

Wes pulled on his sweatpants. The first he'd ever owned. She couldn't afford to buy him designer suits, but he'd seemed pleased with the gift. The loose fabric hung deliciously off his hips, his toned behind so distracting it took three tries for her to slip her foot into her flannel shorts.

They shut themselves inside his sound room, headphones on, beats tripping through the equipment as they experimented. She no longer had to think when splicing phrasing. She felt the rhythmic changes, loved being the conductor of those harmonic frequencies: tones, notes, chords. Beauty through sound. The ease made blending songs easier. She could think ahead instead of playing catch up. Wes pointed to the line fader. She pushed it up slightly, boosted the track to get ready for the incoming beat. He dropped the new song. She tweaked the volume as they popped their bodies in time to the blending notes.

A seamless beat match.

Exactly how Wes and she had melded their lives: perfectly synchronized, stretching and adjusting to fit into each other's worlds, whether bickering or laughing or making love. A harmonious relationship built on years of friendship.

She closed her eyes and smiled.

Wes tapped her shoulder and held up his phone, the lightness in his eyes eclipsed with dark.

She pulled off her earphones. "What's up?"

"It's my father. I'll just be a minute."

He was out the door before she could find out why Victor S. Aldrich was calling Wes at one a.m. She tried to ignore her trickle of worry and focus on the music. She played with mixing in snippets of another song, raising the volume and adjusting the bass, but her attention kept snagging on the closed door.

Concerned about Wes, and not trusting his father as far as she could throw him—which wasn't very far—she removed her headphones and searched for Wes. He wasn't in the kitchen. Or the bedroom. She almost went upstairs when a muffled voice came from the bathroom. She tiptoed closer.

"No." Wes's voice was quiet but angry. More silence, then, "You don't get to control this. I will not leave her."

Her? As in Annie? Was his father suggesting they split up?

"This is my life. My choice. And I choose...no. *No.* How else do you need me to say it? This is not your concern, and I won't...*what did you say?* You can't do that. You have no right."

His hushed tone had morphed from adamant to furious, landing on panicked. Unable to stand there a second longer, she pushed the door open.

Wes looked at her, his blue eyes vacant, like he was lost.

Her inner pit bull snarled. "Get off the phone with him. Tell him you'll call back in the morning, or I'm driving over to his mansion and spray painting penises all over the expensive stone."

Wes didn't laugh. He pressed the phone closer to his ear,

listened for a moment, then laughed, a harsh, humorless sound. "I guess I know where I stand, then."

He hung up and scrubbed his eyes. "He heard we were out to dinner."

"And he'd rather burn your inheritance than have me as a daughter-in-law, right?"

Wes didn't balk at the marriage joke. He leaned into the sink counter. "He has backward views on the type of person I should date, but he'll get over it. I'm sorry you had to hear that."

"It's not the first time I've heard him talk crap about me."

He narrowed his eyes. "What do you mean?"

"The night the Bromleys told me they were getting out of the fostering gig, when you brought me to your house, I was a mess over moving. There was a foster kid there I loved, Clementine Abernathy? I promised her we'd stay together, then a week later June told us she was pregnant."

"I remember that foster home, but you never mentioned Clementine."

"There was lots I didn't mention back then."

His brow wrinkled. "Where did Clementine end up?"

"I don't know." She swallowed through her discomfort. Annie wished she'd kept in touch with Clementine, made sure the sweet girl had ended up on her feet, but survival mode hadn't allowed for pen pals and phone friends. "It was hard for me to talk about. I was scared and sad and stubborn and didn't know what to do. I went to the kitchen that night, too stressed to sleep, and overheard you and your father arguing. I heard what he said about me and my family."

Wes cringed. "You *heard* that?"

"At least I know where I stand with him. I'm trash to that man."

"I could kill him for that." Wes straightened to his full domineering height, but reached over tenderly and tilted up her chin. "You're the opposite of trash. You're creative and smart and are stronger than anyone I know."

She appreciated his compliments, but they weren't talking about what mattered. "There was more to that call than him talking shit about me. He threatened you with something."

He released her chin, a slight snarl curling his lip. "It's my problem. Nothing for you to worry about."

Again with his secrets. "I'm getting tired of you telling me what is and isn't my concern. You need to stop protecting me, or doing whatever it is you're doing. And while you're at it, tell me why the idea of me walking two steps down the street on my own has you in a paranoid tizzy."

He glared at her. She glared harder.

He stood and strutted past her, too damn sexy in those sweatpants. "This isn't a conversation to be had in the bathroom."

Did that mean he was finally going to open up? She hurried after him, her socked feet sliding out from under her as she rounded into the living room. He stopped. She skated by him.

"Your floor's fun," she said.

He shook his head, a hint of a smile showing. "You're fun. Now get on the couch before you break an ankle."

She saluted him and sat. He fell onto the cushion beside her. "My father threatened to fire me."

"Over me?"

"Because I'm out of his control. It's a fear tactic. He was pissed about me splitting with Rosanna, even though Karim was okay with it. Karim actually thanked me, said Rosanna's been more grounded since we dated. None of it matters to my father because it wasn't his plan. And you're a wildcard he doesn't like. He said one more wrong move and he'll give me the axe."

"He can't be serious."

Wes's attention strayed from her, his nostrils flared, red blotches dotting his cheeks as his hand jerked through his hair. He looked furious and slightly worried. "Growing up, he was ruthlessly cruel with the house staff and his in-laws." Wes's tone stayed even, but his eyes held an edge. "It wouldn't shock me, which would be a new level of vicious, even for him. I mean, how does someone end up—" His jaw bulged.

"End up what?"

Frowning, he waved a dismissive hand. "Nothing. I know why he's a tyrant, and it changes nothing."

"We can go into hiding. No more dinners out. Pretend it's over." She wasn't sure why Victor treated his son like crap, but she wouldn't be responsible for Wes losing his job. He'd said Aldrich Pharma was in his blood. Work was a large part of what made him tick.

"That's not up for discussion. He doesn't like us together, but he isn't pulling rank. It's the DJing I'm concerned about. I knew it would be an issue, hence the secret identity. Now it's a ticking time bomb."

"But you've been so careful."

"I have, but a secret this big can't stay quiet forever. I always knew that, but I knew I was close to something with the video feed. I needed to get to that end goal, and I'm there. I don't need to keep performing." He traced a line from Annie's forehead down her nose, tapped his finger against her lips. "You can be our mouthpiece."

She went to bite his finger. He yanked it back.

"That's nonsense," she said. "I'm not good enough. And you love performing. You can't quit."

"I can."

"I won't let you."

"There you go again, being feisty." He sounded playful, but the harsh glint in his eyes hadn't left. "Quitting will be tough.

DJing has become an outlet for me, but Aldrich Pharma matters more. That business is why I put up with my father. It's why I work crazy hours. I love that job and won't risk it, or jeopardize the employees who rely on their paychecks."

"I'm not ready to play for us both." Her voice sounded as small as she felt. He was asking too much.

"You're not ready *yet*, but you will be. We'll do the video show together. I'll even buy you a matching mask. Then I'll fade into the background. I'll still use the studio. Work with you on the music until it feels as natural as breathing for you. And, if I'm honest, this was Leo's dream, not mine. One of the reasons I worked so hard at it was for him, and for my mother. She was always on me to do things outside of work." He studied his fisted hands and slowly released them. "Leo has you now."

Leo had been the reason she'd stayed *away* from music for years. He was also why she'd returned. Playing piano had made her feel closer to him. DJing had done the same. She wouldn't walk away now. If Wes wanted to pass the proverbial torch to her, she'd keep it lit for them both.

"I'll do my best to make you guys proud. But I still want to vandalize your father's house." And help Wes unwind from that upsetting call. She maneuvered onto his lap and straddled his narrow hips.

He palmed her backside, but there was less hunger in the move than usual. "I like it when you get all protective of me."

This was her opening. The perfect time to corner him, locked together on his couch, upsetting call or not. "I like it when you're protective of me, too...*if* I know why you're being impossibly controlling."

He froze.

She pressed her hands to his cheeks and held him steady. "Why have you been freaking out? Why is there a driver taking me everywhere? What do you think's going to happen to me?"

He stared hard into her eyes for several seconds, calculating, unreadable, then he sighed. "A competing company got my phone records. Rosanna overheard a guy outside a party talking about it on his cell. DLP is notorious for underhanded dealings, including blackmail to get what they want, and they want to sabotage our Biotrell merger. Your number was on my phone. They know we're close."

Extracting that intel had been easier than expected, but stickiness coated her belly. "They invaded your privacy like that?"

"They're unpredictable and good at covering their tracks."

"Okay, but...what can they do? Put a hit on me to get to you? This is pharmaceuticals, not a mob takeover."

Wes moved her hips back slightly, distancing her on his lap. "A woman died because of them. I don't think that was their end goal, and it was a while back, but their carelessness led to a car accident that took a person's life. I didn't want to put you at risk. It's also why I delayed taking you out. But I'm done letting them infect our lives."

"I haven't seen anything odd. No one's been following me. Unless there's something else you're hiding."

"There haven't been other signs, as far as I know. I think they're focusing on the business, not personal shots. Another researcher gave notice. Duncan's looking into the possibility of a mole in the office."

She was glad he was sharing this burden with Duncan, but it also pissed her off. "I get your concern, but I don't get why you didn't tell me."

"You were dealing with my lies about Leo." His attention drifted away, somewhere over her shoulder. "I'd never seen you that upset and didn't want to add to your stress. My job is to keep you happy."

"Your job is to lean on me so I can help you. We lean on each other. We're a team."

He searched her face. "Is that what we are?"

Why did he sound so unsure? "Yes, unless we're playing Scrabble, then we're enemies. Same goes for chess. But right now, I'm the Batwoman to your Batman. So you need to tell me everything else these DLP clowns have done."

"Nothing."

"Nothing? Did you have anything DJ related on your phone? Calls to clubs?"

"I use a different phone for that. We're keeping tabs on them best we can, but so far all's quiet. They might have backed off when Rosanna and I split, figured their competition had fallen. But, please, don't worry. It's me they want to sabotage."

Was he serious? "If they mess with you, they mess with me."

"Drop it, Annie."

"Why won't you let me help? I can talk to Vivian's girlfriend. She's a private—"

"*No.*" His cheeks turned his famous shade of furious.

She wanted to wring his neck. "You're impossible."

"This is business, and it'll be dealt with by *me* through work. Now let's get back to this bickering with benefits." He wrapped his arms around her and pulled her against him. His heart was beating too fast. "You smell like honey and sage."

She tried to relax, kissed his chest, right over his racing heart. "You smell like diamond shavings and gold dust. Always expensive. Except when you're Falcon. Then you smell like a secret spy."

He didn't laugh. His hands moved, coasting over her back, gliding up into her hair as he rolled his hips. She lit up in seconds as they kissed and kissed and *kissed*, barely coming up for air. They shed their clothes, sliding against each other, trying to get closer. His movements were strong and rough, more demanding than usual. And the look in his eyes? She'd never seen him this intense, desperate almost as he surged into her over and over, faster, deeper. She'd never climaxed so hard.

They stayed locked together on the couch afterward, sweaty, panting, their hearts racing. He held her agonizingly close, like she'd vanish if he loosened his hold. She couldn't speak through the painful pressure behind her ribs.

Something bigger was growing between them, almost unbearably strong. She suddenly understood his recent vigilance, because she felt the same. Terrified this was too good to last. Scared DLP would hurt Wes somehow. His body shuddered slightly, and he pressed his lips to the top of her head. He whispered something, quiet words she couldn't hear, then he carried her into his room.

She woke later, groggy, alone. Wes's side of the bed was cold, and unease wiped the sleep from her eyes. She padded into the living room, only to find Wes by the windows, staring into the dark, forlorn. Sad. So unlike the Weston Aldrich she knew.

Her unease worsened.

His father's nastiness must have affected him more than he let on, or Victor's open dislike of Annie could have Wes second-guessing their relationship. A possibility that had her clutching her chest. But the way he'd made love to her didn't support that theory, and they'd become so close since they'd admitted their feelings. He'd been extra domineering lately out of fear, his controlling nature plugged into an amplifier. Because he was crazy about her. Just like she was crazy about him. Wholly, deeply *in love* with him. He'd be even more stressed now, worried about the merger, possibly losing his job. Add in DLP, who could be doing God knew what to sabotage him, and no wonder he was having trouble sleeping.

A surge of protectiveness flared behind her ribs. Wes's

phone records had been accessed. People who did that wouldn't hesitate to do worse. At the very least, they could learn about his DJing, and he could not, for any reason, get fired. He may have scolded her for trying to help, but she wouldn't sit idly by and do nothing. Sarah was a private investigator. Duncan had intel on the details. The trick would be helping Wes without him knowing.

22

WESTON'S EYES darted from his Rolex to Duncan, their lunch dragging longer than intended. He had to run the numbers on their latest Alzheimer's studies and prepare projections, then arrange a final meeting with Karim's Biotrell team for next week. The last merger details would be negotiated at that meeting, the papers finally signed. With DLP upping the stakes, he needed this deal done.

"We have ten days," he told Duncan. "Ten days until this wraps up. We can't lose more employees before then, especially on the Alzheimer's studies."

Duncan sipped the last of his espresso. "I sent a memo, asked everyone to change their passwords, just in case. I've had our firewall reinforced, even though it's already Fort Knox. I've been sniffing around, asking random staff how things are, sussing out if anything feels off. All seems clear."

"That doesn't make me feel better."

"Short of asking if someone's offering people cash to jump ship or if they're being blackmailed, there's not much else we can do."

"We can't give Karim more reasons to question our stability."

"Tell me something I don't know. Pretty sure your father will fire me if we lose this merger."

"You and me both," Weston said under his breath.

Duncan signaled their waiter for the check. "What's that supposed to mean?"

"Nothing."

"Bullshit." He winked at a woman at the adjacent table.

Wes smirked. "Do you ever quit trolling for women?"

"Do you ever answer personal questions?"

Annie often accused him of the same. Weston was adept at evading thorny topics. It was a cultivated skill. He may have told her about DLP's ominous behavior, but he hadn't been honest about his father's threatening phone call. *I will never acknowledge her as a member of this family. Leave Anthea or you're out of the will.*

His father could burn that piece of paper for all Weston cared. Weston wasn't a dependent. He earned his living through hard work, and the status of excessive wealth didn't drive him. Accomplishments drove him. Sure, he loved art and architecture and the finer things in life, but the past weeks with Annie had taught him he loved her tiny, messy apartment as much as his elegant loft. He'd take a night with her over a collection of modernist paintings.

That conversation with his father had been disturbing, but for different reasons: it had been a reminder that losing the person you love could ruin you.

When Weston had been upset his father had missed a debate tournament or forgotten a soccer game, his mother would kiss the crown of his head and say, "Your father is a passionate man. He loves you more than you know. More than anyone in this world. He works so hard to provide for you."

She had been right in some respects, but love for his son hadn't driven the man. It had been love for his wife. Singular love for this one, irreplaceable person. Once she'd died, birthdays had been blown off, holidays erased, staff fired while Weston tried to dodge the man's cruel wrath. His father's limited warmth and humanity had burned to ash, all because he'd lost the love of his life.

Exactly how Weston felt about Annie. She was that love: unparalleled. Irreplaceable. He hadn't been able to open up with a woman before her, because there had been no *before her*. She was the one person who calmed him, made him laugh, reminded him there was life outside of work. He loved her more than he'd ever imagined possible. If he lost her, it seemed inevitable he'd end up as cold and vicious as his father, and it was infecting his mind.

Nightmares had woken him most nights since that call.

Annie running and laughing, then tripping and falling off the side of a cliff.

Annie slammed through the windshield of a car.

Annie stabbed by a mugger.

He'd wake each time, sweating, terror gripping his lungs, and she'd just be there, next to him, sleeping deeply. He was spiraling, struggling to get back to where he'd been, trusting in a future where control was out of his grasp and the fear of losing her was less potent. He'd been unacceptably distant with her at times, had nearly asked her for space to see if the nightmares would lessen. But he'd promised her he wouldn't panic and push her away.

"Personal is hard for me," he told Duncan, a delayed reply to his jibe: *Do you ever answer personal questions?* His therapist used to harp on that, too. Tell him talking was healing.

"I get it, but you've been looking rough for months now, and worse lately. If you won't talk to me, I hope you at least talk to Annie."

He hated hearing Duncan mention her name. Despised that they'd ever dated, even once casually. But Weston's perfectly tailored suit felt too tight, the laces of his shoes pinching his feet. "I'm in love with her," he forced out. If talking was healing, maybe this would help. Even with Duncan.

"Now we're getting somewhere." Duncan pushed his empty espresso cup to the side. "Not that I'm surprised. It's been nice getting to know her, and I was happy when she told me you two hooked up. She's beautiful and funny, and she's the only woman you've ever dated this long."

"I have issues in the commitment department. But I doubt anyone else would have lasted the test of time. Annie is... everything." *Irreplaceable.*

"So why do you look like you've lost her?"

"Because I could."

"How?"

DLP could cause an accident. Cancer could steal her away. A stray bullet could rip through her chest. "Life is unpredictable. The possibility of losing her has been messing with my mind, and I've been pulling away from her because of it."

Duncan considered him. "As in nuclear war and climate change could end the planet so we should all quit our jobs, liquidate our assets, and sip margaritas in Bali?"

"Not the same."

"Exactly the same. You're playing hypothetical roulette. It's like you want to pull the trigger before someone else does."

The chicken marsala he'd eaten churned in his gut. It *was* exactly the same. His father's call had set him back. He knew it. That man's harsh bitterness was a byproduct of love: losing it had twisted him. Now Weston could barely blink without picturing Annie harmed, leaving him miserable and alone, more devastated than he'd been after losing Leo and his mother.

If they quit dating, reverted to friends, spent less time together, she'd have less of a hold on his heart. He'd stop having nightmares. He'd return to his simple life where work was enough to fulfill him. All possibilities he'd entertained during his sleepless nights. Then he'd picture breaking up with her, and pain would slice through his chest. All he'd want to do was wake her up and confess how much he loved her.

He had to get out of his head and over this hump. Annie was too important. And he had no clue why he was confiding his distress to Duncan. "I shouldn't take advice from a man who considers monogamy an airborne disease."

"Yet I'm the one who's smiling."

Weston shook his head. "I buy her all these gifts, for her scrapbooking, a dress I knew she'd love, all to show how I feel, but I haven't told her I love her. I physically can't force out the words, even though I love her so much it hurts. I'm terrified about getting in deeper."

"There's nothing wrong with waiting. As much as I've gotten to know Annie this year, I'd guess she doesn't give up on people easily. Tell her when you're ready, but keep doing the gifts. Women love that shit."

He hadn't been around Annie when she'd found her presents, but he'd heard the pleasure in her voice when she'd censured him for the excess. He had no intention of curbing his gift giving. The rest he'd have to figure out, sooner rather than later.

They paid their bill and were out the door when Weston's phone rang. His spare phone. *Falcon's* burner phone. Piss poor timing.

He'd been carrying it on purpose. With his final DJ

performance in a week, e-mailing his electrical and staging needs for the video feeds had proven challenging, and playing phone tag with the club owner, Mick, had been even worse. Weston shouldn't answer the call, not near somebody he knew, Duncan included. With the time crunch, he had no choice.

"Go ahead while I take this."

Duncan nodded. When he was safely swallowed by pedestrians, Weston dodged bodies and nestled by a liquor store window. "Falcon here."

"You're harder to reach than Elvis Presley."

And as dead if Duncan caught a whiff of this call. Or not. Duncan was his right hand. He was becoming an actual friend. One Weston should hang out with more often. "I'm in demand."

"You're something, man. What are those shirts the kids are wearing at your shows? All splattered with your name on 'em?"

A horn blasted. Weston plugged his free ear and tucked closer to the window he was facing. "Freed by the Falcon. Not my doing."

"I could sell some merch. Take charge of printing for a cut."

Not the worst idea. He could put his earnings toward more gun-control lobbying. Or a homeless shelter, if Annie liked that idea. He thought ahead to future shows, how much they could earn, then remembered this was his last show. He wasn't sure why the thought made him antsy. "Go for it," he told Mick.

"You want in on the design work?"

"I'm a DJ, not a graphic designer. Just send me proofs."

"Done. As for your stage requirements, they're gonna be tricky."

Five minutes later, Weston hung up, pleased to have those details sorted.

The rush of pedestrians paid him no mind as he pocketed his phone. Duncan was long gone. He'd dodged a bullet answering the call in public, but this would be the end of it, at least. He'd quit performing after this show. Work behind the scenes. Keep Leo's memory alive by talking about him and raising funds in his honor. Not playing would feel odd at first, but this unsettled void would disappear over time. The merger would soon be finalized, all his hard work coming to fruition.

If he could figure out how to quit worrying he'd lose Annie and end up like his glacial father, life would be looking pretty damn good.

ANNIE WAS ON A MISSION. She would not be deterred, even by a Dolce & Gabbana-wearing man, whose extensive wardrobe made her closet look like a thumbnail in one of those eco-chic tiny homes. Weston was a mess. She'd known him long enough to see the signs. Sullen silences. Distracted wall-gazing. If he wasn't all over her at night, or quick to apologize for his preoccupation, she'd worry he was second-guessing their relationship.

The merger and DLP drama were to blame. The other option wasn't an option.

She strutted down the street, stilettos on, her pencil skirt and red blouse the antithesis to her bohemian style. This was ball-breaker attire. She would sneak into Duncan's office, demand information on those shady DLP jerks. Sarah had agreed to help her find dirt on the men or women behind the phone scheme, use her private eye skills to gather intel, and find enough evidence to alert the cops. If need be, Annie would blackmail the blackmailers. She would prove to Wes he didn't have to handle his problems alone.

A couple of blocks from the Aldrich Pharma offices, she skirted around a sidewalk grate, an acrid gust of wind wafting past her nose. A homeless woman was sitting against a brick wall, her meager belongings shoved into a garbage bag. Annie stopped to put a five dollar bill in her cup.

"Thank you," the woman said, her voice hoarse.

"I hope things turn around for you." Annie made eye contact with her. The woman smiled, revealing several missing teeth. Annie's heart cracked as always.

She straightened, getting her head back in the game, but a man brushed past her, almost knocking her over.

The woman steadied Annie's calf. "Lots of sharks in these treacherous waters."

"Tell me about it." She was about to thank the woman, when she realized the shark in question had been Duncan. A gift from the ball-breaker gods. She wouldn't have to sneak into his office after all, or lie to Wes if he caught her there. Luck had dropped Duncan Ruffolo into her take-no-prisoners lap.

He stopped a few storefronts down, faced a dumpling shop, his face gleeful as he pulled out his phone. Probably calling one of his lady friends.

She thanked the homeless woman while waving at Duncan. Unable to catch his eye, she hurried over.

"If you want to bury Weston Aldrich," Duncan said into the phone, his back to her, "I hit the jackpot. Biotrell is as good as yours."

What in the actual hell?

She must have heard him wrong, misunderstood the context. Duncan wouldn't sabotage Wes. He'd worked at Aldrich Pharma for years.

She grabbed his arm and yanked. "What did you say?"

"Get your fucking hands off—" He spun around, sneering. Then he jerked back. "Annie?"

He looked as stunned as she felt, a hint of distress in the tightening lines by his mouth.

"What did you just say?" she asked again.

"I'll call you back," he said into the phone, not taking his eyes off her. He hung up and pressed some numbers on his cell, then crossed his arms, feigning indifference. "It makes sense now, why you ditched me to hang out with Falcon."

He didn't say more. He didn't have to, not with the calculating gleam in his eye, and Annie's pulse rocketed with the implications: Duncan knew Wes was Falcon. Duncan had been calling someone who wanted to bury Wes, and Wes had mentioned a possible mole at Aldrich Pharma.

Shit. Shit. Shit. What was she supposed to do now?

Duncan didn't speak or try to explain.

Her brain spun in a dizzy rush. "You work for DLP. You're a goddamn spy." She needed to hear him say it. Confirm this lunacy. But he didn't agree with her claim or deny it. "That's why you went out with me and kept texting—to get dirt on Wes. It's why you kept asking me to talk to him."

Again, no comment, and a skeezy feeling slinked under her skin. She'd gone out on a date with this man, had pursued a friendship. She'd considered hooking up with this creep. All that time, Weston had warned her Duncan couldn't be trusted. He'd called him ruthless in business, an attribute he had praised.

She was livid.

"I'll expose you." She would *destroy* Duncan. She didn't have evidence, but if she kicked up suspicion there would be an inquiry. The minutia of Duncan's life would be analyzed under a microscope. "If you breathe a word about Wes to anyone, I'll call the cops. They'll dig into every facet of your life. What you're doing is illegal."

At least she thought it was. This was insider trading, right? Some serious, low-level espionage.

"You won't." His nonchalance was maddening.

"Fuck you, I won't." He was a cretin *and* delusional. Weston Aldrich was her person. Her man. One word about Falcon to Biotrell and the rumor would spread. His father would hear about the DJing, and Weston would be fired.

She'd walk naked down Fifth Avenue before letting him lose his job.

"You won't," Duncan said again. He held up his phone. "I was behind Weston when he was talking to some club guy. He said, and I quote: 'I'm a DJ, not a graphic designer' and went on to talk about the setup for some show. I taped his conversation. One word from you, and I hit Send. The man on the receiving end of the recording will know what to do with it. If you ruin me, I ruin him."

Simple math. One plus one equaled disaster.

It didn't matter that she was in her ball-breaker attire. Looking serious and ready to attack didn't give her superpowers to burst Duncan's head with her mind. "I call bullshit. If you say nothing, you're"—she flung her arms angrily—"screwed? Someone hired you to do a job. They'll be pissed you didn't come through. How do I know you won't squeal like the little rat you are?"

She needed time. A few days to get Sarah on this. Dig up enough dirt to bury Duncan under his own shit. Going along with his idiotic bribe worked in her favor, as long as he held up his end.

He didn't flinch at the insult, just shrugged one big shoulder. "I did what I was paid to do. I got dirt on the key researchers DLP wanted lured away from Aldrich Pharma, with another one not far behind. I've been paid in full. Feeding them Weston on a silver platter was a...last minute request. They asked for skeletons in his closet. I provided."

It would be the nail in Weston's coffin, and Duncan didn't give a crap. Or did he? Something shifted in his expression. A hint of remorse? He could choke on that guilt, for all she cared.

"Fine," she said quickly, surprised her pounding heart hadn't punched through her chest. "I'll keep your secret if you delete that recording and stay quiet." New York's cacophony of horns, brakes, intermittent music, and voices blurred as she studied Duncan's every blink and twitch.

"Deal," he said. "Under one condition."

His conditions would be as slimy as him. "What?"

"You break up with Weston."

"Are you insane?" She was a second from kneeing Duncan in the nuts.

He lifted his phone higher, held it out of her reach. "Then I hit Send."

She tensed, her knee twitching to make contact. "Why would you ask that?"

"Give me some credit, Annie. I know how close you two are. Even if you uphold your end, he'll know something's wrong. He'll get it out of you. Besides, I'm doing you a favor."

"No, what you're doing is screwing yourself. He might know something's off when he sees me, but I can make up excuses. Throw him off your trail. If I break up with him, he won't buy that crap." Wes knew she loved him. She'd admitted as much that one time in his office, had shown him repeatedly with her body. Duncan's plan would backfire in his face.

"That's where you're wrong, Annie. I just came from lunch with Weston. He told me he's not in love with you. Said he buys you gifts, scrapbooking stuff and dresses out of guilt. He loves you, but he's not in love with you and doesn't know how to end things, because he doesn't want to hurt you or lose you as a friend."

The oxygen in her lungs turned to sludge. She teetered on her stilettos. Wes *had* been acting strange since his father's call.

Less present with her, his smiles sometimes forced, and not sleeping well. She'd told herself the merger and DLP had been the problem: worry over her, stress with work, frustration with DLP. Had she been deluding herself? Wanting him so badly she'd been blind to his true feelings?

"Like I said," Duncan went on, "I'm doing you a favor."

Fat freaking chance. He was a lying degenerate who was trying to shove a wedge between her and Wes, ensure she didn't cave and spill his sordid secrets. And it was already working, infecting her mind. No more. The second she called Wes and told him she was done with him, his Spidey Senses—or *Falcon Feels*—would be on high alert. This break-up scheme would bite Duncan in his backstabbing derriere.

"Fine." She matched Duncan's nonchalance, because she was *chalant* as fuck. "I was getting bored of him anyway."

Duncan's amusement upped her ire. "Whatever you say. He's in his office. Call him now, then I delete the recording."

Oh, he was a piece of work, this guy. One who would spend five to ten in a six-by-eight cell. Curling her lip at him, she pulled her phone from her purse and hit speed dial.

She held her breath.

Wes answered after three rings. "Annie, hey."

Not *I was thinking about you.* He hadn't said that in a while, had he? He'd been more friend than boyfriend, when not in bed or sending gifts. And why was she suddenly doubting him when Duncan was the bad guy here, clearly out for blood?

"We need to talk," she told Wes, injecting as much double meaning into her words as possible. *Duncan is your mole. He could expose you. I'm trying to save you.*

Telepathic messaging.

Rustling came from his end. "Okay, shoot."

So much for telepathy. She opened her mouth, bile rising as the words she needed to say got stuck. A cramp seized her stomach. The idea of breaking up with Wes, no matter the phoniness of the circumstances, made her physically ill.

"If I go down, he's going with me," Duncan whispered. "Make it believable."

The choice really wasn't hers. Not when she'd do anything for the man she loved. Even break both their hearts for the short term.

"Thing is," she told Wes, those cramps worsening, "something's been off between us. It's given me time to think, and I realized I got carried away." Her voice cracked and tears burned her eyes. "I think we rushed into things and...and I don't love you the way I thought I did. I think it's better we stay friends, go back to how things were. Not that there's any going back from here, but I don't feel the way I thought I would. And I..." She swallowed another rush of bile and steadied herself. She would kill Duncan for this. "I don't love you. I think I loved the idea of you."

She waited for Wes to raise hell, read her mind, question her sanity. Yell at her and tell her she was just having a momentary freak-out. She'd have to push back, be as convincing as possible. Anything to save his job. She waited so long for some kind of reaction that the phone turned slippery in her shaky hand.

Then he said, "Okay."

Okay? One word? Was he not going to fight for her? Demand answers? "I just, I don't know. I think it's the right thing?" She sputtered out the words, while shrinking under Duncan's steady stare.

"Yeah, fine. I get it."

She didn't get it. She couldn't fathom his neutral reply, the flatness of his tone.

He cleared his throat. "I'll do next weekend's show on my own. We'll take some time apart. Speak when we're—once we've had time apart. I have a Chicago business trip coming up, a few dinners with investors next week. And a golf tournament. I'll be busy. I'll call you when I can." Did he have a hair appointment, too? A manicure scheduled? Another ridiculous reason for why he wasn't begging her to change her mind?

Then he hung up. Just like that. Shut her out.

As though their time together had meant nothing.

Her bones turned dense, heavy with so much *hurt*. Duncan hadn't been lying. Wes didn't love her. He never had. She'd given him the out he'd actually wanted, and she didn't know how to blink or breathe or press End on that sickening call.

Duncan angled his phone toward her, played a snippet of Wes's incriminating call, then made a show of deleting it. "Pleasure doing business with you. And my 'benefits' offer hasn't expired. You know how to reach me."

There was that skeezy shiver again. She averted her gaze from him, couldn't focus through the hurt, but she swiveled back and called his name. "Why'd you do it? Why'd you hurt the man who took a risk offering you an amazing job?"

Duncan's confidence slipped briefly. "DLP has ways of getting to people."

He disappeared in the walking crowd, just another man strutting down the sidewalk, as though he hadn't just exploded Annie's life.

She wanted to sink to the cement, curl into a ball and cry until she was nothing but a salty puddle. But that would mean Duncan had won, and the more she thought about Wes's reaction, his quick jump to cut his losses and run, the more she didn't buy it. He'd warned her he might freak out and bolt, hurting her in the process. This could be his instinct to run from real feelings, protect himself from getting hurt. Protect her in the process. That reasoning made a hell of a lot more sense than Duncan's bullshit about Wes not loving her.

She knew Weston Aldrich, every damaged, infuriating, amazing, loving inch of him. That man would pack his feelings into his internal bomb shelter, building his defenses, precisely because he loved her, not because he didn't.

She knew, and she'd let Duncan prep her to believe otherwise.

She sniffled, wiped the corners of her eyes, and dialed Sarah. Weston loved her, and she loved him so hard it hurt. She wouldn't believe otherwise until she'd explained her call and spoke with him face to face, but that would have to wait. Whatever DLP had on Duncan was a doozy. There was no telling how far they'd push him. Duncan could still find another way to drag Weston down.

When Sarah answered, Annie bit down on her teeth. "The mole's name is Duncan Ruffolo. He's a long-time employee of Aldrich Pharma, Weston's executive assistant, and we need to crush the life out of him."

23

WESTON STARED at his office door, waiting for his father to barge in. It wouldn't take him long to hear they'd lost another researcher. Their final Biotrell meeting was in three days. All Weston's hard work would spiral down the drain, Aldrich Pharma would suffer the consequences, and Victor S. Aldrich might fire his son.

Weston should make phone calls, reach out to Karim and Biotrell and get ahead of this latest cataclysm. All he could do was stare at his office door and wait.

A couple minutes later, it flew open. "Thanks to you, this merger's about to bust wide open." His father slammed the door shut.

Weston flexed his fingers on his chair arms. "I didn't fire Allan. I didn't cut his wages or make his work here difficult. He left because DLP are underhanded bastards."

"Losing Allan Merkur is a blow, but he's not the problem here. Neither is DLP. Karim asked one thing of you, one goddamn thing—to date his daughter. And you had to go and get tangled up with that street girl instead of putting Aldrich Pharma first."

Heat blasted up Weston's neck. All he'd done his whole adult life was put business first. He'd worked instead of socializing, instead of dating and vacationing like a functioning human. Which would have been fine, if he'd felt supported, valued. He lived and breathed this place, had even given up DJing for it, but the words that had Weston wanting to topple his desk were *that street girl*. "You will not speak of Anthea in front of me."

"She's not our people, son. Dating her cheapens yourself and the family name."

Weston laughed, a harsh, bitter sound. "You're right. She's not our people. She's better than us. She actually cares about the people in her life. She goes out of her way to show her love and doesn't lock herself in an office because she's bitter life took a nasty turn."

She was the best person he knew, and he didn't correct his father's misconception that they were still dating.

That reality had slithered around his neck the past week. A python of despair. He couldn't take a breath without missing Annie. He couldn't touch his mixing equipment without hearing her playful voice ringing in his ears. He was performing tonight, his last appearance as Falcon, but he'd barely reviewed his set or the video montage. Thoughts of her were in his bed, his heart, his mind, screaming at him to fight for her. Get her back. But he kept replaying her out-of-the-blue phone call. The distress in her voice.

The way he'd immediately shut down.

He'd been so quick to believe her change of heart. Not just believe. His initial reaction had been *relief*. Selfish, short-sighted, idiotic relief. Several deep breaths free from worrying about how far he'd fall if he lost her down the road.

Then reality had crashed in on him.

"You're weak," his father said. "Always have been. Ruled by your emotion."

"How is working myself to death being ruled by emotion?"

"You don't work to put Aldrich Pharma on the map. You work as an escape. You work so you don't have to feel. Emotion drives that, son. Not determination."

He wasn't wrong, but he wasn't exactly right. "I've used work as a crutch. It's been an outlet for me for as long as I can remember. That doesn't change the fact that Aldrich Pharma has always been my priority."

"Not enough of a priority. Not when it counted."

Weston pushed to his feet and steepled his fingers on his desk, leaning forward just enough. "Do you know why I let you treat me like I'm gum under your Berluti shoes?" His father's left cheek twitched, but he didn't reply. "Because I loved Mom. Because she was strong and kind, and I know how much she loved me. She also loved you, and I know losing her turned what little warmth you had to ash, which always made me sad. I let you behave like a brute because I pity you."

His father's mouth twisted. "Your mother didn't raise you to be disrespectful."

Weston's muscles tensed, a jaguar poised before he leapt. Or a mutant jaguar-squirrel. Thinking of Annie's ridiculous jokes pained him, but his father's jab sharpened his focus.

No, Weston's mother hadn't raised him to be disrespectful. She'd raised him to say please and thank you and to think of the larger world around them. When his life was insular, ripe with wealth and fortune, she'd gifted him with compassion. She'd ensured he'd had outlets and interests to level him, and he'd dishonored her memory by denying how important DJing had become in his life.

He looked at Victor's thick gray hair, his chiseled jaw and

sharp suit, so much like his own. Weston *really* looked at this unforgiving man and said what he should have said years ago, "I'm a DJ."

The lines around his father's aging eyes compressed. "You're a what?"

"A DJ, like Leo wanted to be. I spin music and play in clubs, and I'm pretty damn good. I've been doing it for years and didn't tell you because I knew you'd panic. Fire me, likely. Or the board would get spooked, worried about investor backlash. But hiding my music was the wrong choice. Mom didn't teach me to be disrespectful, as you so nicely pointed out. She taught me to respect *you*, even though you've been an overbearing bully since she died. She taught me there's a bigger world out there than Aldrich Pharma. Which means there are other jobs, too. People who'll hire me because I'm good at what I do, even if I'm in the music scene as well."

Annie left jobs she didn't like, flipped the pages on half-finished puzzles, because they'd lost their fun. Her laissez-faire attitude had frustrated Weston, but maybe his irritation had been jealousy. As important as Aldrich Pharma was to Weston, as much as he'd hate to leave it in someone else's hands and worry about the workers under its employ, losing Annie wasn't the only reason he'd been a mess this week. Work fulfilled him, but DJing did, too. He'd been quick to think he could walk away. Close that chapter of his life. He hadn't accounted for the edgy void growing at the prospect.

"You'll quit that...music stuff," his father said, vehement. "The board doesn't need to know."

Weston rounded his desk with measured steps, walked to his door, and yanked it open. "I'm not changing for you or anyone. I won't date a woman to secure a business deal, or stoop to DLP's level of scum. I won't quit DJing. So you can deal with this reality or you can fire me, as you've threatened. The choice is yours."

His father's nostrils flared. "If you lose your job, it'll be because you screwed up this merger. Even without Rosanna, you should have sealed this deal."

He should have. The failure wouldn't go down easy. But DLP was the culprit, not Weston. "Whatever happens, I'll deal with it. But we're done here."

His father stood his ground, cheek twitching, temple pulsing, the air around him thick with unspoken censure. Weston matched the man's obstinate pose. With a final scowl, Victor marched past his son and out the door.

Weston stared after him, breathing hard.

"I'm proud of you." Marjory appeared in his line of vision. "That was a brave thing to do, and I'm curious about this DJ development."

"He's going to fire me," he said, ignoring her DJ comment. Adrenaline leached out gradually, leaving Weston weary, but no less committed to his decision.

"He might surprise you. But the bigger question is why did you break up with Annie?"

"I didn't." There was that python again, twisting around his constricting throat. He may not have initiated their break-up, but he'd instigated their downfall. The only explanation for her about-face had been his distance prior to her call. His internal freaking out had undermined their relationship. Instead of letting her in, he'd shut her out. He was to blame. Or she truly didn't love him the way he loved her. He wasn't sure which option was worse.

Marjory crossed her arms, sending the shoulders of her orange blazer toward her ears. "Do you keep me on staff as a courtesy?"

He didn't reply.

"Do you think I'm bad at my job?"

"You're the best secretary in the building."

"I am."

"And?" He was in no mood for her games.

"*And*...don't treat me like I'm dense by telling me lies. You're worse off than the last time you two split. The bunny's back, and so is"—she gestured to his face—"*that* look. And Annie wouldn't break up with you."

"She would and she did."

"Did you cheat on her?"

"Fuck, no. She said she didn't love me, that she just wanted to stay friends." Because Weston had pulled back, scared of a million what-ifs, instead of showing her the extent of his love. "I didn't treat her like she deserved," he said.

"Listen to me, Weston Grayson Aldrich. I know that girl. I've seen her grow into a beautiful woman and fall in love with you all from that desk chair out there." Marjory hooked her thumb toward her leather throne. "I've seen you fight your feelings for her until you damn near choked on them. I've spent years biting my tongue so you two could get here in your own time. Annie wouldn't walk away just because you're acting like your emotionally stunted self."

Marjory was short. Five-foot-nothing with big, curly hair, a sweep of nineties bangs, and a pointed nose she poked into everyone's business. Still, when she spoke, she had a way of making Weston feel like the smaller of them. "Doesn't change the facts. She called me and ended things."

"And when you told her no, you wouldn't let her get away, what did she say?"

He glared at his secretary.

She huffed. "Just as I thought. Fix it, Weston. Standing up to your father won't mean much if you're standing alone. And stop bringing that rabbit into work. He smells."

Weston glanced at Felix. Aside from feeding him and cleaning the little guy's cage, he often forgot Felix was there. His only company the past week. A sad state of affairs.

Marjory left and closed the door. He rubbed his eyes and replayed the past week's events. He'd assumed Annie's break-up call had been a reaction to his prior behavior. He'd been so in his head after his father's ultimatum, distant with her at times, but maybe it wasn't so cut and dry. He hadn't been outright rude, and it had only been two weeks of his panic-induced nightmares. They'd already had three insanely good weeks before that. Addictive. Intimate. *Hot.*

And she'd been as on board as him, wild in bed, affectionate, teasing. She'd been the brave one who'd said *I love you.* Only once, but she'd said it. If Annie hadn't broken up with him because they'd had a rough couple weeks, then why? To show him what he could lose? Had she found out about his father's ultimatum to cut him from the will? Thought she was doing him a favor?

None of it made sense, and Marjory was right. Standing up to his father and being a DJ wouldn't mean much without Annie at his side.

His mother's impassioned advice rushed back to him: *If you don't let yourself care about others, you'll only live half a life.*

He'd assumed the teaching had been about philanthropy, not relationships, but maybe he'd been wrong. She could have been nudging him to open up to the idea of love one day—advice he'd warped over the years. Pain of losing her and Leo had distorted good memories into bad, love into fear, so efficiently he'd perverted her wisdoms to protect himself: *If I let myself care about others, I'll live half a life and end up like my father.*

If she were here, she'd probably tell him to open his eyes to what he had, that loving meant living a fuller life, no matter the risks. She'd tell him he was too strong to turn out like his father, even if he lost his irreplaceable person. But, at the heart of it, the outcome didn't matter. Running wasn't living. Letting fear dictate his choices wasn't making the most of his time. He *was* stronger than that, because of his mother's guidance. Because Leo had shown him how music and DJing could fill a person up.

The notions settled in him, awareness he'd somehow missed. Along with how royally he'd screwed up with Annie.

Unsure how to fix this mess, he picked up his phone and called Duncan. It went to voice mail. He'd called him earlier in the week as well, his first time reaching out socially, needing a friend. Duncan had been busy then, unavailable now. Rosanna was on a business trip in London, and there was no way Weston was going to start talking to his rabbit, asking for dating advice.

He needed more people in his life. Friends like Leo. He'd always assumed their connection had been unique, that no one else would understand Weston, get it when he'd moaned about his father and the expectations that had come with his life back then. Maybe he hadn't given others the chance to live up to Leo's memory since losing him. He'd missed his friend so much, he hadn't wanted to move on, get close with others. Not just out of fear of losing. Fear of forgetting. If was time to stop being afraid.

First was Annie. He had to speak with her, tell her he loved her and should have fought for her. Grovel. Crawl on his hands and knees. Explain that his fears had made him a coward in the end, as he'd worried from the start, and find out exactly why she'd ended things. He may not have bolted on her physically like he had with Lila, but he'd done a mental runner.

Furious with himself, he picked up his phone and dialed Annie's number.

ANNIE STARED at her cell phone, at the name *Weston* flashing as it rang, and her heart sped. She wasn't sure why he was calling, but she desperately wanted to answer his call. Unfortunately, it was the last thing she should do. Sarah said she'd have evidence soon. If she talked with Weston before then, she'd cave and blurt the truth. Confess her love and apologize for the ruse. Maybe he'd apologize right back for his cold brushoff. Maybe he'd continue protecting his heart.

Either way, once he learned about Duncan's deceit, he'd tear after that man, ruin Sarah's diligent work, and sink himself in the process.

Annie had to stay strong.

She forced herself to ignore the ringing and finish her latest scrapbook page. The idea for the creation had come to her while drowning in chips and chocolate this morning, sad about her current reality. The page was centered around a photograph of Wes in a suit—*shocker*—with two dogs cut and pasted around him. One pooch was peeing on his leg. The other was taking a dump on his expensive shoes. She'd smiled maniacally while adding the words *you suck*, spelled with cut-up magazine letters, like a serial killer.

She was still hurt by Wes's reaction to her call, even if his flat "okay" had been his issues talking, not his heart. Scrapbooking always helped her work through her discomfort, and he'd find this funny *when* they kissed and made up. Because they would kiss and make up. She'd force him to face his fears. Or she'd been wrong and Wes truly wasn't in love with her in the end.

Her phone quit ringing, and she exhaled. Tried her hardest to ignore the possibility that she was wrong about his feelings.

A minute later, it started again. *Dammit.*

Steeling herself, she glued letters down on her scrapbook page. Her phone rang another five times while she worked, going silent then blaring back to life. Her page ended with her last letter glued at an awkward angle.

When her cell quieted for longer than five minutes, she picked it up gingerly, as though it might explode. There was one message. From Wes.

Her heart resumed racing.

He was likely calling to keep their friendship intact. Wes would never abandon her and walk away, even with his fears. Or he'd discovered Duncan's betrayal and was calling to warn her. Or Duncan had found another way to bring Wes down and Wes needed her help. Or he'd been hanging out with Rosanna again and had discovered they actually cared for each other and he wanted Annie to know before their dating went public.

Swallowing the square of chocolate she'd popped into her mouth, she pressed the phone to her ear and listened.

"I fucked up. I miss you like crazy. I let you walk away because I thought losing you now would be easier than losing you later in some horrific way, like my mom and Leo, which was cowardly and cruel. I'm done being scared. I need to see you. Please let me explain and grovel in person. I can do better, be better. Please come to tonight's show."

Annie bit her lip. She pressed her hand to her chest.

He missed her. He'd realized how wrong he'd been without her having to shove her scrapbook page in his face. He'd admitted it, no matter how scared he'd been. God, she loved him so much it hurt. She was so damn *proud* of him, wanted to kiss every inch of his gorgeous face. But she would not. Not yet, at least. Not until she had that evidence in her hands.

If not calling him before was tough, it was torture now. Good thing she was built of tough stuff. She did listen to Wes's message again, though. Five more times, his deep voice telling her he'd fucked up, begging for another chance. Tears blurred her vision and crowded her throat. She really couldn't wait to smother him in kisses.

Her phone buzzed again, this time with a message from Sarah.

Sarah: *We've got Duncan. Not enough for an arrest, but enough to shut him up and bury him professionally. I can have the files to you this afternoon.*

"Yes!" Annie fist pumped the air and did a seated jig. Things were finally going her way. Soon, everything would be right. This time she and Wes would be free to be together, nothing between them. She moved her thumbs on her phone, ready to call Wes and put them both out of their misery, but she paused.

This was the part in crime movies where things went sideways. The good guys were so close to victory, then they were undermined one final time before the grand finale. A chance she wasn't willing to take. She needed those files in her hand, *then* she'd make her move. She also wanted to see Wes's face when they made up. Gobble up that memory and store it next to one of Leo playing piano and Wes working on his awful scrapbook and Joyce mastering her piano chords.

Bad memories often overshadowed good ones. Unless you locked down the good. Reveled in them. Saved those moments for when things got tough, as things always would. And she knew how to make this memory extra special. At his big show tonight.

24

WESTON PEEKED through the curtains and scanned the hopped-up crowd for Annie but couldn't spot her through the growing crush. The two-level club was filling fast. Neon lights lined the stairs. The balcony was packed, the massive iron-wrapped disco ball illuminating the dancing bodies on the main floor. He searched every woman through the pulsing lights to no avail.

Tons of merchandise flashed up at him from the crowd, though: Falcon shirts, Falcon hats, Falcon glow sticks flashing in pumping fists. Mick had certainly come through with the last-minute merch. Weston's cut would fund local shelters, and his plans to distribute QR-code cards at the exits, with ways to help gun control movements, would touch many hands, as long as his video feed had the desired impact. The turnout and energy couldn't be better. All signs pointed to success. But Annie should be here, and he had no clue if she planned to come.

Agitated, he slipped behind the two sets of curtains, checked the monitors and cables again.

"All good?" one of the stagehands asked. The kid looked nervous, shifting on his feet.

Falcon's reputation had preceded him, his eccentric silences and demands known and respected. Weston wore the same black outfit and Falcon mask he'd worn to his other shows, hadn't alerted Mick or anyone to a change in status. He'd normally nod, not chance speaking, but his father knew the score now. He actually looked forward to telling Rosanna and seeing the shock on her face. She'd always teased him for being a stuffy country-club boy.

He was uneasy about the story leaking to the press, as it no doubt would. *Heir to Aldrich Pharma has Wild Side,* or some other salacious heading. Assuming he got fired, he believed other pharmaceutical companies would hire him, but it wasn't certain. Still, there was no reversing this trajectory.

To the skinny kid, he said, "I could use a glass of water."

"Oh, yeah. Sure. Right on it." Eyes bright, he skittered off.

Thirty minutes later Weston stood behind his mixer, finger on the dial, nervous energy pulsing through him. If Annie didn't show, he'd search her out tomorrow. Fix this. Fix them. Make sure she knew unequivocally she held Weston's beating heart in her small hands. He loved her. He wouldn't mince words. He'd tell her straight and true and make sure she never had reason to doubt him again. But he wanted her to see the video feed's first steps. The audience's reaction. Leo's tribute. Their collaboration. He couldn't have created something this powerful without her.

The sound system cut out. The crowd hollered from the other side of the two curtains, the crescendo rising into a roar. His body vibrated with the thunderous sound, and all he could think was *this. This is who I am.* If he'd quit DJing as planned, he would have missed this unparalleled rush.

He kissed two fingers and pressed them to the photograph of Leo he'd attached to his mixer. "This one's for you, man."

He signaled the skinny kid who'd brought him the water, and the outermost curtain sailed up. Weston was still hidden behind the second curtain, but he felt the descending quiet, the crowd's excited anticipation.

He started the video feed and watched the playback on his screen.

Kids with toy guns, playing and laughing, spliced to a kid hiding under his school desk, crying. A pregnant mother spliced to a woman slumped over a tombstone. Dark images followed, violent and upsetting, spilling from one screen to the next, footage that would distress some club goers. As it should. It was silent in the massive club. Quiet so tension-filled it screamed with the madness of weaponry, guns purchased too easily, consequences ignored. The only sound Weston heard was the hard pounding of his heart.

He unleashed the first fragment of sound. Cello. Plaintive. *Angry*; the instrument lamenting its sorrow for so many senseless deaths. Faster images. Faster music, the growing cacophony gripping Weston's throat in a fiery crush. He closed his eyes. Memories, still so brutal and strong, flashed to life.

Leo yanking him around, pissed Weston had ignored their meeting. Yelling at him. Words he didn't remember.

Then, "Dude, why didn't you—"

The bullet.

Screams.

Blood.

Chaos.

Leo in a crimson heap on the floor.

Weston forced his eyes wide, fought the burn. A few gasps drifted from the club. He knew what was coming next. Hope. Clear, clean water dripping from a gun barrel, irrigating a field.

Growth. Advancement. Belief in the power of change. A rifle from afar, up close a cluster of butterflies that fluttered away. Stringed instruments joined the plaintive cello, a flute, the rumble of a bass. An orchestra, powerful, played together. A larger voice.

Together we can make a difference.

This wouldn't be the first time these people would have seen cries for better gun control. For every person who didn't believe changes were desperately needed, there was at least one who wanted upheaval. The problem was getting people to *act*. He hoped he and Annie had packaged their message meaningfully, through a medium that already resonated with the crowd. Empowered them as a collective.

Unable to see their reaction, he focused on the screen in front of him, the images and music peaking, so loud and bright it silenced the violent images in Weston's mind. He would never fully forgive himself for what happened with Leo, but he would live with it. He would live *better* and be the man Leo's sister deserved. The man his mother had raised. The man he wanted to be.

He cut the music.

The last curtain flew up.

The same three words glowed on every screen: *Your voice matters.*

A decree. A dare to try.

Weston stood tall, flushed with adrenaline. Thousands of faces snapped toward him, some with tears on their cheeks. Fire in their eyes. They had heard him. They had heard Annie and Leo and every other person fighting for progress. For all his and Annie's efforts, at least some would leave here changed.

Wes was supposed to transition now, blast his beats and get this party started. But his sights snagged on the brightest light in the room. Annie, *here*, standing on the bar, brazen, her hand pressed over her chest. She wore casual jeans and what looked like a gray hoodie, zipped up to her neck. Odd style for her, considering her eccentric closet, but she could be wearing a garbage bag for all he cared. She was looking at him, tall and open, letting him see to the heart of her.

He whipped off his mask while mixing the music.

The crowd roared. Annie gawked, the cutest grin slashing across her face. He blasted into his set, pointed at her and crooked his finger. She needed to get her ass on this stage, next to him. Closer. Close enough for him to drag in her scent.

She didn't move. He didn't know why.

Vivian and her girlfriend were by Annie's legs, talking at the bartender and gesturing wildly. Unsure what was up, he adjusted the volume, danced to the experimental electro pop tune, hard against the beat. Abstract, nature-inspired videos morphed across the screens. Annie tipped her head back, popped her hips in time. *His.* That woman was his, and he wanted to leap off stage, say screw it and tear out of there with her in his arms.

As tempting as that was, he was here for a reason.

He dragged his gaze away from hers for a moment. Focused on the crowd. A Freed by the Falcon junkie was dancing, one hand up, his fingers spread in a peace sign as he lost himself to the beats. His huge smile was a gift, infectious and uplifting. This was the definition of music. Inspiring. Empowering. Raw and honest.

Weston faded in the next song earlier than planned, fed off the club's contagious vibe. It was a partnership. Transactions traded in spirit, rising up, up, up until their joy punched through the ceiling.

His eyes jerked back to Annie. She was still standing on the bar, bent over at the waist, having a heated conversation with the bartender. The bartender shook her head and pointed at the floor. Vivian shouted something back. Management wanted Annie down, and Weston couldn't agree more. If she got off the bar top, she'd get up here where she should be, basking in this radioactive energy.

A bouncer moved toward the scene. Weston tensed. He pictured Annie tripping, falling, smacking her head on the edge of the bar.

She turned toward him abruptly, sidestepped the bouncer's grabby hands, and unzipped her hoodie, letting it fall to the floor. The bouncer was on her in seconds, manhandling her into his arms, escorting her to the exit. It all happened in the blink of an eye, but Weston caught a glimpse of her shirt before she was hauled off. Bright yellow. Black lettering.

It read: *I Love the Falcon.*

His ribs constricted, the feeling burning a hole in his chest. She'd said the words to him once before, but everything was different now. Her love. His love. Her willingness to forgive him his failings and risk vulnerability again. Once they talked and he found out what had driven her to break up with him, he'd do everything in his power to make Annie the happiest she'd ever been. He wouldn't lose her again, not for any reason.

He checked the music, gestured aggressively for the skinny stagehand to come over. "The girl who was standing on the bar —her name's Annie. Find her. Get her on stage. Do it now."

Weston's fingers worked the mixer. He danced with the crowd, filled with thoughts of Annie, while trying to stay dialed in to his show. Not an easy task. He glanced at Leo's photograph, thought about how long he'd fought his feelings for his best friend's little sister, how his friendship with Annie had grown organically alongside his love for her, so many random choices pushing him toward one end goal: Anthea Ward.

Always her. There had never been another option.

"Thank you," he told Leo. Call him crazy. Foolish. A believer in signs and portents. Someway, somehow, his best friend had played cupid.

"I won't jump on the bar again. I swear." Annie tried to wiggle out of the massive bouncer's hold. She'd have better luck escaping a straitjacket. "You can't kick me out. Seriously. I'm not some crazy stalker. I'm...friends with Falcon."

He smirked at the writing on her shirt. "Sure you are, sweetheart. And I'm best buds with Chris Hemsworth."

She deflated in his iron grip. *Friends* didn't begin to cover what Falcon was to her. She was being dragged away from her center of gravity, each step making her feel untethered.

"If you hurt a hair on her head," Vivian shouted while trailing them, "I will rain hell on your life."

"I'll investigate you," Sarah added. The bouncer didn't look scared. He absolutely should.

Annie turned while being half-dragged away. "Stay in here. If I don't get back in, find Falcon after the show and tell him I'm in a timeout outside."

The girls got swallowed by the masses.

The bouncer walked Annie outside and deposited her feet firmly on the ground. "You're out for the count. Don't let me catch you in there again."

"Can't you just get him a message? Tell him Annie's outside. He'll be pissed if you kick me out."

A streetlight glinted off the man's bald head. His face held as much expression as a rock. "And I have some magic beans to sell ya."

He lumbered his huge thighs through the entrance, and Annie collapsed against the club's outside wall. She still couldn't believe Wes had removed his mask. *Boom.* Just whipped it off and exposed himself like it was no big deal. Would the reckless move get him fired? Had he *already* been fired because Duncan had gotten to him before she'd had a chance to tell Wes about the evidence in her apartment? Sarah had dropped off the files just in time for Annie to leave for Wes's show. She needed to tell him about those files after he performed, and that she loved him as deeply as ever. She wasn't sure he'd seen her shirt.

That was supposed to be their moment. Her treasured memory with him blown away by her grand gesture, followed by him shouting how much he loved her, too. All she'd accomplished was a G-rated strip show before being dragged off by King Kong.

She eyed the line extending out the door and around the block. A different bouncer was at the entrance. She could sweet talk her way back in. Bat her eyelashes and unleash her feminine wiles. But her yellow T-shirt and jeans weren't particularly wiley. Maybe he wanted piano lessons.

A skinny kid busted through the entrance, out of breath, scanning the street frantically. When he looked at her, he did a little jump and rushed over. "Annie?"

"Yes..."

"Thank God. Come with me. Falcon wants you on stage."

She gripped his upper arms. "You're a life saver, and I'm going to hug you now."

An awkward hug later, he straightened his black T-shirt. "I'm more of a lackey. That Falcon guy is scary."

Wes was undeniably intense when you didn't know him. But she knew him, down to his soft, gooey center.

They pushed their way back into the club.

King Kong stopped them the second he saw her. "What did I tell you, lady?"

She pointed to her savior. "This nice guy was sent by Falcon to *bring me on stage*. Tell your buddy Chris Hemsworth I say hi and that I prefer his hair short."

King Kong's cheeks flushed.

The kid grabbed Annie's hand. "Get moving. I don't wanna lose my job."

Falcon's music pulsed hypnotically, a provocative beat that swelled into a shriek of synthesized keyboards. She wanted to stop and dance. Close her eyes and get lost in the funky rhythm. The club was hot and steamy. On fire. Bodies pulsed wildly, arms in the air, shoulders popping. The same people who'd been seized by emotion during the video intro were euphoric now, as she and Wes had planned. Grip them by their hearts, then set them free. Leave them feeling high. Changed. She and Wes had made people *feel*.

She followed the kid to a door at the side of the stage. VIP access. Another bouncer let them in, then she was being led down a corridor, up dark stairs, into the stage wings. And the view? The crowd was insane from this perspective. Both floors seemed to bounce, the whole club jumping to the intoxicating beats. Lights exploded from the massive disco ball, white lasers cutting through the sweltry air.

She felt Wes's attention before she looked at him. A sixth sense. Her Wes radar. The second they locked eyes, static sparked along her skin. Even without his mask, he looked feral. A bird of prey intent upon her, those chiseled features slashed into a sculpture, noble and savage.

She wanted to jump on him, maul him. Kiss the straining veins along his strong neck, bite his earlobe, mark every inch of him because every inch of him was hers. God, she'd missed him so much. But he was in the middle of a massive show, the entire club plugged into his socket.

She wouldn't jump his bones here, but she could do this.

She faced him fully and tugged on the hem of her yellow shirt, making it easier to read. "I never stopped loving you," she yelled over the music. "I don't think I ever could."

Giddy with anticipation this afternoon, while waiting to get Sarah's files, she'd had the cotton printed with: *I Love the Falcon*. She expected Wes to step away from his equipment now. Give her a brief kiss. Or stay playing while sending her a hungry snarl of possession.

Instead of doing any of those things, he lowered the mixer's volume and faced the crowd. "When you love someone," he said into his microphone, clear and rough. "You never let that person go."

The volume flared back to life. The crowd cheered. Her heart inflated to three times its size as his long legs ate up the distance between them and he hauled her into his arms, twirling her on stage and kissing her breathless. In front of everyone. Hungry. Deep.

Not a G-rated kiss.

She whimpered into his mouth. "I didn't want to break up with you. It was the worst thing, but crazy stuff was happening. Things you need to know."

His face sobered, the chaotic club fading slightly. "Are you okay?"

"I'm fine now. I just love you so much."

His eyes darkened. Another depraved kiss later, he sucked on her neck and bit her ear the way she'd wanted to bite his. "I fucking love you, Squirrel. And I'll never let you break up with me again. You'll have to chain me down if you think I'll ever let you go. Now get over here and make music with me. We'll talk later."

He tugged her toward the mixers, no mask to hide behind, his intentions clear. She felt like a supernova, uncontained happiness and energy exploding through her pores. They played together, alternated like they'd practiced, one of them controlling the volume while the other manipulated the beats. Louder bass. Softer drums. Adding back tracks and merging layers as the songs built into breathtaking peaks. They were in sync with each other. The crowd was in sync with them. She never wanted it to end. But it did. Gloriously.

Images had been drifting across the monitors since the powerful introduction. Wondrous colors and shapes, nature preening its natural beauty. They killed the videos. The lights dimmed as they took the music down low. They stooped themselves and motioned for the masses to do the same. The entire room crouched. They were one creature. One organ thumping together. One crush of humanity that, for this one night, would believe their voices could be heard.

Those three words from earlier flashed on the monitors, one at a time.

Your. Voice. Matters.

A growing chant. The words flashed faster. The music built, the lights, the energy. Dynamism exploded through every set of smiling eyes.

"Don't forget this feeling," Wes called into his microphone, fist pumped into the air. "Take the cards from the bouncers when you leave. Make your voice count."

The answering outcry was deafening, wolf whistles and shouts coming from all directions. Weston didn't stick around to bask in his glory. One hand locked around Annie's wrist, he dragged her off stage into a private dressing room.

He spun around and pinned her against the closed door. "I'm so sorry. I should have fought for you. For us. I was an idiot."

"You should have, but I understand why you didn't." She breathed in his sincerity, their tumultuous history, all the regret filling his declaration, and tossed him a playful smile. "Back massages go a long way when earning forgiveness. As do foot massages."

Amusement softened his stern features. "Am I that screwed?"

"Never hurts to go the extra mile."

"I plan to massage all of you, slowly, with undying devotion."

She blinked up at him, dazed from the show and his sultry promise, unable to reply or make another joke. His temples were sweaty, his hair askew from the non-stop dancing. Utterly scrumptious. She grabbed his hips and yanked all his raw male energy against her. "I missed you so much."

"I was lost without you." He kissed her roughly as they tugged at each other, demanding hands pushing at damp clothes, gasps escaping between filthy kisses. "I love you," he whispered as they slowed down. "Always." His next kiss was soft, gentle and reverent, the thick sweep of his tongue making her moan.

He pulled her to the room's black leather couch, cuddled her close. She nosed his damp neck. "I'm sorry I broke up with you. It was the last thing I wanted to do."

He angled her body toward him, eyes beseeching. "Then why'd you do it?"

"Because Duncan blackmailed me."

"He *what*?" His arm tightened uncomfortably around her.

She confessed about her plan to help him fight DLP, catching Duncan, the ensuing threats and Sarah's private eye work. "I think DLP has something bad on Duncan. That's why he did what he did."

According to Sarah's evidence, Duncan hadn't been uber-stealthy when lurking around Saanvi's apartment. A neighbor's surveillance camera had caught him ambushing Aldrich Pharma's top researcher at her front door, then forcing her into his car. She'd later emerged weeping and had run into her brownstone. She had quit Aldrich Pharma the next day. There were phone calls logged between Duncan and a higher-up at DLP. Sarah had found a dodgy offshore bank account.

None of it was irrefutable evidence. Duncan might not get arrested, but it would no longer be Annie's word against his. There was enough in the folder to burn that man's career to the ground.

"I think I will fucking kill Duncan," Wes said fiercely. "And you know what this means?"

She shook her head.

"You saved the merger. It was toast. We lost another researcher, but once I show Karim your files, there's no way he'll sign with DLP." He leveled her with an adoring look. "I should have accepted your help when you offered it. I shouldn't have pushed you away."

"Lots of massages," she said playfully. She wanted his hands on her, always.

He settled her more firmly on his lap, ran his thick fingers up her thighs. "You'll be begging me to stop."

"Fat chance. But what about your job? You took off your mask."

He quit kneading her thighs. "I doubt I'll work at Aldrich Pharma much longer. My father knows about Falcon."

Had her plan backfired? She'd thought waiting for evidence had been the smart move, delaying Wes from reacting and lashing out at Duncan. The good guys were supposed to win. "I should never have trusted him to keep his word."

"He didn't leak anything. I told my father. I was tired of denying a part of myself to appease the company and realized I didn't want to quit DJing. I'll find work elsewhere."

"But you love Aldrich Pharma."

"I love you, and I love *the work*. Someone will hire me who doesn't care what I do at night."

She hated the slight defeat in his posture, the weariness in his voice. "I don't think he'll fire you, but if he does, you'll take Marjory with you. And you won't have to hide the mutant animal testing going on in the secret underground lair anymore. We can free the animals together. Felix can be with his fellow rabbit-squirrels and star in his version of *Planet of the Apes*."

He smiled. "Planet of the Rabbit-Squirrels."

"You read my mind."

He pressed small kisses along her jaw, up to her temple. "I would shudder to delve into that murkiness." He leaned back and looked at her as though they'd just met. "I love you, Annie."

She touched the sharp slant of his cheekbones, feathered her fingers toward his mouth. "Say it again."

"Only if you say it back."

"Demanding."

"Give me a few hours and I'll show you demanding."

She liked that dirty promise. She liked this even more—them tucked together, touching, nuzzling, adrenaline still high from the show, her heart so impossibly full. "I love you more than I love scrapbooking," she whispered.

He nipped her bottom lip. "Good, because I'm tossing the book you made of me."

She froze, picturing her latest creation with dogs defiling his photograph. "I tossed it already."

He cocked his head and stared at her. "You're such a liar."

"I lost it."

"You added to it."

"What? No. Of course not."

He flipped her onto her back, loomed over her like the sexy beast he was. "Lying comes with penalties."

She would happily take punishment from Wes, her best friend and lover. She might have to add to that book every day for the rest of their lives, just to see this predatory gleam in his eyes, so she could reach for his wide shoulders, feel all that maleness gunning for her, and say, "Do your worst, Herbert."

EPILOGUE

Nine Months Later

"HAVE YOU SEEN MY PASSPORT? I was sure I left it on the bookshelf." Annie tore through her chaotic apartment, bulldozing through stray magazines and sheet music.

Weston leaned on the kitchen counter, enjoying the show. "On your bookshelf, where exactly? In that mess of half-finished puzzle books or tucked between the torn magazine pages that might spill over at any minute?"

She slanted him a dirty look. "My place is cluttered but organized, and I'm tired of you judging it. One more crack, and I'll change the lock."

"I'll pick the lock."

She pursed her lips. "I can't believe Leo taught you that."

"I also know how to jack a car."

"Leo never stole a car. He didn't even have a license."

"You don't need a license to steal a car."

She puffed out a laugh, then side-eyed him. "Did he really steal a car?"

Weston mimed zipping his lips and tossing the key. Annie didn't need to know about the night they'd taken a Mercedes for a joy ride to impress a couple of club girls.

He grabbed Annie's passport from a stack of old phone books and raised it in the air. "Are you looking for this?"

She grabbed a couch pillow and tossed it at him. It landed a foot short of its target.

He sauntered over to her, passport in hand. "What were you saying about your organized clutter?"

She pressed her forehead against his chest. "This was a memory blip, not clutter."

"Whatever you say, Squirrel. But we know which of the two of us is more organized."

"Whatever." She nuzzled closer. "You'd be lost without me."

No argument from him. "I also wouldn't have a pet rabbit I don't hate." The second those words were out, he flinched. He hadn't meant to blurt that confession.

Annie pulled back, squinting one eye at him. "What do you mean I'm the reason you have Felix? You took him from your neighbor."

"Yes. I did." He scratched his nose. "That's exactly what happened."

She stepped fully away and crossed her arms. "You're lying."

He glanced at his watch. "Would you look at the time? We should really leave."

"Explain about the rabbit."

"We might miss our flight."

She didn't budge.

With what he had planned for today, better to smooth this over before he dug himself deeper. "I bought Felix from a pet store and lied about his separation anxiety so you'd quit chasing me at my shows."

She leaned closer to him and cupped her ear. "You'll have to speak up, Herbert. It sounded like you said you lied about Felix to ditch me."

He fought his rising laugh. "I was blinded by your beauty and distracted at my shows and didn't know what else to do. But think about how great it worked out. We have an adorable pet rabbit."

"Because your need for control is so preposterous you're willing to exploit a perfectly innocent animal."

"It was self-preservation. You were relentless."

"That didn't sound like an apology."

"Sorry?"

She rolled her eyes. "No, you're not. You're a control freak who always has to have his way." She pushed to her tiptoes and kissed his cheek. "But I kind of love your evil-mastermindedness, future husband."

Hopefully she'd love today's surprise even more.

He took her hand in his and planted a kiss on the engagement ring he'd given her last week. Proposing had been as emotional and terrifying and perfect as he'd hoped. He'd done it right in front of the Office of the City Clerk, had dragged her up to fill out the marriage license right away. She'd cried and laughed, the two of them kissing and smiling through it all. "This is proof," he'd told her. "My promise to you there will be no freaking out before the ceremony."

She'd loved the gesture, had prattled on about how they'd get properly married next year, during the summer. She hadn't clued into the stunt's ulterior motive.

"Enough about your rabbit games." She bounced on her toes, a thousand-watt grin lighting her face. "Have I told you this trip will be my first flight and that Ibiza is my number one bucket-list destination out of my list of two hundred and twenty-four?"

"A few times." About two hundred and twenty-four.

She skipped over to her bag, grabbed the handle, and rolled her shoulders back. "I am, as of now, a jet-setter. A stylish woman of the world, about to embark on the vacation of a lifetime."

"With the man of her dreams."

She tossed him a wink. "We should pretend to meet in the hotel lobby. You can pick me up. I'll take off the engagement ring."

He grabbed her bag and planted a hungry kiss on those adorable lips. "Not a chance. Every man there's going to know you're mine."

She tossed her arms around his neck, kissed him while smiling. "All yours. And you're mine. Which means I actually have to get my butt in gear and start planning our wedding."

Her joy dipped slightly, a hint of stress in her creased brows. All signs that today's plan wouldn't backfire on him. It better not, at least.

Annie was the first thing he thought about in the morning, at lunch, while walking down the street, when seeing vintage clothing stores or passing a craft shop. He refused to sleep without her, splitting their time between his place and hers. He bought her gifts incessantly, loved toying with her long blond hair while they watched a movie. He couldn't look away from her when she found a new song for their set list, her skin glowing with excitement. She was his best friend. She was the reason Aldrich Pharma had announced their merger with Biotrell and a large part of why he still worked for his family company. She'd even begun to win over his father.

Today better go off without a hitch.

He carried her luggage to the waiting car and slid into the backseat with her.

She linked their fingers and turned to him, her hazel eyes, more green than brown today, brimming with affection. "Have I thanked you for planning this trip?"

He kissed her nose. "You have, but don't hold back. Thank me again."

"Thank you, *again*. I don't have patience for planning. I mean, I will for the wedding," she said quickly. "But I know how crazy busy you are. I hope taking the time off work isn't killing you."

"Not when this is a partial business trip." DJ business was also business. His father had grudgingly agreed to ignore Weston's moonlighting. With the merger solidified, shareholders couldn't argue against his capabilities. And when Ushuaia called asking Falcon to play their massive open-air club, he couldn't refuse. Especially since a trip to Ibiza lined up perfectly with today's plans. "Besides, exploring that exotic island is no hardship."

She fiddled with his fingers while tucked into his side, tracing the length of each digit. He watched her intently, bounced his heel, waiting for her to clue into their driver's direction.

Eventually, she squinted through the window. "He's going the wrong way. Why is he going the wrong way?"

Weston tugged her closer, worried she might open the door and bail out. "I have no idea."

"Yeah, I've heard that before. Always when I ask you about a random gift that appears out of thin air. Where are we going, Wes?"

"Like I said, I have no clue."

"Do you have a clue if we're going to miss our flight? In case you've forgotten, I'm a woman of the world, and gallivanting women don't like missing their flights when they've been counting down the days with stickers and colored markers in their scrapbooks."

"I have not forgotten. Our flight is later than I told you. Enough with the questions."

"*Weston.*"

"*Anthea.*"

She gave him the silent treatment for the rest of the ride.

When the car pulled up to a random curb in midtown Manhattan, she caved. "Why are we still in the city?"

He kissed her ear and murmured, "Don't move."

He stepped out of his side of the car and rounded to hers in several long strides. He yanked her door open and dropped to one knee.

She glanced around the street, then back at him. "What you doing?"

He gathered her small hands in his. "The day I met you was the most important day of my life. Knowing and loving Leo was a gift, but meeting you was destiny. I didn't know it then, but you're the glue and sparkles that hold me together. You're every artwork I've ever admired, captured in a vibrancy I never fathomed. You're the reason I'm living a full life, and why I have a silly pet rabbit. You're my..." His throat clogged with emotion. She was *everything*. "You're my heart, Squirrel."

Her chin trembled, those expressive eyes glossing over. "What's a heart-squirrel?" she asked through her tears.

He laughed. "You. You're the crazy squirrel. And I love you so damn much."

"I love you, too. More than anything. But you've already proposed, and I said yes." She pulled out her left hand and waved her vintage square-cut diamond ring in his face. "We even have our marriage license. What's with the bended knee and gorgeous profession of love?"

He'd gone on a hunch with this next move. A slightly reckless hunch. Annie was taking her own piano lessons, while teaching in her spare time and working on her DJing. She had gigs booked. She'd even started a scrapbooking club for kids at a community center, and she still waitressed a couple of nights a week. All hectic and time consuming, though fulfilling. He'd known she wouldn't love carving time for wedding planning. Planning in general wasn't her forte.

He, however, was a born organizer.

"That was just the preliminary proposal," he said, his voice shakier than he'd like. "This is the official one." He fanned his hand toward the building. "We're having the ceremony today."

"WHAT DO YOU MEAN TODAY?" Annie's voice screeched as her brain struggled to play catch-up. They'd talked about an eventual wedding, sometime next summer. Time for her to figure out the million and one things that would need doing. Now Wes was watching her with wary, shifty eyes. He was nervous, and she was flummoxed.

"The wedding's already planned," he said, casting a glance at the brownstone behind him. "And it's happening now."

"I'm sorry." Her laugh had an erratic pitch to it. "I must have misheard you again. First the Felix reveal, now this."

He stood from his bent knee and held out his hand, palm up, to help her from the car.

She stared at it, helpless. "My wedding isn't happening here. *Now.* I'm wearing an old skirt and a tank top." Printed with the words: *Because I'm the DJ, That's Why.* "And I wanted our friends at our wedding. Nothing big and fancy, but a day we could share with them."

Another moment of perfection to gather and cherish

alongside the millions of others they created daily. She'd worked so hard to build friendships this year. Talk to women. Share her worries when getting together for food and drinks with people like Pegasus, whose real name was Gretchen. Grow a network she could count on, and who could count on her. She'd hate not to have them here today.

Wes stretched his hand closer to her and lowered his voice. "As much as I love our bickering with benefits, which would have been entertaining while planning a wedding, I didn't want the planning to be a burden. You're busy and hate scheduling and research, but I enjoy it. I also wanted to do this for you. Not just the signing of our marriage license. Really show you I'm ready for us. So let me love you the best way I know how. Let me whisk you off your feet and be your prince."

God, this man. All those months of infatuation, yearning, pining, she'd never imagined he'd be this devoted, that a few words from him would knock her sideways. Her dream wedding morphed into this moment now. A random New York street. Pedestrians casting them odd glances. Weston Aldrich offering her the one thing he'd never offered anyone: his unprotected heart.

"Yeah, okay." Her words sounded watery. She accepted his hand and stood. "I can't believe we're getting married today. Do we have time to call Vivian and Rosanna and—"

He pressed a finger to her lips. "Trust me, will you?"

She nodded, too blown away to speak. He signaled to someone in the brownstone behind them, and Vivian and Sarah scurried out. Annie squawked. They whisked her inside, and people were *everywhere*, catering people and makeup people and hair people.

"Whose house is this?" she asked, dazed.

Vivian clutched her hand tightly. "A friend of Sarah's. And no more questions."

"But—"

"No buts." Rosanna appeared from around a corner, as stunning as ever. "You're officially kidnapped. There's no worrying or questioning. There's only smiling and enjoying." She held up a white dress.

Annie screamed.

Rosanna winced. "You broke my eardrums."

"How did he—"

Rosanna tutted and raised her hand. "Is she always this bad at following instructions?"

Vivian linked arms with Sarah. "We usually let her ramble and check back every few seconds to make sure she's breathing while she's talking."

"You're all traitors," Annie said, unable to tear her eyes away from the fashion masterpiece. It was the exact dress from one of her scrapbook pages, layered lace, fitted and feminine with a tiny train. Immaculate. Romantic perfection.

Suspicion dawned, giddy delight that her favorite man had scoured her books for inspiration, pored over the pages, and had created her perfect wedding.

"He's amazing," she said, a fresh wave of emotion shaking her voice.

"He loves you so much." This from Rosanna.

"His research skills would make him a killer private eye." Sarah.

Vivian kissed Annie's cheek. "Now shut up and let us work."

Twined wild flowers were woven into Annie's braided hair, like ones she'd plucked on a Central Park picnic Wes had once surprised her with. The girls changed into dresses in varying shades of green—like her eyes, Vivian mentioned on a sigh. Weston had apparently been quite specific on the tones. Bowls of salt and vinegar chips were brought in for them to munch on, alongside fancy appetizers only Wes would choose. Both their worlds colliding.

That man was more than a prince. He was frustrating and irritating and amazing and handsome and talented and smart and the most thoughtful man in the world. Having this beautiful day imagined by him was better than stressing over choices, worried she'd forget the smallest detail.

When she saw the rooftop garden, as whimsical as any floral dress she'd ever worn, more tears welled. Flowers smelling of sunshine spilled over stone pedestals and sprouted from every inch of the architecturally stunning deck. An arch of wild flowers stood at the far end, poetic in its simplicity.

Marjory had even brought Felix. She kept wiping her eyes, while muttering, "I always knew it."

Annie's new acquaintances were milling with Weston's. He'd made his own friends recently, part of *his* mission to live a fuller life. They wore lovely suits, praised her beauty and kissed her hand. One massive man towered over the rest. Brick Kramarov. Heavy-weight boxer and Weston's spokesperson for their new Parkinson's treatment. He hugged her kindly and leaned his head down. "I wish you two nothing but the best."

Annie glanced behind him, looking for Brick's plus one. "Is Isla here?"

Brick's face shadowed. "No, she..." He swallowed heavily. "I haven't told her about working with Weston on the Parkinson's drug yet. The timing has to be right."

Brick's sadness hurt Annie's heart. He was a pile of goo packed into the body of a warrior, and his pain was palpable. Annie hadn't met Brick's love interest, but he spoke of her often, even confessing that his spokesperson offer was a way to win back the love of his life. Annie hoped his plan worked.

A man stole Brick's attention, talk of boxing taking over, and Annie's favorite piano student, Joyce, gave her a hug and patted her cheek. Pierced and tattooed DJ friends interrupted, offering their congratulations. A motley crew for her and Weston's kaleidoscope life.

Then there was Rosanna's father, standing to the side, chatting with Victor S. Aldrich.

If you'd asked Annie nine months ago if Weston's father would attend their wedding, she'd have laughed herself silly. Then she would have checked for a hidden camera. Fast friends they were not. There were no warm family dinners or engaging phone calls. His name was nowhere on her emergency contact list. But they had an understanding.

Victor had shockingly thanked her for nailing Duncan to the wall and solidifying the merger. There hadn't been enough evidence to convict the creep, but he'd been fired, his reputation ruined. Aldrich Pharma had since thrived. She wasn't sure where Duncan had slinked off to, but he'd be lucky to get a job flipping burgers. The last she'd spoken with Weston's father, after his grudging gratitude, she'd thanked him for having such a wonderful son and had told him, unequivocally, he'd only meet future grandbabies if he thawed his frozen heart.

They made eye contact across the decorated rooftop. Victor nodded stiffly. She replied with a wide smile. The corners of his lips twitched briefly, as though reciprocating the gesture, or maybe he was passing gas, then he returned to his conversation.

She glanced toward the sky and silently thanked Weston's mother for teaching her son how to love, regardless of his father's stony nature. She thanked Leo for being a great big brother and teaching her to be strong and happy and for bringing Wes into her life.

She searched the rooftop for the man of the hour, but he was nowhere to be seen. Another handsome man approached

her with a woman on his arm. Annie had never seen him
before. She'd have remembered those thick eyelashes and his
dashing sweep of dark hair. The woman on his arm, however,
was familiar: the freckles dusting her nose, that strawberry
blond hair, her hesitant yet curious gaze. Something tickled
Annie's memory, a younger version of this woman, with pigtails
poking out of her head.

Annie slapped her hand over her mouth. "Clementine?" she
said through her fingers.

The woman's brown eyes lit up. "I wasn't sure you'd
remember me."

"How could I forget you?" She'd been so quiet in their
shared foster home, reserved, distrustful. For three months
Annie had invented ridiculous stories while brushing
Clementine's beautiful hair, trying to make her smile.

"I was shocked when Weston called," Clementine said, her
face flushed. "I've thought about finding you so many times,
but..." She ducked her head as though embarrassed.

"I did, too. Lots. But everything was so hard back then."
Impossible. Life sending her for another loop. Yet here
Clementine was, because Annie had mentioned her to Wes,
once, almost a year ago. "I had no idea Wes was doing this. I
can't believe you're actually here."

Clementine sniffled and caught Annie in her arms, holding
and hugging her with equal force. She pulled back and fussed
over Annie's dress. "If I ruin this I'll never forgive myself."

"I probably wouldn't forgive you, either." She winked. "Now
introduce me to this hunk of a man."

The hunk in question dropped his gaze and smiled shyly.
"I'm Jack, the lucky man engaged to this amazing woman." He
looked at Clementine, his sweet shyness melting away into
adoration thick enough to taste.

Weston couldn't have given Annie a better gift than seeing

Clementine grown, happy, on the arm of a seemingly sweet man. Speaking of which, where the heck was her prince?

A violin trilled and Clementine clapped. "That's your cue. We'll catch up later."

That *did* sound like her cue. It was the hopeful violin segment Wes had worked into some of his opening DJ sets, but her groom was still absent. The guests maneuvered as though prompted to assume their places. Vivian took Annie by the arm and led her toward the flower arch and waiting minister.

Annie stumbled in her pretty heels. "Last I checked, the groom should be at the end of the aisle when getting married." She came to a dead stop, fear locking her ankles. "Did he get cold feet? Is he on a plane to Ibiza without me? Am I getting ditched at the altar?"

Vivian pinched Annie's upper arm. "What did we say about the questions?"

"Have you no heart?"

Vivian deposited her under the arch and patted her shoulder. "Have faith, young grasshopper."

The guests stood, facing her, eyes bright and eager. Except for Victor. His severe scowl was as predictable as ever. But the rest of them? They left an opening, the type of rose petal-covered aisle a bride would use to float toward her beloved, but *this* bride was at the arch, the groom was a no-show, and their friends were grinning, like this odd circumstance wasn't odd at all.

The violinist switched songs. The small gathering glanced toward where *the bride* should appear. And there he was. Weston. Falcon. Her best friend and lover, decked out in a tux that hugged his lean lines and probably cost a mint. That man and his suits.

He smiled at her, paused and shook his head as he covered his heart with his hand. He glanced up at the sky and mouthed something she couldn't understand. Her eyes burned, her throat turning raw and scratchy. She was going to lose her cool before he walked the short distance to her.

When he reached her, she bit the inside of her cheek. She would not cry and ruin this gorgeous makeup. "You did this," she whispered.

"I did."

"I can't believe you found Clementine, and the dress is beyond gorgeous, and the flowers and everything you planned is almost perfect."

He stepped closer, blocking the gathering from view. "Almost?"

"I'm supposed to be the one walking down the aisle, not you."

He made a soft clucking sound and kissed both her hands. "That was for me, not you. I wanted to walk toward the most ridiculous, amazing, beautiful woman in the world so she knows she's the only person who could ever be at the end of this path. You're the only direction for me, Annie. You're my compass. Everything will always point to you."

Biting her cheek didn't help. Tears overflowed. "Even if I'm standing on the lip of a bubbling volcano about to erupt all over your gorgeous tux?"

He laughed and wiped her tears with his thumbs. "Even then. Now what do you say we get hitched? We have a honeymoon in Ibiza to get to."

Annie had never considered herself lucky. Not with the rough childhood she'd been dealt. But here, right now, amid their hodge-podge of friends, one rabbit named Felix, the New York skyline stretching into the distance, and this breathtaking man looking at her like she was the center of his world, she'd never felt luckier.

Thank you for reading Wes and Annie's story! Stay on the lookout for book 4 in the Showmen series:

Coming in 2021

THE KNOCKOUT RULE
Get swept away with heavy-weight boxer Brick Kramarov as he falls for the last person he ever expected.

CHECK OUT KELLY SISKIND'S OTHER TITLES BELOW!

STANDALONES

Chasing Crazy: "This is one of the best New Adult contemporary romances I've read to date." ~ *USA Today* Bestselling author K.A. Tucker

---

INTERCONNECTED STANDALONES

Showmen Series

New Orleans Rush: "A fun mixture of magic, sensuality, and iconic pin-up girl style. The romance in New Orleans Rush will leave you smiling and filled with optimism." ~ *USA Today* bestselling author Helen Hoang

Don't Go Stealing My Heart: "This book sparkles and sizzles with Siskind's trademark humor and heat. Don't go missing this one!" ~ author Jen DeLuca

The Beat Match: "Fun to read, while also delivering a satisfying, sometimes tear-inducing, and heartfelt love story. Do yourself a favor and *read this book!*" ~ Bookgasms Book Blog

---

Over the Top Series

My Perfect Mistake: "This has easily earned itself a place on my all-time favorites shelf." ~ The Sisterhood of the Traveling Book Boyfriends

A Fine Mess: "Delicious, sizzling chemistry that leapt off the page!" ~ *USA Today* Bestselling Author Jennifer Blackwood

Hooked on Trouble: "...experience the romance, the sexy times, the heartbreak, and the swoons...you can thank me later!!" ~ The Book Hookup

---

One Wild Wish Series

He's Going Down: "An intoxicating romance that lingers like a great Merlot and leaves you with one hell of a book hangover!" ~ author Scarlett Cole

Off-Limits Crush: "...with loads of flirty and witty banter. Siskind knows how to write characters that have off-the-charts chemistry." ~ RT Book Reviews

36 Hour Date: "Kelly has blended a mystery into this compelling love story in a way that keeps the reader flipping pages. I couldn't put it down!" ~ *USA Today* Bestselling Author Ellis Leigh

ACKNOWLEDGMENTS

Thank you to J.R. Yates, Mary Ann Marlowe, and Shelly Hastings Suhr for being such awesome early readers. Your help on this book was invaluable. Chelly Pike, Jen DeLuca, Sandra Fuda Lombardo, and Michelle Hazen have eagle eyes. The book is shinier because of you all! My editor Tamara Mataya is the bomb. Thank you for helping make this book sparkle.

Mary Ann Smith never ceases to astound me with her cover-designing talent. This artwork captures Weston and Annie and their story perfectly. Thank you for bringing my vision to life. Shawn Chartrand's DJ expertise helped me navigate writing the more technical details of the novel. Any errors are my own.

A massive thank you to my readers and the blogging, reviewing, and bookstagramming community: y'all are angels. Every time you tell someone about one of my books or share a picture on social media, my heart takes flight.

I can't wait for you all to meet boxing heavy-weight contender Brick Kramarov and the love of his life, Isla Slade, in my next book, The Knockout Rule, coming in 2021!

ABOUT THE AUTHOR

A small-town girl at heart, Kelly moved from the city to enjoy the charm of northern Ontario. When she's not out hiking with her husband or home devouring books, you can find her, notepad in hand, scribbling down one of the many plot bunnies bouncing around in her head. Her novels have been published internationally.

For giveaways and early peeks at new work, join Kelly' newsletter: www.kellysiskind.com

If you like to laugh and chat about books, join Kelly in her Facebook group, KELLY'S GANG.

Connect with Kelly on social media:
twitter.com/KellySiskind
facebook.com/authorKellySiskind/
instagram.com/kellysiskind/

CPSIA information can be obtained
at www.ICGtesting.com
Printed in the USA
BVHW030959030720
582582BV00002B/9